GETTING HUGE

GUERNICA WORLD EDITIONS 57

GETTING HUGE

A NOVEL

John Young

GUERNICA
World
EDITIONS

TORONTO—BUFFALO—LANCASTER (U.K.)
2023

Guernica Editions Founder: Antonio D'Alfonso

Michael Mirolla, general editor
Scott Walker, editor
Cover design: Nick Young
Interior design: Jill Ronsley, suneditwrite.com

Guernica Editions Inc.
287 Templemead Drive, Hamilton (ON), Canada L8W 2W4
2250 Military Road, Tonawanda, N.Y. 14150-6000 U.S.A.
www.guernicaeditions.com

Distributors:
Independent Publishers Group (IPG)
600 North Pulaski Road, Chicago IL 60624
University of Toronto Press Distribution (UTP)
5201 Dufferin Street, Toronto (ON), Canada M3H 5T8
Gazelle Book Services, White Cross Mills
High Town, Lancaster LA1 4XS U.K.

First edition.
Printed in Canada.

Legal Deposit—First Quarter
Library of Congress Catalog Card Number: 2022942214
Library and Archives Canada Cataloguing in Publication
Title: Getting huge : a novel / John Young.
Names: Young, John, 1959- author.
Series: Guernica world editions ; 57.
Description: First edition. | Series statement: Guernica world editions ; 57
Identifiers: Canadiana (print) 2022028525X | Canadiana (ebook) 20220285268
| ISBN 9781771837798 (softcover) | ISBN 9781771837804 (EPUB)
Classification: LCC PS3625.O95 G48 2023 | DDC 813/.6—dc23

For Lauren, Nick, and Tess

IX

by Wendell Berry

I go by a field where once
I cultivated a few poor crops.
It is now covered with young trees,
for the forest that belongs here
has come back and reclaimed its own.
And I think of all the effort
I have wasted and all the time,
and of how much joy I took
in that failed work and how much
it taught me. For in so failing
I learned something of my place,
something of myself, and now
I welcome back the trees.

Contents

Chapter One

A Lovely Easter

My deacons saw Easter as a business opportunity. So they set before me a BHAG (a Big Hairy Audacious Goal) to break our Easter fundraising record. And now, on Easter morning, their BHAG was getting buried under a slushy snow.

The fundraising record was set by my father on Easter Sunday back in 1976. Yes, my father was minister of the Concord Congregationalist Church before me. Before he called me down from the mountain–from my church in the White Mountains of New Hampshire–to install me in the position he had built into the most-coveted in all the Congregationalist Church. I'm sure he envisioned me leading the flock for forty years like he did–as well as being a community leader and president of the Congregationalist Church of America like he was. Dad was a big man in the church and a big man in town.

Although, I'm bigger, at least physically bigger. At seminary they used to joke: "John Crackstone is closer to God than anyone." That's because I'm six-feet, eleven-inches tall. A skosh over seven feet in shoes. But on that Easter morning, as Concord, Massachusetts filled with snow, I did not feel especially close to God. The snow assured my failure on the BHAG, another financial shortfall by the tallest minister in North America.

As a kid, I was in awe of my father. Impressive in the pulpit and on the street, but more than that, Dad was a hell of a fundraiser. On the record-setting Easter of '76, everything fell his way. Of course, it was America's Bicentennial Year. Easter landed on April 18, one day before Patriots' Day, when Massachusetts celebrates "The Shot Heard Around the World," so we saw record-setting tourists. Then my father leaned on patriotism, devotion, and belief-in-a-cause in his sermon. Another fortunate fluke: a stifling, 93-degree heat wave drove locals and tourists to seek out the nearest air conditioning, and our church had it. Even though I was just six years old, I remember the standing-room-only crowd that Easter. Whether in appreciation for the air conditioning or Dad's sermon, the CEOs (Christmas and Easter Onlys) opened their wallets.

Me? I got snow. So achieving the BHAG was as likely as patent-leather shoes and pastel dresses on a slushy Easter egg hunt. At my father's desk, now my desk, I already knew my defeat. I imagined the next finance report dripping with the deacons' disapproval and word of my failure trickling back to my now-retired father as he basked in the warm Arizona sun. The weight of his disappointment in me pending.

An emphasis on fundraising had been millstoning me, grinding on me since I'd taken over twelve years before. Enough that I felt my grip on the job slipping. Which threatened my family's security. Still, I mustered no zeal for fundraising and even saw it cutting against my vision for the church.

After the fundraising debacle of this Easter day, would the deacons enlist my father to fire me? I was his hand-picked successor, and I had reluctantly accepted, so they might ask him to clean up his mess.

The funny thing is, even a dozen years after Dad passed the mantle of Concord Congregational to me and retired to Arizona, it still felt like it all belonged to my father. Dad's house, the parsonage where I grew up. Any second, I expected to round a corner and collide with my father—forehead bumping his hard Windsor knot, an apology prepared. And it still felt like Dad's job, his church, his congregation, his deacons. Why did I fear a deacon's retort that I wasn't "Reverend Crackstone"? Because I wasn't Reverend *William* Crackstone. I was *John*, the gawky, gangly kid who was either in the way or never there when you needed him.

"John," I heard Nancy call, "where are you?" She walked into the study in flannel pajamas before I could answer, carrying a small package. "Good morning," she said.

"Not so good," I answered. "Did you look outside?"

"Yeah, I know. And I know what it means for the deacons' stupid goal. That's why I brought you this. I planned to give it to you tonight, but I thought you might need it now. Happy Easter." She extended the package.

"But I didn't get you anything," I confessed as I began to unwrap the box.

"We don't usually get each other gifts for Easter," Nancy said. "It's small."

I dropped the wrapping and ribbon on my desk and lifted the lid. "Worry beads? Seems appropriate for today. Plenty to worry about."

She shook her head. "Don't be a goof. They're prayer beads or meditation beads," she said as she lifted them out of the box and raised my wrist. "They're a symbol of protection and good tidings."

With deft hands Nancy encircled my right wrist and snapped the silver clasp, then turned my wrist over for me to see. "These are ancient beads. The three white mother-of-pearl beads in the middle are for your family"—she touched each one as she went—"me, Gordon, and Megan. The white represents stress relieving—"

"I need that."

3

"Yes, you do," she replied. "This turquoise one represents you–for wisdom, loyalty, love, and … and a bunch of other good stuff. You can Google it," she said, waving her hand. "The last one represents the community; it's red jasper, for courage, creativity, and focus. Now, the band," she said, "it consists of three braided pieces of leather for the Trinity, and you can see there's a thin silver cable encircling the center leather piece that goes through all the beads and represents lasting strength of the bond of all of these things in your life." She put her hand over it. "Do you like it?"

"Yeah," I said, "but do you think it's a little too hip-py–dippy for Concord? Will they think I'm trying to be a Yogi?"

"Never mind," she said, reaching to take it off. "You don't have to wear it."

I pulled my wrist back. "No. I like it. I just wonder if I should wear it around the church. You know how people are. Some will think I'm a Buddhist or something."

"Some people are idiots," she snapped. "I have to get ready."

"Wait …"

But she was gone.

It really was cool, the bracelet, a thoughtful gift. But other than a watch, I'd never worn a bracelet of any kind before, and I found it a weird time to start. I decided to take it off, and I could talk to Nancy about it later, but I couldn't figure out the puzzling clasp.

I had to get over to the church to help old Joe, our volunteer, shovel snow. I went upstairs to see if Nancy could help with the clasp.

When I walked in, Nancy was pulling on her Easter dress. Not the colorful one she had set out, which was one she'd worn a few years ago, but something that called to mind a Soviet–era housing complex. Concrete color and shapeless in drape, it featured big, medium–gray buttons down the front like a row of tarnished silver dollars. For a moment I considered asking her to change, but the only time I'd ever asked her to wear something different, she'd taken offense. With the pressure of the snow assuring my fiscal failure for this big day, I had enough to worry about. Like getting to the church to help Joe shovel and salt the sidewalks.

I went downstairs, thinking about Nancy's dress choice, and bundled up to go shovel snow. Pulling on my gloves, I remembered the bracelet. Hell, it would be fine. If their minister was a little more hip on this day, so be it.

Still, while I trudged through slush on my way to the church, I imagined the nattering of old church ladies about Nancy's dress. I didn't need a wardrobe kerfuffle heaped on my worries. But why had she selected the Soviet uniform? Was it some sort of punishment for my bracelet reaction? I pondered it more while shoveling and salting the church sidewalks with old Joe–could Nancy's dress be a sign of depression? A cry for help? But Nancy had always been strong–the fortitude of a fourth-grade teacher. If she were depressed, I would know. There'd be more signs.

Then I heard a cat–like cry and turned. It was Carol Baker, my neighbor and the wife of our youngest deacon. She'd fallen on a patch of ice, sprawled in her red wool coat, blonde hair a muss, with Easter flowers scattered around her. As I went to her, my brain took a snapshot of the momentary still-life–the only splash of color on the bleak, blue–gray snow. In the center of it, Carol struggled to re-gather herself, and I helped her back onto her pumps, brushing snow off her and noting the fit physique under the red coat. She rubbed her knee, and I bent for a look. Her hair brushed my face, and in that instant her perfume rose to my nose. Though cathedral–like on my oversized face, my nose is not especially sensitive to scent. Yet Carol's subtle fragrance, combined with touch, made me pause to take in this lovely woman.

About then Shelly Andersen, our associate minister, hustled out in her snow boots to see if Carol was okay and took her from my hands to escort her inside, leaving me to gather flowers while Joe re-salted the offending stretch of ice.

In the end, the meager Easter crowd and its financial results lived down to expectations as if foreshadowed by Nancy's dour dress. The day brought only two uplifting events, the first marked by my brief interlude with Carol Baker. The second was the last thing I did before bed: quietly I planted pumpkin seeds in our basement. Hunched like a mad scientist in a secret lab, I prepared seventy-five Dixie cups with potting soil and one seed per cup, lined up in three rows under grow-lights.

The seeds were for giant pumpkins which I had planned to grow with my kids, Megan and Gordon. Just a fun father-and-kids project which also might teach them a little about nature, and about the responsibility of caring for something alive, ending with giant jack-o-lanterns in the fall.

It sounded simple enough, but it quickly grew into something big.

* * *

The first Friday night after Easter, Nancy and I walked to the 1746 house owned by old Caleb Bradstreet, a deacon who'd served with my father. Once again, Nancy had selected something blah to wear: a brown skirt and jacket with a beige blouse and minimal makeup. The Bradstreets' historic house had been expanded over the centuries to both sides. Its four bedrooms represented a downsize from their previous mansion. To show off their new kitchen addition, Caleb and Nikki Bradstreet hosted the annual "Deacons Dinner." This dinner also marked the deacons' first-quarter financial review, a chance to see how the Easter fundraiser went, how Easter had contributed to the nest egg.

Caleb met us at the front door. "Reverend Crackstone." Caleb's hand extended in a formal but warm way. "And Nancy," he added, taking her hand in both of his. "Please come in."

I ducked under the eighteenth-century door and kept my head low to avoid the chamfered beams overhead. With their collection of fine antiques, the interior presented like a museum. Nikki left the other guests and caterers in the kitchen to welcome us. When I turned to greet her, my hair brushed a chandelier, giving me an instant to duck before I crashed into it. That's why I wear this conservative version of the curly bush I wore in college, just barely respectable enough for a minister. While at Boston University, I grew my curly hair into a full shrub, and I discovered how it acted as both an early-warning-device and a furry bumper pad. My father hated my hair, but I kept it. Too bad, Dad.

Even with the early-warning-device hairdo, I bump my head more often than I want to admit. New England's old houses feature low doors, low beams, low ceilings, low light fixtures. It's crazy. If a six-foot-tall man bumps his head on a low-hanging light fixture, the host or hostess is quick to apologize, but when you're seven-feet tall, you get a look like, "*Watch where you're going, you big oaf. Don't you know how tall you are?*" And I caught that look on Nikki's face for an instant. Of course, the Bradstreets—both small at 5'8" and 5'3"—never thought of the lamp, or the beams, or the low doors. Me? I followed Nikki's historic house tour, ducking and bobbing like a Central Park pigeon.

When we arrived at their beautiful kitchen addition, it glowed like something out of *Architectural Digest*. Though they were left blond, the beautiful beams referenced the antique house. Of course, the kitchen gleamed with bright lighting, top-shelf Euro appliances, and dramatic stone countertops from Iceland. The room ended with a bank of windows overlooking formal English gardens. It all befit one of Boston's august investment gurus. Most of the other deacons were in the kitchen with their wives—yes, all twelve deacons were men.

I thought of our kitchen in the parsonage, last updated decades ago, with its stained Formica counters and sputtering Kenmore refrigerator. I'd like to update it, but with the Easter earnings, I knew not to request any changes. I'm sure all the deacons and their wives enjoyed impressive kitchens.

Though large, the Bradstreets' kitchen grew crowded. An odd dance played out as the caterer cooked and servers squeezed among us to offer hors d'oeuvres and wine, while we guests clogged the flow like rush-hour traffic on Route 128, and I noticed the catering crew was all Latino, while we were all Caucasian.

Then Matt and Carol Baker made an entrance, and it was an entrance. They stepped into the bright new kitchen exuding youthful vigor and wealth, like JFK and Jackie O into the White House. Nikki asked Carol for her coat and marveled aloud at the figure cut by the form-fitting, if conservative, ivory-colored dress. "My dear, you are lovely."

She was.

The board meeting at the dining room table was short and not-so-sweet. Thank goodness everyone was hungry, so we only lingered briefly over the bungled BHAG. As expected the deacons placed blame with me, though not overtly because they're masters of the blame game as well as ducking responsibility for failure. Anyway, I missed the BHAG by a mile. Shelly Andersen, our associate minister, and the only woman in the room, chimed in that no one could control the weather. But Caleb Bradstreet, who directed the finance committee, was deep into the spreadsheet. Long, disapproving looks fell my way—as if my personal shortcomings had permitted the snow.

These guys made me want to get out of the minister game, like Jack Corbett, my best friend from seminary. After he escaped the pulpit–or, rather, was tossed from it–Jack founded and sold three or four tech startup companies, becoming a multi-millionaire.

Afraid of what I might say, I asked Shelly to give a prayer to close the meeting. As we left the room, I heard Nikki ask us to bring our chairs into the great room, but I pretended not to hear and went to the kitchen for a large glass of red wine.

The caterer had set up two long tables in the great room, one of the additions from sometime around 1840, and large enough to handle the crowd of twenty-seven: all twelve deacons and wives, me and Nancy, and Shelly. I stood, stooped, and said a brief prayer before we ate.

Carol Baker sat right next to me. I'd never been in such proximity to her. Two bites into dinner, Carol turned to me and said, "So, Reverend–John. Is it okay for me to call you John?" I assured her it was. "Just how tall are you?"

I don't know how many people come with a life question, but that's mine. I looked at her and very straight faced said, "No one's ever asked me that before."

She started to say 'Really?' but then smirked.

"Carol, my altitude is six-feet, eleven-inches. Barefoot. Seven-feet in shoes."

"Amazing," Carol said. "I've never met anyone seven-feet tall."

"Most people have never even seen someone this tall. There are only about three thousand people this tall in the whole world," I told her.

"Wow," she said, "seven-feet in shoes, and your shoes, John, I noticed, they're huge."

Usually height questions and observations of my out-sized self, especially about the size of my ears or nose, hands or feet annoyed me, but I liked Carol and decided to tell her a quirky tale of the too tall.

"Yeah, my feet are oversized. Weirdly, from the age of

seven until the age of seventeen, my shoe size matched my age." She laughed. "No kidding, I was a first grader in men's size seven. Age twelve, size twelve shoe. In high school, I worried my feet might not stop and imagined myself in size forty-eights by now, but my foot stopped at age and size seventeen."

"Size seventeen?" she said and kind of chuckled.

"It's a hassle to find shoes, and they're expensive. Another joy of being extremely tall." I didn't go into it with Carol, but clothes are a pain too. With a 42-inch inseam, you don't just stop by Gap for a pair of khakis. Ever see a shirt with an 18-inch neck and 28 sleeve? Not at Macy's, you didn't. Rather than stylish, I aim for inoffensive. Which is harder than you'd think. When you cover as much visual real estate as I do, a bad jacket blares above the crowd for blocks like a billboard for a used car dealer.

In high school, my mother made most of my clothes, and though she did a respectable job, home-made clothing fed derision in style-conscious Concord High.

Once, in my freshman year of high school, I glued an Izod alligator to a shirt my mom made. It didn't look too good, even to me, but I thought it passable. Then, in the crowded lunch room, one of the jocks confronted me. "That's no Izod," he said, and quick as a finger-snap he snatched the alligator off. "Did you really think that would fool anyone?" And he stuck the alligator up his nose, held the other nostril, and shot it back at me like a booger. The lunch room exploded in laughter, and left me, the tallest person in the building, tallest in town, feeling like a freak.

As he turned away he declared: "The stork is a dork."

And it stuck.

I don't know how many times I heard that phrase in high school. None of it helped my confidence with girls.

Of course, the inconveniences don't end with shoes and clothes. When your height makes you an extreme outlier, a lot of things get difficult. Think about it. Sleeping bags. Tents. Folding myself into folding chairs with knees jutting into the air like playground equipment. Wedging into cars, airplane seats, restaurant booths. Urinals too low. Turnstiles threaten castration. And bending, the backache of constantly bending and stooping.

"Hey, hello, Earth to Reverend Crackstone," Carol Baker said, smiling and drawing me back into the conversation. "I have a question for you, John. You probably played basketball. Would you be willing to give our older daughter some pointers? That girl is just mad for basketball."

Despite what most people think, not all the super-tall play basketball, which gets to the second question of my life. Many times I've wondered, does every short guy get asked if he's a jockey?

"I know it's hard to believe, Carol," I said, "but I never played basketball."

Well, not since my sophomore year of high school when I walked off the court during practice and told Coach Garrett to buzz-off. While little Bob-o Garrett was in mid-scream, I saw him anew. A calm fell over me as I looked down at his red, vein-popping face screaming up at me, and he went silent in my head. Nothing this little monster said or did appealed to me or motivated me, especially his boundless passion for rebounding. I never liked sports and was never good at them. Including basketball, where I had the ever-important, un-coachable talent of being insanely tall. When I was a freshman, this idiot, Bouncing Bob-o Garrett, made me stand up at an all-school assembly and in front of everyone proclaimed that I would be an all-state center by my senior year, perhaps an All American. Kids roared their approval. When I failed to thrive at hoops and quit, some kids hated me. Teachers too radiated resentment, as if I'd squandered some momentous, God-given talent. In my freshman year, when an opponent drove around me for a lay-up, I was booed by my classmates and teased in the halls the next day. Opponents loved the challenge of pounding on me and shooting over me as if I were Jabbar or Shaq. And I just didn't care. A lot of kids are not interested in sports, but if you're crazy tall, you'd better be. If you possess huge intellectual potential and pass on being a physicist, architect, or microbiologist to make a boat-load of money on Wall Street or in commercial real estate, no one minds. Have perfect pitch, but decide to attend law school? No big deal. But our society loathes wasted athletic potential.

I wondered how it would play out for my own basketball-mad boy. Gordon, ten years old, stood tall for his age, but not the way I did. Still, coaches gave him a lot of attention, and Gordon got ticked off when I refused to be an assistant coach. But even if I had the time, I knew nothing of the game.

"I'm sorry I can't help with basketball, Carol," I said. "I don't know the game, despite my height. But I know a retired basketball coach named Bob Garrett, who lives in Woburn. He might help your daughter."

I admit suggesting Bouncing Bob-o Garrett to crush the spirit of their daughter registered on the mean side. I guess I wasn't feeling charitable toward the Bakers. Because of Matt, not Carol. The youngest of my deacons, I'd recruited Matt myself, thinking he'd be my ally. But no. The former quarterback quickly sided with the old guard, joining the finance committee, and he had locked in with the head-waggers during the presentation of my Easter fiasco. It was an all too common experience with these twelve men.

"It must be hard," Carol said, leaning close.

"Humm?" I asked.

"Being so tall. I imagine it must be hard, especially as a minister. Even without standing seven-feet tall, you already live in a fishbowl. Everyone watches you, judges you, and a lot of them, no doubt, look to catch you up in a mistake or hypocritical action."

My eyes went to the tablecloth.

She continued: "Do you feel that way out in the community? A burden of being measured?" I looked at her, and she cocked her head at the thought. "It sounds isolating."

She knew.

"Yes," I whispered. "That might be the hardest part."

For the first time in a very long time, I felt seen. Carol Baker understood me.

* * *

At the end of the Deacons Dinner, Carol and I joined Nikki and the caterers to clear dishes as the staff poured coffee. Part of me didn't want to assist, as if I were "the help," yet "serving" was supposed to be my life's mission. Looking down at the dishes, I remembered the low door but forgot about the antique light fixture hanging above it and ... whack. It went swinging against the wall and spilled a wild circle of light around the room as I rubbed my stinging forehead.

Nancy blurted out, "Another gaffe by the giraffe!"

Yes, it was funny. The first five hundred times you heard it. But I still had to laugh every stinking time; otherwise she appeared mean-spirited, or I came off as a humorless, brooding jerk. Besides, her recurring wisecrack diverted attention, giving me a second to dab an eyebrow for blood or rub a bump at my hairline.

"Another gaffe by the giraffe," one of the women at the table snickered, and they all tittered again.

Well, I thought, it's a little annoying but better than "the stork is a dork."

In the bright lights of the new kitchen—a stark contrast from the moody, colonial-period great room—Carol turned to me. Her eyes flashed alarm. "John, you're bleeding."

Before I could even look for a mirror, she reached up to dab my forehead with a paper towel. "Sit down here," she said, pulling out a chair. "It's not bad, but let me wash it out real quick."

She pulled my head forward as she washed it, turning my eyes toward her breasts, trim waist, and flat stomach. Inches away. I noted her perfume again.

"We've got to stop meeting like this–" she said, and my imagination leaped, and then, "–over accidents and spilled blood. First my knee, and now your head." Carol vanished for a moment, returned with hydrogen peroxide, and put a band-aid on my forehead. Then she laughed.

"What's so funny?" I asked.

"Come and see," she said, and I followed her into the bathroom. There was a bright orange, Snoopy band-aid on my forehead.

"Good color choice," I said, smiling.

Carol bent to put the hydrogen peroxide under the sink.

There was something kind of sexy about being in a bathroom with a woman other than your wife.

"Hey, that orange reminds me," I said. "Did you guys plant your giant pumpkin seeds yet?"

"I found some seeds in Matt's suit coat before I dropped it at the dry cleaner," she said. "Were those from you? I thought they were a snack. I almost ate them!"

"I'm glad you didn't," I said. "I gave them to Matt because I thought you and your girls would enjoy growing them. Following the Old Farmer's Almanac, I planted mine on Easter Sunday, inside, and I'll move them outside in mid-May. I've got extra supplies if you want."

"Yeah. Let's do it," she said.

Chapter Two

Planting the Seeds

The next morning–after the kids hoofed to school, Matt headed off to the law office, and Nancy plugged away at the church preschool and daycare–I ducked under the trees between our neighboring yards, pushing a red wheelbarrow of supplies. When I arrived at Carol's back door, reaching out to knock flashed a sense of risk, of danger.

Carol opened the door, wearing a ratty red sweatshirt and tight jeans, hair pulled back in a blonde ponytail, with little or no makeup. She looked spectacular. Somehow I'd forgotten her beautiful blue eyes and saw them as if for the first time. She held an off-white coffee mug that looked like it was chipped out of a rock.

"Reverend Crackstone! Come in, come in," she said, and I wondered why she used my title instead of my first name. To keep me in check? I imagined her in high school or college, using Doctor or Professor to keep the relationships professional with men. "How about a cup of coffee?"

I pointed to the crude mug in her hands, "Do I have to drink it out of a rock?"

She laughed and held up her mug, "Summer camp project. And you should see the ashtray, almost enough to make you take up smoking."

We had a cup of coffee at her kitchen table, and yes, the kitchen was well-appointed with weapons-grade appliances.

"What's this?" she asked, looking at the bracelet on my right wrist. "I never noticed this before."

"Oh, it's new. Nancy got it for me. It was an Easter gift."

"Very cool," she said, leaning in for a closer look.

"It's kind of growing on me. I wasn't sure about it at first, never been much for jewelry."

"It's almost not jewelry so much as a small piece of art. Or like a symbol of something bigger, some larger connection to other religions or spirituality." She shook her head. "Listen to me, I'm reading so much into it. Sorry. I think it's really cool, whether it has any special meaning or not."

Before I could say the bracelet did have special meaning, and that Nancy had designed it making deliberate choices, Carol was on her feet and pouring us more coffee. She changed the subject and asked how I got started in pumpkin-growing, and I told her about the Topsfield Fair the previous fall where we saw the giant pumpkin weigh-in and ordered the seeds.

"The winner tipped the scales at about 2,000 pounds and set a new world record. New England usually produces the world's largest pumpkins," I added, "something to do with low pH in the soil and abundant water."

The winner also had taken home about $35,000, between prize money and selling seeds, but for some reason, as I told Carol about the fair, I withheld mention of the money.

* * *

Back in March, a nearly weightless UPS delivery about the size of a shoe box had arrived at my door. I set it aside for the kids to open when they got home from school. Gordon stabbed a knife into the box and slashed the tape.

Inside, packed in Styrofoam peanuts like fine china, was a little brown bag of one hundred seeds. I took the knife from Gordon and split a seed open to show my kids the pale pupa in the middle and told them about how the embryo grew into giant pumpkins, a miracle of nature. (Though during the summer, I would frequently reflect on my spontaneous seed splitting and wonder if I'd killed a world-record prospect.)

I counted out twenty-four seeds and put them in a plastic sandwich bag for the Bakers. Did I intend to get close to Matt? To Carol? Perhaps my own fear of approaching Carol and risking my marriage explained why I watched for Matt to come home. Or was it fear of rejection? Whatever the reason, when his Jeep Grand Cherokee splashed into the driveway, I crossed the backyard boundary to offer my attorney neighbor, my deacon, my almost-friend a plastic sandwich bag of giant pumpkin seeds. Like a six-foot two-inch Swiss Army knife, Matt Baker unfolded from the seat in a well-tailored suit. So professional and polished looking that it left me–in my endless khaki pants, and baggy brown sweater–a gangly stick figure.

"Hello, John, what's up?" he said.

Unsure if this was one of the tired jokes about my height (how's the weather up there?) or merely a figure of speech, I let it lie. I extended the bag, suddenly feeling like a child holding out the clay coffee mug made at summer camp. "Pumpkin seeds. For giant pumpkins."

I folded my arms over my chest, pausing to let him ascertain the gift and to let me reclaim the authoritative resonance of my minister's timbre. "Last fall, we saw the giant pumpkin competition at the Topsfield Fair. Pumpkins as big as a bathtub." I let the elongated image settle over the lawyer, wishing I'd landed on something more spherical. I told him we ordered seeds and thought his kids might enjoy growing some too. I scanned the property for a glimpse of Carol. I realized the situation begged a mother's enthusiasm more than a father's return-from-office exhaustion. Then I began to explain. "You plant them in early-to-mid-April, indoors—"

"Pumpkin seeds, huh?" Matt interrupted, peering through the plastic bag as if he were just beginning to understand what was inside, and jostling the seeds.

"—and then move them outdoors mid-May," I continued.

"Yeah, the girls'll love it," Matt said, grinning. "Thanks, John."

I lingered an awkward moment, unsure what to say. The beginnings and ends of conversations often fumbled ahead for me. Had I been dismissed by Matt? My father—Reverend William Crackstone—was never dismissed. Nor did he ever seem at a loss for words. He quickly defined the lay of the land in conversations and determined the end of discussions. For a long time, I hoped this knack came with age and practice; though, at forty-eight, I knew better.

So I took up where I'd left off. "Okay then, just plant the seeds in early-April, inside. And move them outdoors in mid-May."

"Early-April in. Mid-May out. Got it, Reverend," Matt delivered with a grin and stuffed the bag in his suit-coat pocket.

The title Reverend sounded like a knock, though I registered minimal reaction. Matt and I had soft-shoed the dance of reverend-deacon-neighbor for several years.

* * *

Whatever had held me in check back in March when I handed Matt the bag of seeds, I now stood in Carol's kitchen with a warm coffee mug in my hands. "Ready to plant some seeds?" I asked.

"Let's do it," she said.

And so we did.

It was fun to work next to Carol. At one point, she tossed her gloves aside. "Sometimes, I love to get my hands dirty," she said. "My girls, not so much. They're still in the pink tutu stage. Except for basketball in a clean gymnasium."

I laughed and thought of my daughter, Megan. I think she'd be willing to sink her hands in the soil. Though I hadn't given her or Gordon much chance yet.

"For that matter," Carol continued, "I can't see Matt digging in the garden or yard either. He avoids it."

"Well, you have beautiful landscaping," I said. "We're not much for gardening or yard work."

"My flowers and landscaping might be beautiful, but my hands?" She held them up for me to examine. "Not so much, right?"

I just laughed, but to be honest, her hands looked like an old farmer's—dirty, wrinkled, split, and veiny. Yet, they attracted me.

When we finished, she had filled a shoe box for each daughter with a dozen Dixie cups. Each one loaded with potting soil and one seed. Carol didn't need a grow-lamp with sunlight from a south-facing bay window, and her girls could keep an eye on the sprouts and learn to water them just a little each day.

Carol held up a planted Dixie cup in a toast. "To these little wonders which will produce giant pumpkins."

I took one up, and we tapped our paper cups together like wine glasses. "To little wonders," I said, thinking more of her than the pumpkin seeds.

Chapter Three

Into the Light

As soon as the infant plants emerged from the black potting soil, I knew the Lord had blessed me with tremendous gourds. A mini-miracle right there in the musty parsonage cellar. The cellar was practically a crawlspace for me. I hadn't been able to stand erect down there since I was eleven, the year I reached six feet. And I normally avoided going down there. Yet during April, like a chain smoker sneaking out for another nicotine fix at the door of an office building, I slipped down six times a day to check on my infant pumpkin plants. And a remarkable thing happened when I did. Down there, away from my father's large, walnut desk, the weight of the job eased, another miracle.

For the first time, I understood fanatical orchid growers–one of whom was a prominent member of my congregation–paying thousands for a single bulb, building greenhouses, spending hundreds of hours to grow and tend fragile flowers.

There I was, bent under the grow lamp, breathing through my mouth, dripping water around each pale green stem, my kids hovering at my elbows. "Get back. Get back," I ordered.

"Can I do one?" Gordon asked.

"Me too," Megan chimed in.

"No. You'd kill them with too much water," I warned.

From across the cellar came an assertive crack of wet pants. Nancy, doing laundry, had pulled jeans from the washer and gave them a hard shake before thumping them into the drum of the dryer. She looked my way but said nothing.

"Soon you can water them," I said. "But let's give them time to grow. Okay, kids?"

Another snap of pants before Nancy sent the kids upstairs to wash for dinner.

I didn't like what was coming. Nancy dropped the laundry basket heaped with clean clothes at my feet. For a second I thought about how over the last few years she no longer folded my laundry or balled-up my socks, just piled them on the bed for me.

She spoke in a harsh whisper: "What's with you, John? We bought those seeds for the kids, and now you bully them aside like–like a toy train collector who won't let his kids touch a caboose. Loosen up."

"I'm trying to assure a good experience by getting the seedlings to a place where the kids can help." The excuse sounded lame even as I uttered it. "Besides, a lot of money is at stake. First prize won over thirty thousand dollars last year."

"Oh, John ..." Nancy rolled her eyes and then rejoined with her one-two-three points argument, ingrained from high school debate training. "First of all, you're a minister, not a gardener. Second, we'll survive without the thirty thousand dollars. Third, there's a relationship with your kids at stake."

"You exaggerate."

"Think about it, John. How many chances do you get to connect with them? I mean *really* connect?"

Point made. And she read the recognition in my eyes.

"This is a chance for you. Connect, honey." She picked up the laundry basket. "Don't blow it."

She bumped me with the basket as she passed. I believed it deliberate but let it go without a word and yielded, my shoulder blades thumping an asbestos-wrapped steam pipe.

Nancy made sense. Nonetheless those seedlings whispered to me, and I could not help but listen.

* * *

I was about to come in the back door after work when I heard a woman holler. "Hey, John!" I turned and saw Carol waving from our mutual property line. "Our pumpkin seedlings are up."

"Well, ours are about a week ahead of yours," I said. "Practically growing pumpkins already."

"This I've got to see," she said, stomping across our backyard. She wore black tights and a flannel shirt, like a Vermont yoga instructor. Even her makeup was perfect. It didn't matter if she was working in her garden, going to the gym, or going to dinner.

"Just a minute," I said. "I'll open the bulkhead."

Seeing Carol called to mind a Saturday in the previous summer. With the kids off to sleep-over camp, I'd invited Nancy to go out to a special breakfast, hoping to connect with her. But she wore a baggy T-shirt and baggy jeans, no makeup like she'd just rolled out of bed. Then acted meh about the outing. When she got home, Nancy put on her makeup to go out to the grocery.

I opened the metal bulkhead doors and held out my hand to help Carol Baker down the steep steps. We gripped each other just above the wrist, hers thin and muscular. That wonderful smell I'd noticed when I helped her up on Easter morning and at the Deacons Dinner wafted over me. Nothing more than a hand and a subtle smell, but the instant registered as dangerous, exciting, even illicit. She let go of my forearm when her feet hit the floor, and I released her arm.

"Like that bracelet," she said, tapping my wrist. Then her eyes went past me. "Look at this setup," she said of the workbench with grow lamps. "You are more than a casual botanist, Reverend."

After surveying the layout and the progress of my seedlings, she nudged me with an elbow and a shoulder. "So were you, like, one of those underground pot growers in college?"

"No, no, nooo."

"I think you were." And her index finger pecked me in the chest.

"No, really, I've never even smoked pot." Which was true.

"Okay, Preacher's Kid." She let out a little snort. "Whatever you say ..."

I just laughed.

Carol asked about the soil-filled cups without seedlings. Eleven of the seventy-five had failed, which put me a tad better than the eighty-percent germination rate for finicky giant pumpkin seeds. Carol sprouted twenty of her twenty-four seeds, which was also right on target.

"Yours are a week ahead and taller than mine, but we will catch up, John. We will. You're not always going to be the tallest, you know."

When we left, she walked up the stairs right in front of me, her shapely butt in the tights visible from below. Outside, she asked where I planned to put the pumpkin patch. I hesitated to show her because it was in the back corner of the lot near their property, where there was plenty of sun and I could see her tend and nurse her flowers. Carol decided to put her pumpkins just across the way where, she said, I could keep an eye on hers, and she could keep an eye on mine.

"Speaking of that," she said, "want to see our seedlings?"

I wanted to say yes. But I glanced toward home and noticed Nancy watching out the window, and I demurred.

Why? What did I fear? Did I think something could happen with this alluring, gorgeous woman to unravel my life like what happened to my friend Jack?

* * *

Jack Corbett, as I mentioned, was my best friend at seminary.

The story of what happened to him unfolded as a classic tale of our times. Like me, Jack got married at the end of seminary to a lovely Christian girl and landed a job as an assistant minister in a West Texas town. As soon as they arrived, his wife focused on her career, expecting him to focus on his. Meanwhile, as Jack struggled to grasp the football-mad parishioners, he met another woman through the church. She'd been uprooted from California by her husband, a minor but ambitious oil executive. And she didn't understand the West Texas culture any better than Jack did. Also like Jack, she felt set aside by the spouse.

Long story short, they had an affair. It lasted less than six months, but when Jack's wife found out, she packed her bags to move back to Rhode Island and told a deacon on her way out the door. It didn't matter that the affair had ended. The church deacons demanded Jack's resignation. The whole process from job start to getting sacked took about eighteen months, and it shook Jack's faith in God and man.

Once booted, Jack headed for Dallas. He took a job in sales for a software company, got interested in business and technology, and went to the University of Texas Business

School in Austin for a tech–centric MBA. You'd never guess he'd been a minister, and he avoided sharing that part of his life story.

After business school, Jack clawed his way up at Ernst & Young in Dallas, eventually becoming a partner. Solving all of these problems in tech companies was like post–doc work. He learned how to run a company. Then one day he realized that, despite making great money (he once let it slip that he'd socked away over a million before he turned forty), he was grinding seventy– and eighty–hour weeks and traveling twenty days a month. In an effort to keep him on board, Ernst & Young had provided him with a well–furnished apartment in a Dallas high–rise and had given him a house–keeping and shopping service to stock his refrigerator and pantry. But the arrangement had all the charm of the hotel rooms where he spent most of his weeks and felt nothing like a real home.

So eventually Jack quit and decided to start his own company in Austin. First a web hosting and web development firm which he sold for a bundle. Then he launched a second business in e–commerce software and a Customer Relationship Management system, and he sold that company too–made a killing. Always at the front edge of the next trend, Jack Corbett became Capitalism personified.

* * *

Recalling all that in my backyard with my lovely neighbor an arm's length away and my wife at the window, I told myself my imagined (but potential?) affair with Carol Baker would vault over Jack's pitfalls. Somehow. Miraculously, we could achieve passion and blissful happiness, without the misery of splintered marriages and shattered children.

And through all the noise in my head, those young pumpkin plants whispered to me, whispered something of an ancient truth, an incantation, one that I had not yet learned to interpret.

* * *

The second Saturday in May was rototiller day. I went to Concord Hardware and rented a red rototiller with tractor tires and the name "Sodbuster" painted across the front. I felt like a real farmer. With my trusty Sodbuster, I applied the chopping blades of the rototiller to hacking the mix of weeds and grass in my backyard.

My front yard flowed like a weedless rug of turf, but not the back. My deacons allocated funds for Chemlawn treatment on the front yard only, which, according to the finance committee, was pretty common in Concord. As with our white houses and black shutters, we Concordites Disneyed up our front yards. Anyway, the rototiller jumped and jerked like a mechanical insect, jarring me to the bone as it churned up hunks of sod, gnawing a forty-foot by twenty-foot area. Despite the strain on my bent back, the process was oddly, deeply pleasant. I stopped to rake out hunks of grass and weeds. Then, to prime the soil, I mixed ten 40-pound bags of humus (aged turkey crap) into the pumpkin patch. Over and over, I tilled the soil into a grit as fine as ground coffee. And that Sodbuster, with handles designed for someone five-foot-eight, gave me a hell of a backache which lasted three days. But it was worth it. The smell of soil filled me, opened me. It opened in me a sensation I'd never known and can't easily express, something hard and strong, something antediluvian. Yes, antediluvian. Another whisper of the ancient.

When I finished, a competitive edge flared, tempting me to race the rototiller back to the hardware store. But I took it to the Bakers for Matt to use. Instead of my elbow jerking method, Matt barely touched the thing, letting it bounce a couple of courses over a corner of his manicured lawn and went back inside. Then Carol came out and wrangled the machine over the patch. It didn't appear a fair fight from the way it shook her small frame, blonde ponytail flopping in all directions. But she locked on with an elbows-out, monkey-like grip. She hacked those clumps into smaller clumps until the thing ran out of gas. Then I heard her calling Matt. I kept out of sight. Next thing I knew, Matt pulled it backward into our yard and knocked at the back door. After we manhandled the rototiller into my station wagon, Matt offered thirty bucks to help pay for the rental. I wanted to refuse, but he had the extra cushion, so I accepted. And it neatly covered the half-day rental.

The next day was a glorious Sunday, and it held all the promise of spring. After church services, I couldn't wait to get home and transplant my pumpkin seedlings. I did the usual good-byes, shaking hands with congregants and smiling, although I'm sure I was a bit abrupt with some of those who hang around to ramble on and on every week. Rather than shoo the pigeons off the steps, I took another tact.

"If you'll excuse me a moment ..." I said, leaving Shelly Andersen to perform the grip-and-grin with the faithful. I reentered the sanctuary, waving to and ducking a couple of choir members who hoped to hail me for an opinion, and slipped out a side door. I hustled home, changed into work clothes in record time, and headed for the cellar.

Emerging from the bulkhead door with the baby plants evoked a pure thrill of birth. I raised the pumpkin plants up high as if an offering to the warm sun. Then as I lowered them, it dawned on me that the tray of seedlings also carried the portent of a cash register drawer, a glimmer of thirty-five grand.

Briefly I imagined buying a BMW or Lexus like my deacons drove. It would have to be a used one, but it would still be the best car I ever owned, and no one needed to know I bought it used. My old Ford was an embarrassment.

Then my daydream morphed–took root if you will–what if the prize money was just a beginning? I had found a website that sold giant pumpkin seeds–from a grower in Oregon. He charged ten bucks per seed! Now I was a rookie, but you didn't have to be too smart to see if I won the Topsfield Fair Great Pumpkin weigh in, and especially if I could set a new world record, I could easily launch a company. Think about it. Each giant pumpkin carried hundreds of seeds. The world record holder's family of giants would demand a premium price. Even at the Oregonian's rate of $10 per seed, one giant could produce 500 to 1,000 seeds, or $10,000. If I had twenty giants–they might produce $200,000. And if I had forty? Then I'd cash out big time, putting me right there with the affluent crowd of Concord, right with my deacons–probably above Matt Baker. A giddy laugh bubbled up, and I told myself: John Crackstone, it would take work, full-time work no doubt, but the rewards gleamed–a beautiful new house, two nice cars, college funds. First things first, I told myself, *Grow pumpkins, ones that will rank among the world's greatest. Ones that will put me among the world's greatest growers.*

Chapter Four

A Little Black Magic

Gordon and Megan, once excited about the pumpkin project, had surrendered interest. After my cellar skewering from Nancy, I set up the kids with some pumpkin plants of their own, but I just couldn't risk the plants fully to my kids and helped them. Despite Nancy's solid, three-pointed argument, I mostly restricted Gordon and Megan to hands-off observation.

The kids watched me place the fragile seedlings in the ground, maintaining a distance just beyond the sweep of my mitts as if I might swat them. I scooped out a small hole in the moist, rich mixture of humus and topsoil, supported the soil around each seedling with a finger on each side—the way prongs in a ring support a diamond—and turned over the small cups. On many of them you could see the white roots, thin as a thread and trying to expand beyond the cup. A very close look revealed tiny, hair-like roots, finer than a human hair, extending beyond the obvious ones. I placed each seedling into its hole just so, then gently tamped the soil down with two fingers, and allowed my kids to dribble a touch more water around each plant. After I had most of the seedlings in the ground, we heard the neighbor's back door slam.

"We're planting our pumpkins," Gordon called to Matt, Carol, and their girls. Carol, still tan from their spring break vacation to Florida and working outside, looked sporty in sweatpants and a yellow, cap-sleeve T-shirt.

"Us too," said one of their girls.

"Ours'll be bigger," Matt boasted in a teasing voice. Or was he serious?

I couldn't resist. "Wanna bet?"

Matt and Carol laughed.

My primitive spirit spoke: "A friendly wager," which I admit came out a little too forcefully, and I noted Carol's ample lips go horizontal.

"Okay, Reverend," the one-time quarterback replied.

"How much, Deacon?" I sensed the blood rising in my face, warming my ears.

"Fifty bucks?" Matt said. Carol whispered something. Probably told Matt to stop, saying I couldn't afford to lose that much money.

But I wasn't going to lose.

"Make it a hundred," my voice spiced with playground bravado.

"You sure?" Matt said.

"Two hundred then," I said. I could just hear Nancy telling me to cool my jets and get a grip. But she was grocery shopping.

"Hold on, you two," Carol said. She and Matt took in the faces of the children.

I noted anxiety in the kids' eyes, but that antediluvian spur wouldn't let me laugh it off or sling a comforting arm around my kids' shoulders.

"A hundred then. Until the Topsfield Fair in October?" Matt stated, establishing rules, ever the attorney. He'd probably want to draw it up and have it signed before a notary.

"You're on, Deak." I'd never shortened "deacon" to "deak" before, but I liked the sound of it. Liked the click off the back of my tongue. Also liked the way deak evoked: geek, meek, weak, freak. Did I detect irritation around Matt's mouth? If so, good. The man had had too much come too easily as it was. A little needling was not such a bad thing in one's life.

To be honest, I was at once repulsed by and refreshed by my behavior. Seldom had I tossed off ecclesiastical trappings and let my gut emotions bubble up unchecked. Reared in the shadow of my esteemed father (a preacher's kid—a PK), I'd stymied boyhood enthusiasms, adventures, and yearnings under Concord's watchful eyes. As a fair-skinned boy, quick to blush, who towered first over classmates and then over everyone in town, I felt so conspicuous that I believed any wrongdoing, even the thought of wrongdoing, would be read on my face like a billboard. Did I recognize the adolescence in my brassy tone with Matt? You bet. But it felt good. Cheeky. Good God, John Crackstone, acting cheeky. Clang the bell! Perhaps the Lord wanted to teach me something about myself, or my neighbor, or essential humanity.

Whatever it was, I resolved to leave the channel open.

I looked from Matt to the blue eyes of Carol and down to her breasts, noting her nipples excited by the confrontation beneath the onionskin of congeniality.

Or perhaps it was just the cool spring breeze.

* * *

Back to the pumpkins. Sixty-four seedlings went into the soil that day. Spread out across the plot of turned earth, they looked so vulnerable. Later that night, leaving them to go to bed felt like abandoning newborn infants to fend for themselves out in the yard. Nightmares of skunks, rabbits, squirrels, groundhogs, goats, sheep, dogs, cats, kids—a whole parade of pestilence—eating, uprooting, and squashing my precious little pumpkin prospects bedeviled my rest. And the next morning, there were fifty-three. No kidding. Eleven of my seedlings vanished overnight. All from one corner. The attacker left hardly a trace. Were those small footprints or not? Perhaps a rabbit or some small rodent. Perhaps my neighbor? No, Matt wouldn't stoop so low. Right?

For longer than was reasonable, for longer than I can explain, I mourned those eleven plants. (I resisted calculating the cost (in the thousands) if they had produced giants full of precious seeds.) I drank a large mug of coffee as I stood over their little absent spots in the rows. I'll admit I even said a prayer for them, which, when you take into account my upbringing in the church where one heard frequent suggestions to pray for and about everything, it was not so very crazy. (I mean, I was asked to pray for a hang-nail cure more than once.)

Without hesitation—and ironically, forgetting to call and cancel my first morning meeting with a group of gardeners in the congregation who wanted me to review and approve their exterior beautification plan for the church with summer flowers—I raced to the garden center to buy rabbit fencing to put around the pumpkin patch. When I returned, Nancy informed me the gardeners had stopped by to see if I'd forgotten, so she sat in on the meeting for me. And she wasn't happy about it. Monday was her cherished day off.

Nancy had given up teaching elementary school when we had kids and had taken on the part-time, low-paying task of co-managing the church's daycare/preschool operation. I apologized and thanked her without much compunction or conviction. Although I did feel a little silly for letting my concern over the infant pumpkin plants blind me from checking my calendar. Given my desire to get the fence set up right away, I hustled out after my half-hearted apology to Nancy and hammered the metal stakes into the ground and hung the fence.

What if it was birds? I thought. Did I need to combat air-borne attacks? I scanned the trees. Were they watching me?

Even after the fence, I lost a few young pumpkin plants for reasons I didn't understand. Could it be birds? Moles? Mice? I'd read that these hybrid pumpkin plants are more fragile than traditional seeds. A farmer's fate. Regardless, I still had plenty of little friends to go forward. And they did. Boy, did they take off! The leaves, once tiny as the end of pencil erasers in my cellar, exploded into paddles nearly the size of my palms–palms the size of a lunch plate–and those leaves grew to the size of a car's wheel. Wee stems became vines, and they stretched out in every direction, growing longer and thicker by the hour. Soon small buds formed, tiny things at first, which quickly grew and blossomed into big, beautiful yellow–orange flowers. And at their bases, the first sign of true pumpkins, little orbs smaller than ping-pong balls.

Long before the blossoms, I had read the sparse but seminal works on the succor of giant pumpkins and scoured the Internet for tips. In addition, I plowed through volumes from renowned horticulturists, checking most of these books out from the beautiful red-brick Concord Library near home. These librarians knew me and thought they knew my tastes, so I surprised them, passing by the busts of local eminent writers Alcott, Emerson, and Thoreau, with one horticultural book after another. I took notes on gardening tips and advice–some of it bordering on the black arts–filtering it through my soulful simpatico with the pumpkins and weaving together my own wisdom, forming a little alchemy, a vegetable voodoo. Slowly I forged a plan for the pumpkins. The first order of business: water. Water above all, water first and last, was the secret to giant pumpkins. Once the vines reach a young–adult size, it was almost impossible to over–water a giant pumpkin. Yet standing water will kill them with root rot or mold.

Chlorine, the carcinogen we drink down from our earliest days, could harm the pumpkins, so I bought a ceramic filter to remove it from the outdoor spigot.

Beyond a hefty flow of H_2O (moderately soaking at mid–morning and mid–afternoon, heavily soaking in the evening), I fed them a special fertilizer, a secret potion of my own design, and poured it over my plants at noon each day. This concoction combined the best of the published secrets as well as a twist or two of my own. My growth potion consisted of milk, aged cow dung, peeled banana, eggs (with shell), a scoop of sugar, two teaspoons of fish food, and clippings of human hair. Into the food processor these items went to form a creamy, verdant–colored soup which had a fecund smell both sweet and sour, an odor that more than once nearly drew my lips to the edge for a taste.

* * *

The only item in my special potion that caused consternation was procuring human hair. I imagined a white–collar posse calling me a witch and running me out of town. I mean it. This is New England after all. The Salem Witch Trials were a mere 325 years ago. So I searched out hair styling shops, avoiding Concord Center, until I found "Curl Up and Dye" on a side–street in West Concord, perhaps the most middle–class street in the whole town. When I went inside, it was done up like a vintage men's barbershop, including old, red–vinyl barber chairs, post–war era pin–up girl posters, Butch Wax promotions, a black–and–white 1950s TV against the wall, and a spinning barber's pole. It was just like places my old man took me when I was a little kid. (They kept *Playboy* hidden under the TV, or so the rumor went; I never got to check.)

But the twenty–something girl who ran Curl Up and Dye was hardly vintage. First were her tattoos: Celtic symbols and flowers, and a bit of frayed rope with a feather tattooed around one skinny arm. (Why not a real rope and a real feather? I don't know.) She also wore an eyebrow ring, silver stud in her tongue, and short spiky hair, which didn't jibe with the styles of Concord, so she was her own worst advertising as far as I could tell. This girl you'd expect to see in Davis Square. Hardly a Concord preppy. When I said hello, she had a semi-sexual way of facing down and then turning her dark eyes up with a slight tilt of her head. At just over five-feet tall, I'm sure she wondered how she'd reach the top of my head. But I wasn't there for a cut.

When I requested she set aside a bag of hair for me at the end of the day when she swept up, she took it in with the aplomb of a baker asked for day-old bread. She only asked how much and how often. I wasn't sure myself, so I said a grocery bag full twice a week. Color and texture didn't matter. I didn't know her. She didn't know me. And neither of us wanted that to change.

I noticed how this little spit of a girl stared up, up, up at me and at my hair and agreed to put a bag of hair out for me. A part of me worried I had intimidated her with my size, but I got what I wanted, so I didn't let myself care. At times my size was an asset.

"How 'bout I give you a bag now?" she said.

"Sure, great, kid." Did I sound like Humphrey Bogart in *The Big Sleep*?

She brought me a plastic Stop-n-Shop bag full of hair clippings, practically weightless. I took it, and for some reason I thought of my father. I couldn't picture him in this position—no way, impossible. So I slinked out of Curl Up and Dye hunched like some sort of spy. A very, very tall and conspicuous spy.

* * *

Why did I think of my father when I clutched the bag and slinked out of Curl Up and Dye? As a PK, you feel watched by the community, by the congregation, by your father, like I said. But my father wasn't just any old minister, and my family history in New England wasn't just any old history.

Dad not only guided his flock through this desert of a historic, prosperous town for forty years, he also held the title of President of The American Association of Congregationalist Churches for twenty years, and he swore in four state governors, like a modern-day Cotton Mather. He was no less skillful at navigating political minefields as a community leader. He was made for it. Brilliant, ambitious, distinguished, savvy; tall (six-feet, four-inches) and handsome, with powerful timbre and a tremendous mane of white hair; Ivy League educated; aristocratic in his carriage; determination of a bull, yet a gentleman. At home, he could be a colossal jerk. (Greatness carries side effects.) Mostly I was awed by him, as I mentioned. True when I was a kid, of course, but even more now with my experience facing the demands of the job.

My sister Susan knew the PK pressure too. Enough that after college, she ran from view and settled in Denver, where she still lives with her husband and three kids. She avoids Concord, and since my parents moved to Arizona, we hardly ever see Susan.

Adding to my father's considerable shadow, stretched the long history of Crackstones in America. We Crackstones sailed over on the Mayflower–literally–and we've been in New England ever since. My namesake John Crackstone was on the Mayflower with his son, also named John Crackstone. The elder died the first winter of 1621; his son died six years later. That might have been the end of the American Crackstones, but my direct-line, multi-great-grandfather William Crackstone (younger brother to the elder John) landed in Salem, Massachusetts in 1625. Because of our link to the brother and not a direct descendent, my father was snubbed by the General Society of Mayflower Descendants (GSMD)–also known to some on the South Shore as the Pompous Asses Club. Anyway, he was a man–of–action, old William Crackstone of the seventeenth century, and he helped settle Beverly, Massachusetts, just across Salem Harbor, in 1626, and died at the age of eighty–two. You can still see his gray slate headstone in the old cemetery behind the police station in Beverly. It was after this man–of–action, this William, that my father was named.

Our ancestry connects to The Commonwealth beyond the curious name Crackstone. We are also related to Richard Mather, who founded New England Congregationalism, which was carried on by his son Increase Mather. (Yes, Increase was his real name.) Increase's son Reverend Cotton Mather took a hard right turn, a Puritan turn, and became a driving force for evil in the Salem Witch Trials, a topic we Crackstones seldom bring up at parties.

This line, this weight of history, burdens me, haunts me. So you might imagine the intimidation of family, of filling the shoes left by my father and forefathers. Even though my size–seventeen feet are considerably larger.

Speaking of shoes, when I first arrived back in Concord as the Senior Minister, I thought Dad's success might be tied to his sartorial choices. First, I ordered Dad's shoes, wingtips in black and cordovan. (Mine were special–order, of course.) With the thick leather rim around the sole, my size–seventeens looked like bumper cars. Like full–sized bumper cars. But I wore them, and they were well–made, which meant I wore them for years, clomping around town like a clown.

Next, I splurged on new suits from my father's tailor in Allston, across the river from Harvard. The tailor was a small Jewish man from Poland. I ordered a set of conservative, year-round wool suits: one black, two gray (one light, one dark), one navy blue, one brown, and one a tweedy green.

The tailor kept saying, "Fifty years, and 'dis is the longest suits I ever made. The longest!"

Shoes, suits, I was all set to be a senior minister in Concord.

* * *

And with my bag of human hair, I was all set to grow the world's largest pumpkins.

Chapter Five

Meeting Otto and Shelly

The second time I stopped to pick up a bag of hair for my special fertilizer–under the cover of spring dusk–I slid up to the side door and bent down for the white-plastic grocery bag. Just as I grasped the bag, I heard: "I could fix that for you."

I about leaped out of my ribs. It was the girl.

"What?"

"Your hair. You know, it doesn't have to look like that."

"What's wrong with it?" I asked, knowing perfectly well what most of the world would say, but curious what this girl thought. It also gave me a second to regain my mental footing and rise to my full height over her.

"Well, I don't know what you do for a living, and that's where I start with most of my clients who want a hair consultation."

A hair consultation? This was a new concept to me. I imagined what this punk-rock pretender in the land of yuppies would suggest. "I'm sure your image could be improved with an appropriate cut," she said. "Who cuts your hair now?"

I didn't have the courage to admit that Nancy cut my hair and had for over twenty years. Before her it was my mother or my sister. I hadn't been to a barber, let alone a hair stylist, since eighth grade. This is a little weird to admit, but for the first batch of special fertilizer I made in my kitchen, I made a witchdoctor's decision to use my own hair. Nancy had just given me a cut the day before, and I'd fished the plastic bag of clippings from the trash. So more of me lived in those pumpkins than my energy, effort, and passion—my size was, in a small way, part of them. My DNA lived in them. And after the initial first mix, I added a little snip of my own hair to every batch. To add yet more of myself to the potion, I pondered adding my kids' hair clippings, but that would be too much. It would make me a true shaman of some sort to add my progeny to the concoction. No, I couldn't. Besides, Nancy would kill me. But maybe if this girl cut their hair ...

"Thanks for the hair advice," I said, bending close to her. She was a puny little thing. Cute in a way. "But I came to pick up some hair, not to have mine critiqued or styled. I know it ain't pretty, but it serves a purpose." I didn't want to intimidate her, just end the conversation and maintain some professional distance.

"Whatever. It's your hair, man. I just had a few ideas."

"Not interested in a Mohawk." I smiled at her.

"Hadn't thought of that," she said with a grin, "but it could be pretty cool. If you're a weathervane."

Clever kid, I thought.

She held out her hand. "I'm JoAnn Naurotto. People call me Otto."

My instinct was to manufacture a name for myself. I didn't need another woman in my life and wanted to limit this interaction to picking up a white plastic bag a couple of times a week—but I couldn't think fast enough and took up her little paw.

"I'm John."

"What's your last name, John?"

I didn't want to say, didn't want to be rude, didn't want to lie: "Crackstone."

"Crackstone? What an awesome name, Crackstone. Pleasure to meet you, formally, John Crackstone."

"Thanks, Otto. And thanks for the hair," I said over my shoulder as I turned away. But it vexed me a bit, wondering what she had in mind for my hair. She's a curious creature, I thought.

Although my curly, sometimes wacky hair gets attention, perhaps because it can be changed or sculpted, at my height with a Mohawk, I'd end up on the front page of *The New York Times*.

* * *

Otto, JoAnn Naurotto, made another woman I had to deal with in my life. Women surrounded me. My wife Nancy, daughter Megan, the hot-mamma-next-door Carol Baker, and Shelly Andersen, our Associate Minister.

I haven't said much about Shelly.

I remember the day I met her. She was the last of four candidates for Associate Minister I interviewed. Oh, yes, this followed the sudden and joyful day in November when Daniel Mutan—my father's Associate Minister—took his Harvard Divinity sheepskin and decamped to Somewheresville, Virginia. His exodus lifted a gorilla off my back after two years of his passive-aggressive undermining, which made for a wonderful Thanksgiving. Anyway, after dear Dan departed, I posted the job and received more than three dozen resumes to sift through after Christmas.

Shelly's leaped out of the pile. After teaching English and religion at a Catholic high school in Milwaukee, Wisconsin for a decade, she started seminary at Yale in her thirties. She was raised by lapsed Catholics—so lapsed they became what Shelly called "accidental Congregationalists" or "Congregationalists of convenience" because that church was down the street. Shelly rediscovered her Catholic heritage as an undergraduate studying abroad in France. Awed by ceremony and ritual in an old cathedral, she experienced a dramatic conversion. But in the Catholic church, all paths to leadership for women ended at teacher or nun, so Shelly turned back to the Congregationalists–deliberately this time–and we were the beneficiaries.

Another candidate I interviewed was a brilliant young scholar from Harvard Divinity who carried himself like a young version of my father (Harvard Dignity) and like Daniel Mutan. He fit the historical mold of our church too well. Then came a young man I really liked out of Berkeley's Pacific School of Religion, a first-generation American, family from Mexico, but he withdrew after looking at our lily-white community.

On the day I met Shelly Andersen, it was snowing like crazy. I assumed she would email or call to reschedule, and I settled in at my father's desk, wearing slippers and an old polar fleece. Then I got a call from our maintenance man, who was shoveling sidewalks with old Joe, our ever reliable volunteer, when Shelly showed up ten minutes early in a snow-and-salt caked Subaru.

When I arrived ten minutes late–after I registered the old Subaru as a positive–stomped the snow off my boots, and walked into the conference room, Shelly stood to shake my hand. Her eyes rose up, taking in my full height, and she said: "Reverend Crackstone, I'd heard a bit about you, but no one told me you were the world's tallest Congregationalist Minister." And the ice was broken.

Really the ice was broken the moment I saw her. She wore snow boots, and her parka was piled on the chair next to her. She dressed in a practical wool skirt and sweater like a high school teacher and a girl whose grandparents were Scandinavian, Wisconsin farmers. Which, it turned out, they were.

In appearance, Shelly Andersen was average height, average weight, average looks. But that was the end of average. Battling a snowstorm to arrive ten minutes early for her interview was just the start of exceptional. In her first two years, Shelly revamped the teen program and tripled its size. She created urban-outreach projects the kids loved and which gave them a sense of accomplishment. For example, they went into the worst Boston neighborhoods twice a year on a block-by-block, week-by-week litter pick-up project. Next came an urban home-repair project, matching students with volunteer carpenters to replace and repair windows, paint rooms, and so on; old Joe joined the volunteers as always. Then Shelly organized a school-supplies project. And then she launched a multi-generational project, "A Mission for Mittens," where older women taught kids to knit scarves and mittens for poor kids, and that expanded to include a coat drive with seniors and teens collecting more than three hundred coats a year for the poor. Shelly even created a teen reading group of about forty Tolkien and C.S. Lewis fans to discuss fantasy fiction, which soon expanded to include about twenty adults.

One day she asked me to go over an error she found in the spreadsheet from the finance committee. She showed it to me, and to be honest, I tend to glaze over at the sight of a spreadsheet. The more rows and columns, the less attention I pay. She said we needed to bring it to the deacons' attention, and I asked her to go ahead, keeping in mind the personalities and egos in the room.

At the deacons meeting, when Caleb Bradstreet reviewed the finance committee report, Shelly spoke up: "Excuse me, Mr. Bradstreet, I believe there's a problem with the spreadsheet."

Old Caleb went stone-faced and raised an eyebrow in Shelly's direction. He had long ago risen above questioning. But not to Shelly.

She calmly, slowly, guided attention to the line and column in question. "I hope you don't mind," she said as she opened a folder and pulled out copies for everyone in the room, "but I took the liberty of correcting that line and highlighted how it changes the overall picture. Unfortunately, the overall picture is a little less rosy now, but the numbers are what they are."

Shelly waited for her information to sink in.

"Yes, I see," Matt Baker said. Then another agreed and a third.

Caleb looked at Shelly, took off his glasses in a dramatically slow way, and looked at her before he said, "Nice catch, Ms. Andersen. You're absolutely right. Thank you for calling the error to our attention and for your very clear correction."

I saw then a look of admiration in the old money-man's eye. In one deft move, her stock skyrocketed. For a minute, I worried Caleb might try to hire her away from the church to work in his investment firm.

What most endeared Shelly to others were her laugh and her smile. Every Halloween, because she had gone to the University of Wisconsin, she dressed in this crazy badger costume for the kids' party at the church. When preaching, she made people laugh over a self-deprecating story of slipping around the woods of Walden Pond during mud season only to see her first robin of spring, and then she'd brilliantly bring back the everyday story and connect it to Moses wandering in the desert only to find the rock that produced water for the Jews.

By the Pumpkin Summer, Shelly Andersen proved ready to take on her own congregation. As I increasingly focused on my pumpkin patch, she stepped up to run more of the church. While I dreaded losing her, I recommended she start looking for a senior minister position. For her career growth. But she demurred and said she would know when to look. In addition to being fun and clever and just plain brilliant, she was supremely organized. Spotting that error in the spreadsheet was no anomaly. I don't know how many times she caught a typo in the newsletter just before it went to the printer, or she reminded me of a meeting with one of the deacons or a community leader, or covered an appointment due to a double-booking across my multiple calendars.

Speaking of my multiple calendars, rather than organize me, they began to ensnare. It clicked one afternoon when Gordon called me into his room. "Dad, this is so awesome. Can I get one of these plants?" Then he played a YouTube video of a Venus flytrap catching a fly. Those little eyelash gates close around the fly, and you see recognition hit the fly in the prison, that "Oh, no, I gotta get out of here," but too late. The fly scrambles around and then, with all the peace of sunset, the flytrap slowly eases down the rest of the way. Lunch.

Never thought I'd have empathy for a housefly, but I wanted to pry open that evil plant. I knew that "I gotta get out of here" moment. My work, my schedule had become a 24-hour-a-day, seven-day-a-week trap, all documented by numerous calendars. The never-ending reverend-mode left no room for the John Crackstone I once was. When did I last go for a walk in the woods? I couldn't even remember where I'd stored my hiking boots. When did I last go sit at the ocean's edge? Watch a river flow? Birdwatch? Or visit an art museum?

I couldn't recall.

Calendars guided my life. I managed four of them—no five. Or rather, they managed me: a giant white-board wall-calendar at the office to wipe clean and refill each month. A paper calendar hung next to it (with lighthouse images) for advanced planning. The family home calendar in the kitchen used a different color for each of us and brown for all-family events. Then a computerized one synced with my smartphone calendar and supposedly united all the others—but only with plenty of effort—and it beeped warnings of my next obligation. That one was also available to staff, so they could see where to inject their own little block of pain into my day.

Calendars waited at every turn, yet time vanished around me. Eventually I had to schedule "think time" and "sermon building" into those calendars each week. But it's hard to wedge spiritual inspiration into a time slot. Ruth Stone, the former Poet Laureate of Vermont, said she'd be out working the fields where she grew up in Virginia and could intuit a poem coming at her over the hills like a thundering train. She had to race to the house to get a piece of paper in time to catch it thundering through her or the poem would continue across the landscape looking for another poet. While I'm no Ruth Stone, I do know that sense of a message rumbling out of nowhere, and you have to catch it when you can. So I kept a pad with me, but you can't step out of a hospital visit to jot notes for a sermon. Those inspirational flashes rolled in my direction less often in Concord—much less often than when I lived in the White Mountains of New Hampshire, in Worthington.

Gordon played the ninety-second video a second time. "Isn't that cool?"

"Awesome," I said.

Then, like one of Ruth Stone's poems, an idea thundered out of nowhere: add pumpkins to the calendar.

I went back to my desk and started with the computer calendar, going back to Easter Sunday, and added an orange gift box with just "PP" for planted pumpkins. Then I leaped forward to mark the big day in October, the date of the official Pumpkin Weigh-in at the Topsfield Fair. Then back to add the date of first sprouts, then outdoor planting day, then first blossoms, and on and on. Suddenly this grew rich, a joy, a kind of simplified diary, each event coded in orange boxes. Next I went to my paper calendar and added in these milestones with tiny, symbolic illustrations. (I admit they looked more like blobs, but I liked them!) My little scribbles of joy gave meaning to my calendars for the first time ever.

Chapter Six

Misconnections and Miscues

On a Friday night after ten o'clock, I ducked under the back door frame and into our dark house. I'd been at the hospital since six o'clock after Helen Balch, one of the older church members (an OCM), had suffered a heart attack. As her family arrived, Helen asked me to stay, and the evening wore on. Finally home, I loosened my tie and opened my collar with one hand and flicked on the kitchen light with the other. Two of our nice dinner plates sat on the counter, along with an open bottle of red wine, one glass waiting.

Then I remembered. Nancy had made a special dinner of Cornish game hens with Moroccan rice pilaf to celebrate our anniversary a week early since the kids were both at sleep-overs. Now two humps of aluminum foil guarded the cold, Cornish corpses.

I'd forgotten our plan and hadn't even called—just sent a lame text about being tied-up at the hospital with an OCM, and I'd be late.

Where was she?

I passed the dining room, placemats and silverware set up, candles burned half way down. Not good.

On to the living room where I found Nancy stretched out on the couch asleep in her nice black dress, pearl necklace and matching earrings. Her wine glass empty beside her on the coffee table. Shoes, black high-heels I didn't even know she owned, flopped over on the floor like they'd given up. I didn't want to wake her, but of course I had to.

I then prepared to eat crow, not Cornish hen.

I sat on the floor next to the couch. "Honey? Nancy?" I rested my hand on her shoulder.

She stirred. "My dinner's ruined."

I tried to explain about the hospital and getting caught up with the Balch family, but it sounded hollow even to me.

"I'll warm up dinner," she said.

Her gesture swept me back, and she got up, taking the wine glass. Her foot scooted the pumps under the coffee table. I told her not to bother. "No, come on," she said, "Let's get this over with—hate to waste food." As I followed her toward the kitchen, I heard her talking, but I didn't know if it was to me or to herself. "That's just the way it is. Duty calls. Duty first. Duty always. Reverend Crackstone forever dutiful to his flock." She smirked: "Never mock the flock."

In the kitchen I put my hand on her back and leaned in to kiss her, but she turned and bent to open the oven, dropped the birds on the rack, and slammed it shut. She lifted the Moroccan rice as a congealed lump with a single spoon and dropped it into a large bowl by the microwave.

She poured herself another glass of wine. Then she poured me the last of the bottle, a short glass.

In an over-the-top English accent, she said, "Darling, I waited to eat with you, but not to drink with you."

"I'm really sorry, Nancy. I should've called."

"It's okay, John. It's always okay. I'm kind of used to it. Your dedication is admirable," she said and slammed the rice into the microwave.

"Nancy, that's enough."

She turned slowly, "Yes, Reverend, that's enough. I've done enough, had enough, and I'm going to bed. Your dinner's about warmed up, and I'm turning cold. Turning old. Both." She took up her glass of wine as if toasting. "Happy anniversary, Honey." And she went upstairs.

* * *

A few days later, on our actual anniversary date, I tried to make it up to Nancy. I went to a dress shop, a Concord boutique I knew she liked, and bought her a beautiful, burgundy dress. I'd checked the size of one in her closet. I knew this purchase was a little risky, but the shop manager knew Nancy and assured me of my choice.

When she opened the elegantly wrapped package, she gasped with joy. Until she saw the size.

"This won't fit me," she said. Before I could explain about checking one in her closet, she shot at me: "Is this your way to make me lose weight?"

I was stunned. First of all, she still looked thin, not much different than before kids.

"Well? Is it?" She threw the dress down on the box in a heap.

"No. You don't look bigger," I said. "I'll exchange it for the right size."

"Don't you dare." She stormed out the front door and drove off.

* * *

I went out and puttered around the pumpkin patch and kept an eye out for Carol Baker to be working in her garden. Before long, there she was in gray tights and a white tank top. Looked like she was about to go for a run, but she was pulling weeds from her flowers. I did the same around my pumpkins, setting aside little piles.

Four hours later, Nancy still hadn't returned. I'd imagined her wearing her new dress to dinner at Jeffery's Pointe

Restaurant with its view of Boston Harbor and islands, but now I had to call and cancel our reservations and then cancel the babysitter.

Eventually Nancy came home, but she didn't want to talk. She said she'd gone for a walk in Boston, went to the Museum of Fine Arts, and had done some shopping, though she had no bags. I didn't say much, just got the kids ready for bed and went to bed early myself to read.

* * *

A week after the dress snafu, the first Wednesday in June, we had Couples Bible Study at the church. Among my many duties, I led two weekly Bible studies–the Men's Bible Study and the Couples Bible Study. For Couples, Nancy always attended with me. Always. It only made sense, and she'd been a great foil and great help. She kept things light and kept me on the participant path and off the preacher pedestal.

But on that night in June, as we neared the end of the study, Nancy announced: "Before we dock the boat on tonight's discussion, I wanted to let everyone know that this is my last Couples Bible Study." There was a small gasp of surprise. "I've decided that after twelve years, it's time for me to take a break."

I knew nothing of her plan. Nothing.

Back at home, I got ticked off. "You can't just drop out of the Couples Bible Study," I said.

"Sure I can. Just did."

"We didn't even talk about it. How am I supposed to be part of Couples Bible Study without you there? It's good for the community to see us together."

"Look," Nancy said. "I've done it for a long time, and I'm finished. If you can't do it without me, let somebody else run it. You don't have to run every function. Wouldn't you like a couple of hours back in your week? Well, there's two hours, a gift from me to you."

With that she turned and walked out of the room.

The next morning over coffee and while she made the kids their lunches (the kids were upstairs getting ready for school), I broached the subject again, but Nancy stood firm.

"I need a break from the church, John, a little break. Your faith has to be in public view. Mine doesn't." She paused and scoffed. "Don't give me that look. I'm not taking a break from my faith. Just from a building down the street with all its demands. I'm tired all the time. I'm never *not* tired. It's like I just go, go, go from the minute I get up, without a chance to catch a breath." And then she rattled off her routine: "I get the kids ready for school, make lunches"—she gestured to the Spiderman and Princess Leia lunch boxes before her—"and then I get them out the door on time. Then I rush to the church to wipe dirty butts and runny noses at the daycare. On days off, I race around doing errands for the family or to help you. Then the kids are back home, and I'm making dinner while trying to do a few loads of laundry. Then it's homework supervision and bedtime routines. And I'm exhausted. I collapse into bed at night and the next morning there it is—my life, my routine, your church—waiting for me to do it all again as soon as the alarm goes off.

"And there's no time for me, John. Not a single hour in the day is about me. On the rare occasion when I try to do something for myself, like when I went to the Museum of Fine Arts last week, I feel guilty for not doing something for you or the kids." She paused. "It's been like this day after day for years." She sighed a huge sigh and added: "Sometimes, I just want to run away."

Same here, I wanted to say. Nancy's proclamations resonated for me too. The details were different, but the exhaustion, exasperation, and undercurrent of hostility bubbled right there. Yes, yes, yes! I wanted to bellow. So let's get the hell out of here, head for the tall and uncut (as my Texan buddy, Jack, liked to say) and find peace and time for ourselves. Precious time to reflect and dream again. Let's do it while we still can. Let's become pumpkin farmers, I thought.

But in her next breath Nancy said, "Of course you'd never understand. How could you, John? You sit at your desk day after day, thinking and writing about the meaning of it all, expressing yourself and your vision, setting the course for the church. You have mountains of time for yourself," she said. "And you've got Shelly to help you."

I couldn't even bring myself to reply.

* * *

There was a time when I used to think about the meaning of it all. When I grappled with the big issues and ideas.

Back in my second year, struggling to lead the Concord Congregationalist Church–though I knew it was a stereotype even as it coalesced in my mind–everywhere I looked, I saw the crowning principles of wealth, materialism, and white liberals shielded far from urban struggles just twenty miles away, turning a blind eye to those in need. All of this swirled in a cloudy contradiction to Christian faith as I viewed it–obscuring my vision of an action-based faith.

In the course of the year-two grind, I selected a spring Sunday to challenge the congregation. I spoke of how Jesus, who could have walked with kings, chose to walk among the poor. I spoke of the obligation of the rich to reach out, tried to spur some noblesse oblige, tried to awaken the congregation to the systemic oppression so ingrained in us that we Americans see it as a birthright somehow ordained by God, as if Jesus had prescribed capitalism as a Christian model for the world.

But Jesus had shared the fish and bread! He shared.

In a flash of inspiration, and going off script, I pointed to the grand organ, installed a few years before I took over for Dad, and I asked: "What if the church had raised $400,000 to build a home for welfare mothers instead of buying an organ?" The congregation stirred, and I knew I'd finally struck an emotional chord. But at the end of the sermon, parishioners filed past me as if I did not exist.

The following Sunday, a third of the congregation stayed home. A silent protest. A passive-aggressive rebuke.

At the next deacon's meeting, two of the old guard resigned (which made room for Matt and another other wealthy conservative). The other ten lined up to blast me. Unknown to me, the $400,000 for the organ was donated by one Richard Ames, a life-long and fourth-generation church member, who'd been a close advisor to my father. I was embarrassed, and I apologized. "Don't apologize to us," said one old bulldog. "Apologize to Richard Ames and his family privately and then publicly to the congregation for your brash and insulting behavior." Then another of the old guard piled on: "You need to remember, young man, who pays your salary."

Still idealistic in those days, I tried to articulate what I believed, how I saw parishioners as souls to be saved.

One of the deacons leaned forward, and with the aplomb of a man pushing the button to drop the bomb, said, "Hard to save them if they aren't there, wouldn't you say, Reverend?"

Then another of them, a good guy who'd tried to mentor me in the culture of the Concord church leadership, joked, "Just because you're the tallest man in town doesn't obligate you to be a lightning rod." It was the only levity in the evening, and it passed faster than a spring storm.

The deacons made it clear that, for me to keep my job, I had to support the community. The way my father had.

They explained, as if I didn't know, that the good people of Concord loved their children, worked hard, and donated to charity–which, the deacons believed, included my salary. Members of our congregation were more deserving of commendation than a simple–minded attack. They did not attend church to be reformed. If I wanted to change the world, I could start by changing churches. Simple as that. The deacons expressed dismay that any of this remained unclear to someone who'd grown up in this town, especially to the son of Reverend Crackstone.

I wanted to stand, to tower over these men, perhaps mount the table in a single stride, and pound out the declaration: *I am Reverend Crackstone!*

But my tongue seized up as I imagined their retort: *Oh, how we wish you were.*

Plodding the few blocks home from the meeting, I stewed. I knew I was lucky to have this prestigious job. Wouldn't have it but for my father. Wouldn't have survived that meeting either. Once ousted by deacons, it was hard to land another church. Nancy and my kids loved Concord: historic, beautiful, prosperous, safe, good schools. The weight of failure daunted, of disappointing my dad, of disappointing and uprooting my family.

And so I decided to bend.

Then a voice: "What'd you lose, Reverend Crackstone? Can I help?"

It was a neighbor boy on his bike.

"No, I didn't lose anything."

"The way you were looking down, Reverend Crackstone, I thought you were looking for something you lost."

Out of the mouths of babes, right? He stayed alongside me, sitting on his mountain bike, not pedaling but pushing off the pavement with black sneakers, toes worn thin. After a minute he said: "You okay, Reverend Crackstone?"

"Oh, sure, I'm fine. I just have a lot on my mind."

"I figured you did, looking down and rubbing your neck like that. If you didn't lose something, you were for sure thinking about something."

Sweet kid. Observant, I thought. "Yes, I've got plenty on my mind. How about you? Are you okay?"

"Yeah, I'm good. Got a big tooth coming in up front." He pulled back his lip to show the white tip promising to flood the gap in his smile. Next stop: orthodontia.

"Nice. Looks like it'll be a dandy," I said. "It'll probably be in before corn on the cob season."

"Hope so." We were almost to my front walk. "Well, see you later, Reverend Crackstone." He rode off only to do a fancy skid and look back my way. "See you Sunday."

I assured him I would.

* * *

Since my fateful meeting with the deacons ten years ago, I had locked into my maddening routine. The *routine*, it seemed, had become more important than faith. That and the mental gymnastics of trying to anticipate and predict the deacons' demands. Despite what Nancy thought, I asked myself when had I last reflected on what it meant to be a man of Faith for more than three minutes?

From the pulpit I still longed to shout: Who among you would unplug your cable TV, hand over the keys to your four-wheel-drive grocery getter, or send your children to a mere community college if it meant saving one African child from starvation?

But then, what did that have to do with Faith? Humanity, yes. But Faith? Connecting the dots eluded me in this time when I needed it. When I *really* needed it.

Again I blamed the day-to-day. My routine had become maddening.

Nancy grabbed her break—at least from Couples Bible Study—and I wondered if a break waited for me out there. Maybe a big one. What could I reach for? The pumpkins? An inkling rose in the back of my mind, moving forward, asking whether my pumpkins would point the path to something new, something great.

Chapter Seven

Remembering Worthington

There was a time and a place where I didn't feel like I had to bend. That place was Worthington, New Hampshire where I began as an associate minister.

It's a small town in the White Mountains. Life was simpler there; the congregation and deacons were simpler to be sure. Nancy and I were closer too. And I was less bottled up than ever. When I thought of Worthington while sitting in Concord, it played in my mind like a movie montage. One of those old New England towns, Worthington has had its ups and downs. Mostly downs over the last century and a half. Not counting get-away cabins or ski houses for the Boston and New York crowd, the population hovered around 3,500. Before the Civil War, it exceeded 6,000; but after the war, westward migration pulled farmers to the prairie states, and the Industrial Revolution drew still more.

Twenty-first century Worthington featured two post-card-perfect white churches with towering steeples jutting above the maples—bookends for the commercial district. As the largest town on the western side of the Presidential Range, it offered a classic, New England Main Street with a triangular village green, a granite post office and town hall, a couple of brick banks and a public library. We kept mobile homes off Main Street, but they weren't hard to find. Just outside town we had Tall Pines, a family-run ski mountain, as well as other businesses. Not much in Worthington but enough, and I liked it.

What's more, I loved my boss and mentor, Dennis Cliff.

* * *

Though a friend of my father's, Dennis little resembled my old man. Here the movie montage swivels to the character of Dennis Cliff. Physically he was as unremarkable as I am remarkable for my height. Short and a little paunchy, balding, he looked so average, you'd never notice him. But he exuded a physical energy that flowed from a warm and generous emotional core. He could turn the tenor of a confrontation or a trying day with a quick story, a joke, a wink, or a walk. People remembered the day they met Dennis Cliff. He was the best listener I've ever known. His little gray eyes took you in, weighing and measuring anything you said, and a year later he could quote back to the word something you'd said. He had a jaunty yet forceful stride, and I saw his physical power a number of times on our walks, which frequently turned into hikes up one of the local mountains.

Walks were critical to him, something he'd adopted years before while reading Thoreau, and he held them as sacred as Buddhist meditation. He spoke at length of how walking cleansed the mind of clutter, removing you from a rat's nest to focus mental and physical energy to subconsciously unravel a problem. The physical and mental were not separate. Not for him. Frequently our one-on-one meetings, even the short ones, meant tromping along the River Trail or into the foothills and more than once to the top of Mount Worthington. Sometimes in snowshoes, which never worked very well for me.

On these walks or hikes, Dennis seemed to tie his shoes a lot. I assumed the energy of his stride loosened the knots. Then I noticed he did it during office meetings. Even around the deacons. Especially around the deacons. I observed this over the first two years I worked with him.

One beautiful June morning, we walked along the River Trail, discussing how or if we should help a family take the car keys from their stubborn old father who had reached the dangerous stages of dementia. Dennis stopped for a second time to retie a boot.

I finally asked why he tied his shoes so often.

"Do you need me to teach you how to tie a double knot?" I said.

He chuckled and finished tying. "Okay," he said, "let's go."

"Wait a minute," I said. "You do that a lot, stop to tie your shoes. And I don't think you do it because your shoes are loose."

"You're right." He headed down the trail.

"Hold on there, Reverend," I said, catching up in three long strides. "I'm not letting you off the hook that easily. Tell me why. Is it a nervous tick or something?"

"No, it's a measured response."

We walked a few strides. "And ..."

"And before I go on"–his tone very serious now–"I'd like to ask you not discuss this with anyone in my lifetime."

This gave me pause. Could there be some sort of scandal with knotting up your shoelaces? "Okay, I won't tell anyone," I said.

We continued along the trail.

"It's my simple, stupid device to get a moment to think. Over the years, I've learned that, when you pause to tie your shoes, the world pauses with you. People who are hot and bothered wait a few seconds. They breathe. They calm down. And so do I. Or at least I get a little time to think."

He stopped talking as we climbed a short rise. I thought it was to catch his breath, but past the ridge he kept silent as we approached the spot where we always stopped to enjoy the view of the river and the town. Our church spire jutted above the fresh summer green of June. I waited. He added nothing. We sat, and I opened my water bottle and handed it to him.

"And …" I said.

"And what?"

"What else about the secret of shoe strings?"

"That's it."

"There's got to be a story here," I said. "Who taught you this secret? The Dalai Lama?"

"I doubt he wears Asolos," Dennis said. "Nothing more to it. It's something I noticed and started using back in seminary. You know how it is, people ask us hard questions. Many of which we can't answer, or at least not easily. So rather than stand there looking like an idiot, I tie my shoes."

"Like a half mile back, when we were talking about how or if we should help take the keys from the old man."

"Exactly," he said. "Sometimes one shoe. Sometimes both." He smiled. "Depends on how hard the question and who's asking."

* * *

Dennis Cliff was the kind of man who still climbed ladders to help clean the church gutters each fall–I hope you can visualize my montage as I tell it–and he helped shovel snow off sidewalks, and took up a spade to assist the ladies in the Trowel and Error Garden Club each spring. On our daily walks through town and into the woodlands beyond, he always packed a plastic bag to pick up trash. I saw him stop to help a woman heft a downed limb from her driveway. Many times I saw him shoulder a car out of a snowbank. Watched him pore over the clay figures, ashtrays, and bowls lining the windowsills of his office, items made by and given by children from the Joyful Noise Summer Camp. I saw him relieve a young man, a stranger, of his snow shovel to give him a breather. Then he handed me the shovel to share the load. The following Sunday, that young man and his wife joined the congregation. Through hundreds of such actions, Dennis quietly shaped my notion of the Christian life by living it, and his model of other-centered action resonated with everyone who met him.

In short, Dennis Cliff mattered.

He also mattered because he followed his conscience and led with it. I never saw him stifle a dissenting voice. Instead he drew out dissent, listening and remaining open to change, and sometimes he did change his position. But he could also unravel a fool's argument like a debate ninja, until it frayed to pieces against Dennis's sound logic. If being respected ever entered his conscious goals, there was no show of it. Yet he was the most respected man in town.

While Dennis was the centerpiece of what I appreciated about Worthington, he was not the only thing. Nancy and I lived in a terrific little three-bedroom bungalow at the edge of town, painted a black-brown to match the trunks of the pines around it, making it blend with the woods. We called it "Cottage in the Copse," and it was as peaceful as it sounded. (Now that I think of it, with all of those trees and the shadow of the mountain, our plot would be a lousy place to grow pumpkins.) An impressive hunk of granite four or five times the size of the house rose out of the backyard and marked the foot (the big toe, as I referred to it) of Mt. Worthington. Yet we were less than a mile from church and town center.

A river ran through town, a torrent in spring, a trickle in August, a mill pond for skating in winter and swimming in summer. Every season was full there, screaming colors of autumn, winters with waist-deep snows (for average-height people anyway), slow-arriving springs, and cool summer nights. And mud season—elsewhere known as April. (April was also pumpkin planting time.)

The size of Worthington was comfortable; you didn't know everyone, but you recognized most. Certainly all residents came to recognize me pretty fast—hard to miss "The tallest man in New Hampshire" as the Manchester *Union Leader* once called me; and statistically speaking, I was probably the tallest man in the three states of Northern New England. But Worthington could get too close. Gossip boiled about an ugly divorce, or about a child abuse case, or a love affair with the lid blown off, or the guy who vanished for eight months doing time in the state clink or rehab. Opioid addiction was a problem, and it had gotten worse in the dozen years since I left. People carried mistakes a long time in Worthington. Some sank into their reputations: the nasty drunks, the misanthropes, and the gossips. I avoided eye contact with known troublemakers. It's weird, but there is a certain kind of man who needs to fight me—as if taking down a Goliath made him a hero or something—and I've had to walk away from many challenges over the years.

For all the bad and all the good—one thing abided to me: honesty. Worthington was what it was—good and bad, ugly and beautiful. It made sense to me.

* * *

My day in Worthington began with an early walk from Cottage in the Copse down the tree-lined road, through part of town, to the church. I made the coffee. Dennis showed up, with his large cheese Danish in a small white bag, and we started the day with a short prayer and mug of hot coffee. We discussed sermon ideas, debated Bible interpretation, and took daily walks. I ran the youth ministry and made a lot of visits to people with Dennis and alone.

He instructed me on how to handle difficult members of the congregation as well as the deacons, sent me off to do battle, and gently helped me learn from mistakes.

Then, after about four years, my father said, "So when do you think you'll be ready to take on your own church?" I told him I was still learning from Dennis. "He's a good man," Dad said, "but I hope you're not becoming dependent on him, or getting too settled, too mired–or marooned– in a pathetic little backwater town." After a brief pause he added: "Complacency can ruin a man's future."

Complacency. The word rang in my ears. Next thing, I found myself surfing online for Senior Minister positions. With no plan to apply. Just looking. My preference was for a small or mid-sized city, certainly not a wealthy Boston sub-urb. Maybe there was a Worthington-ish place out there.

* * *

And then bam: Dennis had a heart attack. No one could believe it, this tireless fireplug who walked or hiked every day. I'll never forget the morning Amy, his wife, called me from the hospital. When I got there, my energetic friend looked as white and pasty as the Pillsbury Doughboy. This was not Dennis Cliff.

During his recovery–and it was a long one–I took over the church. It felt good to lead. Dennis had readied me to take the reins. As interim minister, I blossomed, con-fidence growing, and I became comfortable standing up there before my neighbors delivering a sermon. For all their concern for Dennis, the congregation also appeared to root for me, wanting me to succeed, clapping me on the back on the way out and saying I'd done a fine job, and I appreciated it. No one took more pleasure in my growth than Dennis. While he encouraged me, he kept a distance to let me stand on my own, often skipping the Sunday service, minimizing his coaching. He made occasional visits for coffee (minus the cheese Danish). If we went on a walk at all, it was short and slow. At times shuffling. It was painful to see him frail. I wanted to carry him. Though Dennis got better, he never returned to his former vigor. His hikes faded, but the daily walks around town resumed, albeit slower paced and shorter.

At the deacons' meeting before he returned to full duty, Dennis surprised all of us by insisting I be named co-senior minister and that we share the duties fully. The proposal passed unanimously. At the celebration dinner over the weekend at Dennis and Amy's house with Nancy and me, Dennis raised a glass a second time: "And if it all goes to hell, we can open a granite quarry: Cliff and Crackstone."

Nancy piped up, "Or maybe you should call it Blockheads."

A few minutes later, Dennis said, "What did William say about the good news?"

I had not told my father yet. I didn't know how to tell him and sensed he would be disappointed. But Dennis was so excited he insisted I call my father right then.

"Good," Dad said. "I'd begun to wonder if you'd ever get there. It's about time. You were overdue, John."

Classic Dad. Disappointment filled his voice, and I knew it was because I hadn't moved on to break new ground and remained tied to Dennis.

Dad ended with, "Congrats, son." Not even granting me the full word.

I hung up, rendered doleful in what should have been my crowning hour.

When I told Nancy—and I'd waited until Dennis and Amy were in the kitchen—she got hot. Already peppered with a couple glasses of wine, she let fly. "That son-of-a-bitch! For such a big-shot, your father can be a small, small man."

Dennis's head poked around the corner, "Everything okay?"

"Yeah," I said with a shrug, "just Dad's reaction was a little less than expected."

"Your dad is a jackass," Nancy hissed.

Dennis came up to me. "He can be a funny guy, your dad. He has high hopes for you, and I'm sure he didn't mean for it to sound like it did."

In these matters, I knew my father better than Dennis did. To my well-trained ear, Dad's calculated use of language, both in word and tone, always connected as he intended. Especially with me.

"By morning, he'll appreciate how this is a big moment for you," Dennis said.

"I doubt it," Nancy muttered, and though she was right, I wished she'd button it.

* * *

The next few years as co-minister with Dennis Cliff were the best of my life. I imagined this being my career stop, and Nancy and I began to talk about starting our family.

Then one afternoon, the phone rang. I was at Cottage in the Copse working on a sermon.

"Hey, John." It was Dennis. "Guess who stopped in the office today to see you? None other than Reverend William Crackstone, President of The American Association of Congregationalist Churches. Yes, our Grand Poobah."

I could hear Dad laugh in the background. It wasn't like him to surprise me like this, especially on a mid-March day when there was still a foot of snow on the ground.

"Is everything okay?" I asked. "Is Mom okay?"

"All is well. He just wants to see you," Dennis said. "Can I send him down? Or do you want to come up here?"

"If you two are finished–I could use a few minutes to pick up around here–then send him over."

"No problem. We'll finish catching up, and I'll send him packing in your direction in half an hour."

I buzzed around the house, picking up. Gathered the Sunday *New York Times* and stuffed it under the couch. Dad never understood why anyone in New England would take the Sunday *Times* when the *Globe* had everything you needed. (I never bothered to point out that the *Times* owned the *Globe* for many years. And I could just hear his reply: "Until it was rescued in 2013.") In my rush to clean up, I failed to duck under the kitchen door and whacked the top of my head, whacked it hard, no blood, but the pain radiated across my scalp.

"Son-of-a-bitch!" I yelled out loud, then surprised myself with a bellowed: "*God*-damn-it!" which reverberated in the empty little house. Then the old high school refrain echoed in my aching skull: The Stork is a Dork.

A pot of coffee was nearly finished brewing by the time I heard a knock at the door. I took the bag of frozen peas off my head, feeling the bump, and tossed them back in the freezer before letting Dad in. He wore his tweed suit and nice cordovan slip-ons.

After small talk over coffee, and after he assured me twice that he and Mom were in good health, he finally came to the point of his visit.

"Son, you know what? I will have been the minister leading Concord for forty years this May."

I recognized the significance of forty years. Like Moses leading his flock through the desert. I waited.

"I'm going to retire in May, and I'd like for you to take over."

He paused.

I paused.

I became aware I was holding my breath.

He went on: "I don't have to tell you that Concord stands as the topmost position in the entire Congregationalist Church." He paused briefly. "I've already cleared it with my deacons. They are prepared to appoint you." He paused again, but I waited. "There will be perfunctory interviews. But the job is yours, Son."

I could hear the pride in his voice. His voice halfway through had shifted into his ministerial timbre. I knew this tone and used it myself. It is a professional trick, like a special gear we shift into to hide our emotions.

To remain quiet any longer would be rude, so I spoke. "Wow, Dad." I ran my hand over my head, over the painful lump. "This is a lot to take in."

Now it was his turn to wait.

"First of all," I said, "congratulations on your forty years of leadership and on your retirement at the top of the profession. Your service, your work, has inspired many—including me. Second, I almost don't know what to say to the job offer."

That was a lie. My instinct was to run. The fear-driven flight instinct sprang up, but I suppressed it. "To be perfectly honest, Dad, I never imagined this happening."

This too was a lie. I had feared it for years. Returning to Concord was a nightmare—literally—I still had dreams of sitting in a high school class as the outsized adult I was, wearing only my underwear. There I'd be with Dad's deacons.

"John"—again I recognized the bubble of suppressed pride in his voice—"this is a once-in-a-lifetime opportunity."

We both paused. I drank down the last of my coffee. It was cold now.

Then I looked into the mug and lifted the empty vessel to my lips again.

He spoke first. "You've earned this opportunity." Now it was his turn to lie. We both knew I had not earned it. I was a pretty good minister now, thanks to Dennis Cliff's tutelage. But I was not at the level one expects for Concord. And we both knew I wasn't cut out for it. Yet, here it was, placed at my feet. The king handing the crown to his son. How could I say I didn't want it? How could I disappoint him? How could I say no to all it brought? He knew I couldn't turn it down.

I hesitated, but I finally said: "I need to think about it, Dad."

"Really?" He was genuinely stunned, no hiding it, and he shook his head. "I thought you'd leap at the chance to get out of this backwater and be in Boston with all it has to offer, all Concord has to offer." His tone turned toward annoyance. "John, do you grasp the importance of what I'm saying?" He spoke slowly as if to a ten-year-old. "I am handing you the opportunity of a lifetime. This is Concord. This is huge."

"I know, but I'm pretty happy here, Dad."

"Happy? John, you know what happy is for men like us?"

My brain leapt at his statement—"men like us"? I was nothing like the old man. But he was on a roll and kept rolling.

"Happiness in this profession is the size of the audience and the reach of your voice. You're stuck up here in the woods where you squeak like a mouse to … to … what? A couple hundred people? On a good day, three hundred? In Concord, you will reach more than two thousand every Sunday, counting Internet downloads. Plus those people matter in Boston. And Boston matters in America, in the world. John, I'm offering you a place on the world stage. How can you hesitate?"

His face was red now, and it reminded me of my childhood where he would exhort me to work harder in math.

He took a deep breath, let it out slowly, and then went on, the force in his voice rising as he went: "How can you mumble about being happy here in the middle of nowhere, while I offer you a chance to preach to people of real consequence in Concord?!"

"I know, Dad," I said, both hands up as if they had the power to calm. "But you can't expect me just to say yes on the spot. I have my own church–"

"Dennis's church!" he interrupted, index finger punching the air.

"Dad, I recognize this is important." Important to you, I wanted to say, but held my tongue. "No matter what, I cannot make this decision without talking to Nancy first."

He gathered himself, calmed himself. "Yes, talk to Nancy. She would love to be back near Boston, I'm sure."

"We will talk, Dad, Nancy and me," I said. "And I'll have to talk to Dennis."

"Dennis will understand."

"What about Daniel Mutan?" I asked.

"Mutan? What about him?" Dad snapped.

"He's been with you a long time. He probably expects to be considered for the job."

"Daniel's a grown up. He may not like it, but he'll play ball. Or he will move on," he said. "The job is yours."

With dismissal of that point, we covered some small talk. I offered for him to stay the night, but he said my mother expected him back home. I told him I appreciated the offer and the effort he made to drive three hours up here to make it in person.

He paused on the front porch and looked around. "We're probably a month ahead of you for spring. No snow in Concord."

"What a shame," I answered. "Isn't it beautiful?"

* * *

Why did I leave Worthington, New Hampshire, a community where I was comfortable and felt wanted and needed, for Concord, Massachusetts, a place I'd always found inscrutable and judgmental? I have wrestled with that question innumerable times over the last dozen years, the way one over-scrutinizes the oddly shaped mole on a shoulder blade. I don't even know the order of my rationalizations anymore.

Getting my own church was part of it. My father had convinced me I was ready. If it were a prestigious church, so much the better. It marked a once-in-a-lifetime opportunity. On that point, Dad was spot on. Financially, the higher salary appealed to me. But I had no idea how my income—a fraction of what my Concord neighbors and deacons made—would make me feel like less. Like a lesser man, like I didn't measure up to my deacons or my congregation.

Of course, there was a desire to please my father, despite my efforts to separate and stand alone. When the President of The American Association of Congregationalist Churches calls (especially when he's your father), you answer. Finally, as Nancy and I had discussed, there remained a sense of obligation when the father hands over the reins of the family business to a son. The stack of reasons made it hard to refuse.

So I took it.

But like I said before, it still felt like Dad's job, his church, his congregation, his deacons. Then I got off on the wrong foot with the Associate Minister, Dad's Associate, Daniel Mutan, who came with the job. My concern about him turned out worse than I feared. Two years older than I, holding the Ivy League pedigree, Mutan found himself like the dutiful vice president passed over for the CEO's son in a private company. Mutan (or Mutant as I thought of him) was unfairly leapfrogged. He had assumed the job was his, and his resentment seeped out in all directions. He undermined me at every opportunity, resisting the simplest requests—like "forgetting" to visit a congregant in the hospital when I had another meeting, or making a point to use every sick day when needed to sit in on a dull committee, or accidentally not inviting me to a dinner held in honor of a major benefactor.

The day Mutan left was a good day for both of us.

Of course, in taking the Concord job, I left Dennis Cliff behind. He said he understood, even said I *had* to take the offer, but I could see disappointment in his face. I remember lying in bed, unable to sleep at three o'clock in the morning, thinking about what leaving would mean for Dennis. He had come to rely on me in his reduced capacity and had groomed me to take over, a match for his congregation and his community. I knew it. And Dennis, my mentor and friend, needed me, the job growing too difficult for him alone. Yet I left. I also lay there in bed in the middle of the night fearing the known and the unknown in Concord.

What did I miss most about Worthington a dozen years on? I missed the camaraderie I had with Dennis, of course. I missed feeling vibrant and vital, like I mattered to my community. I missed moving in an organization with confidence, owning my decisions, in collaboration with Dennis often, but they were my calls, without the pressure of toiling under my father's thumb or the measures of success he left behind. I also missed—mourned might be a better word—the easier pace of life and how Nancy and I existed in it. Nancy taught third grade at the elementary school as well as English as a second language. Back then, BC—before children—I had her all to myself. She wore her hair in a long ponytail back then. She was happier, easier going. Things had changed. A lot had changed.

I too was easier-going back then. Not measured—financially or against my father's successes. In those days, I hungered to learn my trade and experience life. And that's what I missed most: "the thrill of the new" as my friend Jack called it. The thrill of the new surrounded every day in Worthington. For Nancy it was about teaching; for me about learning the ministry from a master, from Reverend Dennis Cliff. And trying to catch on paper those sermon ideas that thundered down out of the White Mountains.

How I longed for "the thrill of the new" and the joy of sharing it.

Chapter Eight

Fulfillment, Fatherhood, Family

Did "the thrill of the new" drive my attraction for Carol Baker? A thrill that sex with my alluring neighbor would bring? Of course, but there had to be more to it, more than I could see yet. This tale of desire was not new–the commandment "Thou shall not covet thy neighbor's wife" attempted to extinguish a human hunger that ignited disastrous results. Yet it burned hot among ministers. I read the divorce rate among ministers simmered around sixty–five percent, and frequently a sexual affair burned down the house. Did Dennis Cliff ever lust after a neighbor or a member of his church? I never saw any sign, and he never spoke of it. Was it his private, burning secret? My desire for Carol, known to no one, flickered at my soul, kept in check more by the fear of rejection than Biblical commandment or moral righteousness. That, and fear of losing my family and losing my job. But a longing for "the thrill of the new" chipped away at my fears. What tipped the balance for those many divorced ministers? What carried them over the edge to reach out and touch the other woman (or man) for the first time?

What's amazing was how my pumpkin passion, yes, back to my precious pumpkins–all must orbit the pumpkins–once they infused my life with their own "thrill of the new," one would think it a mitigation of my infatuation for the lovely Carol Baker. But no. These two passions blossomed together. As I turned my energy to the soil and vines and growing orbs, the pumpkins somehow stoked a natural craving for Carol, and they brought us together since our pumpkins vined and swelled not thirty yards apart. On two stages a wonderful challenge, an opportunity, growth, even a slowly unfolding drama—all awaited each day in my backyard pumpkin patch.

With the pumpkins, something new and full of promise filled my life. Under my care bloomed measurable change, growth, improvement. Those little sprouts I put in the ground, shorter than my little finger and fragile as a butterfly, grew and grew. The vines bulked up, developing a kind of animal sinew, a strength conveying water and nutrients—the water and nutrients I provided. I measured the vines against myself, growing thicker than one finger, than my thumb, and then one day I called Carol over and measured them against her thin and muscular wrist. Then her ankle. Then my wrist. And when the buds swelled and bloomed I actually blushed when Carol came over to look at the flowers, as they so imitated the feminine reproductive zones. Above all, these lovely yellow–orange flowers also looked like a trumpet blaring hope.

I know these are grand words for pumpkin blossoms, and I don't expect you to fully understand. But for me, these were not mere plants, not merely a break from the well–worn routine (which would have been enough), not an escape from the eyes of Concord (which would have been enough), and not a new–found hobby (which also would have been enough). They were all of that and much more. Over the deafening din of the mundane, over the rabble of Concord politics, over the petty consternation surrounding compensation for a muddling minister, over the drifting apart between Nancy and me, over some hundred other distractions and inactions–over all of this, I could see and hear and feel the clarion call of my pumpkin blossoms. A Louis Armstrong solo. A moon shot. The first cry of a child. Hope, man. I mean, holler from the rooftop, HOPE! The authentic article. Colossal, alive, and growing right there in my backyard.

Yes, I did mention the first cry of a child. I have experienced this great exaltation three times in my life. Twice for my own children and once with a woman in my congregation because her husband was out of town. Of course, there's nothing like your own child's first cry, a spiritual event that ripples–that screams–across the cosmos announcing to the universe that everything is a touch different. A cry proclaims for all that here a small, vital force has arrived to stake its claim.

Oh, yes, I was fully connected to those moments, drank them in and relished them. I loved my children deeply, love them still. In the pumpkin summer, Gordon was ten years old, Megan eight. Hard to believe the fact of the cliché "how time flies." As much as I loved my children, I admit I grappled with a certain discomfort among them, a growing discomfort as they aged, because I felt unsure of myself with them, as if they were emerging as strangers from whom I must hide my weaknesses and comport myself in a proper fashion. I wished I could still sit down and read *Thomas the Tank Engine* to them, but my kids were no longer interested. It was similar with my father. I don't think I ever really knew him. Or maybe I did, and he really was that stiff, proper, emotionally restrained (emotionally constipated?) man so admired from afar and respected up close. (He was the very model of a modern major minister.)

But I knew he wasn't me, with his emotional restraint and distance. For a while, I struggled to maintain the public face of restraint and the façade of the wisdom of a man of God; privately, I lay open more emotions. Many times from the pulpit, passion bubbled up in me, squeezing my throat, threatening to spill tears from my eyes, or burst from a strained voice box, or yowl to denounce or extol, but I had learned the professional tricks of the trade–like that other gear I mentioned–to choke back emotion. To buttress Yankee restraint. The long pause. The drink of water. The clearing of the throat. Even asking for a spontaneous pause for silent prayer. And in these moments, like a method actor, I remembered painful times from my life: when I had to decide to put the family dog to sleep at age sixteen, when my first college sweetheart dumped me, when a dear friend from church died. These grounded my upwelling and allowed me to continue as the somber minister.

At home it wasn't my proclivity to be distant from my children, and yet I wrestled with how much to let them in and how to connect. Should I really let my children know me? Could they? Can a child know his or her parents before they are also adults? Even then? I don't know.

These were big, scary questions, questions I've tried to answer in counsel for many people in my congregation. Questions which had easier answers before I had children of my own. Clearly one withholds certain things from a child, the strife and frustrations of marriage, the small (or large) resentment of sacrifice that comes with having a child, the sexual desire for a neighbor, the passing fantasy of running off with the twenty-four-year-old bank teller.

* * *

Gordon had a pretty bad bike accident last March, just before I planted the pumpkin seeds. It was one of those warm March Saturdays to herald the coming spring, and Gordon rode his mountain bike for the first time of the year. Coming home from playing basketball at a friend's, with a ball under his arm, he tried to take a corner at high speed and lost traction on sand left behind after winter snows and slid right into a parked dump truck. Broke his collar bone. Whacked his head against the truck, which broke his bike helmet, but he escaped with nothing more than a bad headache, thank God.

When Gordon came home with his friend pushing his bike (Gordon carrying the basketball), I sat at my father's desk polishing a sermon for the next day. I heard his painful bellowing for his mother, and I ran out the door and hugged him.

He screamed as if I'd thrown boiling water on him. I had hugged him around the shoulders, putting pressure on his broken collarbone. I leaped back, taking his wail as a rebuke. Until I saw how he held his arm and shoulder and noted the ruined shoulder of his new Celtics jacket. By then his mother was on the scene, dropping to a squat to be at his level. (Why hadn't I thought of that? Why hadn't it occurred to me to get down at his level?) In seconds Nancy surmised the situation and said we needed to get him to the hospital for X-rays–both for the shoulder area and the nasty bump on his head. I played chauffeur, Megan at my side, while nurse Nancy sat in the back seat holding an ice pack to Gordon's head and whispering soothing words to his whimpering.

"I ruined my new Celtics jacket," he blubbered.

"Don't worry about it," Nancy whispered. "We'll get you another."

* * *

When I was eleven years old, I had a nasty bike crash too.

Summer after fifth grade, I rode my Schwinn Stingray Apple Crate everywhere. Loved my cool little five-speed with a sports-car-style gear shift, high handlebars, and banana seat.

One night I raced down our street, rushing home late for dinner–I was often late that summer, and my father grew angrier with each occurrence and each lame excuse (I couldn't set my watch back again and get away with it)–so I chugged full-speed when out of nowhere a bear-sized golden retriever bounded right in front of me, not chasing me, just suddenly smack in the way. Wham! I hit him broadside. Hit him a ton. And over the handlebars I went. Landed right on my chin. Broke my jaw, tore the hell out of the side of my face, scraped up my arms and legs. I left my bike in the street, limped the last couple hundred yards home, crying. Wailing when I got close to home, calling for my mom.

My dad burst out the door, his napkin still tucked in at his neck to protect his tie, projecting a harsh yelling whisper. "Quiet. What's all this racket?" His eyes searched the neighbors to make sure no one was watching. Then he actually saw me. "You okay, son?" he said. He led me, hand at the base of my neck, toward the house, "Okay, that's enough crying," he said. "Stop the crying. I know you're hurt." By then my mother and sister were at the entry. "We all know you're hurt," my old man said. "Now be a man and stop crying." This as my weeping increased when my mother reached for me. At this my father insisted. "I said, stop crying!"

"William," my mother said firmly–to stop my father as she led me down the hall arm around me. Then she added, "Go get his bike."

"Where's the bike?" he barked. "You just left your bike out there? If it's stolen, I'm not replacing it."

"I'll help," Susan said and ran out the front door ahead of my father to find my bike.

* * *

I don't know if the bike accident was the cause, but for the rest of summer, my father seldom spoke to me. He told me to cut the grass; take out the trash; bring something to the church; pass the salt. But little more. Now that I think about it, he never really communicated with me again—not in real terms, never sat down and had a conversation, a heart-to-heart exchange. Later, he lectured me, asked questions, even joked around a little—but something changed that summer. Did he wash his hands of me at the age of eleven because of my behavior over a bike accident? Was it a last straw? He had told me he'd take me up to a fishing camp in Maine during summer, but my broken jaw cancelled it, and we never rescheduled. In previous summers, we went to a couple Red Sox games, but not that year. And never again. I'm sure I whined about the pain in my jaw and about not being able to play for weeks, complained about doctor visits, the scratches on my bike, and was a general pain in the butt as an eleven-year-old boy can be—struggling to reach back and stride forward—one minute crying for momma and the next sneaking off to steal a *Playboy* magazine from a convenience store with a local juvenile delinquent.

The adolescent struggle between boy and man was exacerbated by my size, already six-feet tall at age eleven, people (and perhaps my father) expected me to act like an adult. Or maybe it was because I was a PK. Either way, at home, to my father, I came up short. As never before, my father had no patience for any goofy behavior from me. Susan could be silly with her girlfriends, screaming or giggling, and he'd smile and chuckle. When I got loud with the guys, he'd shut it down, embarrassing me to a point where I quit bringing friends home.

During that period, I also backed away from wanting to follow Dad into the ministry. When I was young, becoming a minister gleamed like the right choice, the only choice. I saw how people respected Dad, how they listened to him. I wanted similar regard. Whenever I spoke about becoming a minister, he encouraged me—until the time of my bike crash.

When the idea of me becoming a minister resurfaced during college, Dad suggested I go into business, get an MBA, study finance. By the end of college, I decided to pursue the ministry, and I thought he'd embrace it. But he remained tepid.

* * *

At the Hospital Emergency Room with Gordon, it was clear we'd have a long wait. I thought of running upstairs to check on a couple of the OCMs who were patients there. It could save me time in the week ahead. Then Nancy's frustration rose, and she went to see why this was taking so long.

I moved over to sit next to Gordon. I looked at his Celtics jacket with the shoulder shredded, and I wondered why he loved basketball so much. He was okay at it, but he'd never be as tall as me. I wished he would pursue something else, something more lasting, and something he and I could connect over.

"Still hurting?" I asked.

"Yeah, but not as bad."

We were quiet for a minute.

"Hey, do you ever think about what you want to be when you grow up?"

"Not a minister, if that's what you're thinking," he said.

"Wow," I said, laughing.

"No offense, Dad."

"None taken. I don't want you to be a minister either. There are so many ways to make a living and contribute to the world."

"It'd be a little weird. First Grandpa, then you, then me. I don't think so."

"Maybe a lot weird," I said. "No, I don't want you to be a minister. Not unless you really wanted to be. But I think there are better options." I paused for a second. "You know, my grandfather, Grandpa's dad, once said to me, 'I hope you do three things with your life no matter the career: take care of your family; find joy in your work; and give back to the community.' I always liked that. It was simple, but it keeps you on the right track."

"Yeah, that's pretty good," Gordon said. "But I still don't want to be a minister."

I started to reaffirm I didn't either, but Nancy came back and said, "'Soon' is all they'd tell me."

Megan found the waiting as interesting as watching concrete set. So Nancy finally asked me to take Megan to a friend's house. We rode in the car without conversation. I wanted to talk, but I didn't know what to say to my daughter.

Finally, I turned off the radio. "So, Megan, what are you into now?"

"Huh?"

"You know, what do you find interesting? What gets you excited? Couple of years ago, you were into Angelina the Mouse and you liked soccer."

"Dad, I never liked soccer."

Then I remembered her looking for four-leaf clovers while the other kids clustered around the ball. "Right. I know. That was just an example," I said. A few seconds passed. "What are you reading these days? Harry Potter?"

"Mom says I'm too young. She's reading it with Gordon."

"Okay, what are you into?"

"Dad, why are you asking me all these questions?"

" 'Cause I want to know what's cooking in that little head of yours."

"What's cooking?"

"Just thought we could talk."

"Why?"

"You know, people talk. You're my daughter, and I love you, and I want to talk to you."

"Okay," she said. "So, Dad, what's cooking in that great big head of yours?" She cracked a wry smile.

Practically a teenager, practically her mother, I thought, and had to laugh.

Then I turned the radio back on, and we rode the rest of the way to pop music.

* * *

On the way back to the hospital, alone, I thought about why I unplugged from my family. What if I kept driving and vanished, would there be much notice? Would I be missed? Other than financial support—and I didn't bring much of that; actually, I brought in plenty but not compared to the rest of Concord—what did I really bring to the family? It would be easy to lie to myself, to you, and say I was always there for them, the stolid presence. Such self-deception was as common as water. I wanted to be a good father.

Life in Concord pulled my attention in too many directions, striving to "be" and "do" what was expected by the deacons, by the congregation, by the community, by my father (or what I imagined of him), and last, by my family. And all the while seeking to excel somewhere. There was always another demand in the queue, waving its hand, distracting from the now.

I thought about my hug with Gordon. How I'd blown it. I really wanted to comfort my son. Was I a lousy father? Was it bad instincts? Not all fathers were as inept as me and my old man. Was it something about fatherhood that made one–or made Crackstones–have the right impulse yet do the wrong thing? Was there something in my freakish height making me obtuse to life going on below my chin?

Even as I intended to plug in and be central to my family, my instinct for how to do it tilted in the wrong direction. With the pumpkins, I initially imagined us all together, working together, but the pumpkins had become my focus alone, functioning to separate rather than unite. I asked myself: Did I draw sustenance from the pumpkins because I didn't know how to do so with my family? The pumpkins demanded so little and returned so much–no one expects a pumpkin to know them or understand them. No need to withhold or impart. Although, I believed I came to know myself better in pumpkin reflection as those buds grew into hard green pumpkins the size of ping–pong balls. Swelling, plumping, burgeoning into green baseballs, then basketballs, then larger and larger. And all the while, I tended them with water and my special fertilizer potion. My care and feeding led to their immense growth.

It also led to one of the hardest decisions in my life.

Chapter Nine

A Budding Obsession

What I'm about to tell you will be difficult. Difficult for me to tell, and difficult for you to understand. But please try. It's not that you need to *understand* it. Because, honestly, I don't understand it myself. Who understands how a person got wired for plants or astronomy or fishing or amassing money or doll collecting or any of a million other human passions?

When does an interest become a passion, and when does a passion become an obsession?

And why are the first two good things and the third bad?

So you may not understand what I say, but perhaps you can *empathize*.

Either way, I ask your forbearance. Please stay with me. And, if possible, suspend judgment.

I'm talking about my pumpkins, of course. Mostly. They were positively burgeoning. Yes, burgeoning. Becoming huge. If you got down close, you could almost watch them swelling the way, if you really study the hour hand on a clock, you can watch it move ever so slowly. Same for the vines. My pumpkin patch was thick with vines, huge leaves, and rapidly growing pumpkins. Cause for celebration, and I'd reveled in it. Except, the success of the many limited the success of the few.

I knew it was coming. I'd read about the need for it. To achieve the pinnacle in pumpkin growing demanded it. I had to cull the weaker ones to let the strong thrive. I emerged from the shed wielding a rusty machete like a vengeful prophet from the Old Testament and waded into my pumpkin patch. Summoning the brute within, I rapidly took the smallest pumpkins, chopping the cords of their lifeline with a single hack and rolling them into the grass—klonking into each other like oversized bocce balls. Then I hacked their vines back to the branching point and piled them up. By lunchtime, I'd cleared out eighteen pumpkins and a knee-deep mound of vines.

My imagination took in the heap of green and spun out a monster rising to my height, composed of vines and huge leaves with a hard pumpkin head to battle over the remaining greenery. Me, The Massive Minister, armed with my machete, facing down The Gourd Monster with whip-like vines. Obviously, I read too many comic books growing up.

The easy work was done.

Now it got hard. But I couldn't launch into it just yet and went inside to eat lunch—for sustenance. I plowed through leftover meatloaf and mashed potatoes cold from the fridge. Then I went back to the shed and took out the pruning shears and a tape measure. Moving with military precision, now I morphed into the master-mind villain, and I went from one large pumpkin to another, measuring the circumference and height, identifying the top fifteen. Some came up but a quarter inch short. A few of these, because of their beautiful shape, I simply had to keep. To the rest, I turned a murderous eye. They had to go. They were mine; I had created them, had fed them, had tended them. Now I had to kill them.

I took my pruners, severed the vines, and rolled out the pumpkins to bump against the others.

* * *

After the pruning, I was thirsty, as thirsty as I could ever remember being. I downed a large tumbler of water without
taking it from my lips and was halfway through a second
when the phone rang, three, four, five times. I didn't answer. A minute later it rang again while I sat at the kitchen
table, and I let it ring, six, seven, eight times before it went
quiet. And it went quiet gently, leaving a faint, lingering
sound that, as it faded, eased out of the room like a cat,
opening a vast silence as it went. Then, in this framed silence, a small guttural wail rose up from me. I let it out. I
sat at the kitchen table and cried like I hadn't in years.

As I lay in bed that night, unable to sleep thinking
about the pumpkins I'd cut out, it occurred to me: While
the pumpkin patch appeared to exist in a large-leafed vegetable peace, what in fact lay before me was a slow-moving
civil war. These plants battled their brothers for sunlight
and space and soil. Like my skirmish to find sun beyond
my father's shadow. Below ground, a pumpkin war waged
even more fierce as roots intertwined, slowly choking each
other, sending out veins, tentacles, and root hairs to compete for precious water and nutrients.

With this vision of war, I rose from bed with new courage. I had not finished the job. Taking a flashlight I went
out and cut out more marginal pumpkins and cleared
away their vines. After leaving most of the pumpkin patch
in ruin, all that remained were eight strong plants, each
freed to focus its entire energy on feeding one potential
champion pumpkin.

Then I heard the back door close at the Bakers and in-
stinctively dropped to a knee, hiding behind one of my
pumpkins. I saw Carol Baker standing by the pool in a white
terry-cloth robe. She studied the water. Then, as graceful as
a dancer, she bent one knee and swept her other foot into

the water, testing the temperature. Crouching lower, my head near one of the spared pumpkins, my chest burned from holding my breath, and I let it out, breathing through my mouth in short chops. Carol paused at the shallow end, looking around. Did her gaze fall on me and linger? The look of desire? Then she dropped her robe, and lifted her nightgown over her head. For an instant she paused naked in the moonlight–thin, small–breasted, muscular–and then lowered herself down the steps into the pool.

I suppressed the urge to lick the smooth, firm skin of pumpkin next to my face. Perhaps she knew I was there and wanted me. What if I walked over? "Oh, it's you. I thought some kids sneaked into your pool." What then? Might she invite me to join her? And I would.

I lay flat now, pressing my growing erection into the ground. Fear held me there.

Soon Carol emerged from the pool, the water flowing down her body, glistening in the scant light. How I wished for more illumination. She squatted to lift her robe and drew it around herself. Then she retrieved her nightgown and went inside.

Had she put on this display for me? Her gaze had lingered in my direction.

I crawled out of my pumpkin patch and, hunched like a chimp–a very tall chimp–scurried to the back door. In the kitchen, I pulled off the dirty sweatshirt, and the first wave of guilt hit me in the gut. What had I done? Nothing. I checked the clock. It was 2:12. Had I witnessed a routine? An invitation? My mouth dry, I poured a glass of water and sat at the table. I prayed for forgiveness in six quick words. Then I polished off the water, went to my desk and marked the fateful, murderous pumpkin day in my computer calendar (with a C++ for seeing Carol in the nude) and marked the culling and seeing Carol on the paper calendar in a little hourglass illustration and a series of circles with a line slashed through them for the murdered pumpkins. Then I went to bed and slept like a baby–an extraordinarily long baby.

* * *

Even after reducing the patch to eight impressive pumpkins, they demanded more of me than you'd think. And a lot more water. They sopped up water like sponges. My three-times-a-day soakings took longer and longer. I continued my mid-day fertilizing with my special concoction, still picking up my twice-a-week bag of hair, avoiding Otto at Curl Up and Dye, and filling my twenty-gallon tub of cow dung once a week from a farm in Acton. All of these details checked off in the calendars and booked ahead for the next week or two. But it was the need for water that got to me. I finally broke down and bought a couple of soaking hoses, the big ones, and left water oozing around the clock.

I had pulled an old beach chair from the basement, one of those low ones, in faded red-and-yellow striped canvas. I built a low table from an old piece of plywood and spare concrete blocks and set up shop among my pumpkins. I read and took notes. I tried to work on sermons, but I found myself calculating and recalculating the prospective numbers of my giant-pumpkin-seed empire. Based on the seed sellers I found online, the idea began to take shape. If I could pull off a world record, or even win first place, the cash could launch a business. A top-five finish would mean more work, bootstrapping, but still, I thought $300K was within reach–after a few years. With continued growth, I could be rich like my deacons, own a beautiful house like theirs (something Carol would admire). Or I could get out of Concord. Either way, it was a path to being my own man. I looked up how to write a business plan and started to outline my three-year strategy.

* * *

One morning I came home from a meeting to see a brown plumbing truck in the driveway.

"What's with the plumber?" I asked Nancy when I came into the kitchen.

"Matt sent him over when he saw our water bill," she said.

Matt Baker, our deacon neighbor, sat on the Finance Committee, so he held the church purse strings. Each month I sent him an update on all bills from the church expenses, including those of our parsonage. I'd buried the bi-monthly water bill on the spreadsheet, hoping it wouldn't get noticed, but obviously it had. When Matt saw it was six-times higher than normal, he assumed we had a leak in the main or something and called out the troops rather than ask me.

I went down to the basement where the plumber walked around, cigarette hanging from his mouth, two other butts smashed out on the cellar floor, tracing pipes with his flashlight.

"Hello," I said.

"Hi-ya," the plumber bellowed even though we were about eight feet apart, and I wondered if he was hard of hearing. "Well, I haven't found the problem yet, but don't worry, sir. I'll find it. They can't hide from me." All of this in a jaunty, chummy, good-buddy tone before he looked at me. When he did: "Whoa, wow, you really have to scrunch down to move around down here, don't you?"

"A little," I said.

"You know of any wet spots down here or in the house? Seen any change in your water pressure? Anything like that?"

"No, but ..."

"You must have been a hell of a basketball player in your day. Where'd you play?"

"I didn't." And I didn't like this guy. I could smell an insincere invitation to the Saturday night poker party coming.

"Too bad. With your height, I'd have been in the NBA."

How many times had I heard this?

"There's really no problem," I said.

"Bad coaching? Injury?"

"What?"

"You said there was no problem, so I figured you meant you didn't hold a grudge, you know, you've moved on. Like that. Focused on your new career."

I wanted to clobber this guy with a sock full of horse manure.

"I meant there's no problem with the water. I'm growing a garden, and it requires a lot of water."

"For crying in the beer. Why'd you call me? I'm gonna have to charge you for the service call."

"First of all, I didn't call you. One of my deacons did. I'm the minister of the Congregational Church, and one of my deacons assumed we had a leak when he saw the higher water bill. There's no problem, and you'll be paid for your time. Leave me a bill."

"Congregationalist, huh?"

"Yes."

"Methodist myself."

He packed his tools, banging them into the tool box for emphasis and stomped up the steps. I followed. When we arrived in the kitchen, he turned and measured my height.

"You're even taller than I thought. How's the weather up there, buddy?"

I grinned, longing again for a sock full of horse crap. From 'sir' to 'buddy' in two minutes.

I followed him out to the truck to get the bill.

"You know, I would have been a good minister."

From NBA star to minister just like that.

"Yeah, people open up to me, tell me their problems," he said. "I'm just there to fix the pipes but here come the deep emotions. The stories I could tell. It'd curl your hair." Then he paused and laughed like he'd struck comedy's gold. He pointed to my curly hair and said, "Looks like you've heard some hair-curling stories yourself."

He tossed the last of his tools into the milk-chocolate van.

"Yeah, I hear their life stories while I got my head under their sinks," he said. "The stuff these ladies say, mostly it's ladies, mostly old ladies. Too bad for me, right buddy?" He chuckled. "So I try to make them feel better. Tell them how it could be a lot worse, that sort of thing, offer some comfort. That's why I say I'd make a good minister. I'm just naturally good at the pastoral stuff." He paused, "That's what you call it, right? Pastoral?"

"Yeah, 'pastoral stuff' is what we call it," I told him.

He ripped the bill off the pad and handed it to me. "Too bad I don't like going to church. Haven't been in years, a lapsed Methodist."

"Thanks," I said before I could stop myself.

"No problem."

I looked down at the bill, eighty bucks.

Items under fifty dollars could be lumped into a general maintenance line cost and passed through without question. Now this had to be added to the whopping water bill. Just how whopping was the water bill? Let's just say the bill for June and July nearly equaled the entire previous year. So I'd have some explaining to do at the next deacons' meeting.

* * *

There sat Caleb Bradstreet hunched over the spreadsheet: "John, what's this big water bill for June and July? You got a leak?"

"Were you filling Matt's pool for him?" another deacon said, chuckling.

"While I know it's not a drop in the bucket, so to speak"–I paused, but no one laughed–"water for our new garden can't be much more than those of you who have automatic sprinkler systems." I saw their fitful brains picturing their own sprinkler systems, spewing over their two–acre lawns. Which made short work of the snare. A bit more discussion followed, and they agreed if future water usage stayed at similar levels, I'd have to pay the difference.

To further shift the subject, I brought up the topic of affordable housing in Concord, or the absence of it, and suggested we consider joining the Concord Affordable Housing Coalition and take it on as a local mission. Perhaps we could buy a few of the large, old homes in town, expand them, and turn them into multi–unit, low–income housing. In addition, I floated the idea of building a shelter for battered women to help them escape communities where they were abused. With these hot topics, I could hardly get a spark, let alone glow an ember. The ideas were dead–on–arrival, buried under statements like:

"Yes, these are real problems, but we have issues of our own at the church."

"We committed to rebuild and expand the patio for outdoor events."

"And expand the dressing room and restroom facilities for weddings."

"Before long we'll need to replace the roof ..."

But the water bill bubble popped–which was the whole point.

Money always dominated mind–share with these men, my deacons (and they didn't see a reason to bring women into the group when I floated the subject once). They measured themselves and each other and the church by money. Though I hate to admit it, it was infectious. As the calling became more toil, I trudged through knee-deep snow steadfastly but without any sense of destination in my assignment to guide these rich people, these master rationalizers and exploiters, through the eye of a needle. In weaker moments, I waxed for a bigger piece of the pie myself. And I had more weak moments all the time. Like calculating the prices of pumpkin seeds. Those reveries certainly lasted more than three minutes.

Over the course of the summer, while my pumpkin life flourished, and while I grew painfully aware of my desiccated professional dedication, I figured the least they could do was compensate me better. Perhaps a financial incentive would rekindle my passion for preaching–and it might be a hedge for the pumpkin business. So I reached for a piece of the pie and requested a $20,000 raise from the deacons, a fraction of what these twelve, well-heeled men who owned my fate drew in annual bonuses. I pulled out my laptop computer at the deacons' meeting and, using a nifty PowerPoint presentation, displayed statistics showing Concord ranked among the most expensive cities in New England, making it one of the more expensive in the nation.

Matt, the big-shot Boston lawyer on the Finance Committee, led the rebuff. Though not really a numbers guy, I remember Matt Baker's points well because they rolled off his tongue like a practiced attorney.

"John, as I recall your salary plus full health and dental for your family exceeds the average for a minister of your experience." He didn't wait for me to confirm the point or try to turn the ship. "Housing was the lead indicator in the cost-of-living index you used in your presentation. But you pay nothing for housing. Not even your heating, electric, or *water* bills. To say nothing of real estate taxes. Nothing to live in a home worth more than a million dollars. At current interest and tax rates that equals approximately a $6,500 monthly mortgage payment, which translates into more than $75,000 per year, tax-free.

"So in real terms, Reverend Crackstone, you must calculate all of these things into your compensation. Overall, it's a generous compensation package for your profession."

His term "for your profession" clanged in my ears. For *my* profession. Not for his. Not for the other deacons. It kept me under his thumb.

I might have argued the benefits of the house. The drafty old barn needed a lot of work–outdated kitchen and bathrooms, sagging porch, floors in need of refinishing, ill-fitting windows, cracks in the plaster ceiling wiggling corner to corner like an ancient river, and so on. I also missed the investment opportunity of home ownership. But Matt, the marksman, had already blasted my hope out of the sky. Nothing but a puff of feathers drifting earthward. Leaving the other deacons to stomp whatever life was left in the idea.

Old Caleb Bradstreet hunched over his pocket calculator, his troglodyte fingers pounding the buttons before he rose up and announced (in a gruff tone full of outrage) my request constituted a 29.4 percent raise.

In the end, I got a four percent cost-of-living increase.

And I thanked them for it.

But it didn't keep me from doing math in my head as I walked home. Okay, $10 per seed like the Oregon farmer. Bags of 50 seeds, $500 each; bags of 100 seeds, $1,000 each. Each giant pumpkin produced about 500 seeds. Twenty giant pumpkins for about 10,000 seeds. That's $100,000 gross in year one.

I took off my striped tie and started to throw it on the ground, but thought someone might see me litter, and stuffed the tie in my pocket.

Year two, grow 200 giant pumpkins for 100,000 seeds, and we're at the cusp of a million bucks. That's gross revenue. Year three, rent a plot of land in Acton and grow 1,000 giant pumpkins for 500,000 seeds to gross five million bucks. Repeat.

What I hardly let myself think about was: the world's best growers sold their seeds for $20 to $50 a pop! And I'd read about the world record holder, whose champion pumpkin tipped the scales at over a ton, sold his seeds for $400 per seed.

When the greenbacks start gushing in like that, why quibble over $20K?

Chapter Ten

The Mystery of Size

With thoughts of a winning seed business, I began tending my pumpkins like a startup entrepreneur. Watching, waiting, testing, planning, measuring. I wished I'd planted a much larger pumpkin patch so I might have twenty giants instead of eight. "But eight is great. Eight is great. Eight is great," I chanted quietly to myself like a cheerleader.

Speaking of cheerleaders, I hadn't seen my cheerleader neighbor that day.

When they moved in about eight years ago, Carol was pregnant with their second daughter, probably eight months along. Even pregnant, there was no mistaking her beauty and ease of movement. Her pregnancy was all in front and no width. Nancy was excited to have a young family move in behind us because she'd just given birth to Megan and saw years of play dates ahead.

One day, Nancy brought home a *Glamour* magazine, and I thought it was Carol on the cover–with more makeup. Thank goodness I didn't say anything. Women watched Carol Baker pass, studied her–even more than men did. For some reason, it wasn't until the pumpkin summer I focused on her.

When you go into major cities—not places like Worthington, New Hampshire—you see these women on the streets around luxury retailers. Hollywood's image of the USC cheerleader grown up. The thick, bouncing blonde hair, the lithe athleticism, the bright eyes and straight, white teeth. Match Carol up with Matt, add the two great-looking girls, and the Baker family was just too pretty—the handsome quarterback, his cheerleader, their future cheerleaders, Amherst College and Harvard Law School, the whole picture of perfection.

If they held a couples beauty contest, the Bakers would be crowned Mr. and Mrs. Concord.

I remember one summer Saturday, the Bakers invited us over to swim. Megan and their youngest were toddlers; Gordon and their older daughter were five or six. Nancy wore a modest, blue one-piece suit, and she looked good in it. Then Carol came out in a two-piece, not a bikini exactly, but it didn't matter. She was stunning—muscular like an athlete. I noticed Nancy looking at her too, and there was no missing the look of—I'm not sure of what. Envy? Loss? Annoyance?

At one point Carol brought Nancy a lemonade and tried to engage her in conversation about some flowers. Nancy crossed her arms, drink in hand. Carol squatted down at the flowers to show Nancy, but Nancy's eyes were on Carol, not the flowers. Then Nancy moved away and sat at the table. Nancy didn't stay long. She made some excuse to go home and wrapped herself in a beach towel when she got up to leave.

When I brought the kids home a little later, I asked if she was okay.

"I just have to do some laundry before church tomorrow."

I was sure Carol didn't wear her two-piece suit to compete with or shame Nancy. But I didn't know how to talk about it. "You seemed a little upset when Carol came out,"

I said. "Were you upset by what she wore? Or how she looked?"

"If you got it, flaunt it, right?" Nancy said.

"I don't think she was flaunting it."

"Sometimes you're an idiot, John." And she marched out of the room.

She and Carol were never close after that. Nancy was polite, but not friendly, and we never swam at the Bakers' again.

One time, I decided to sign up for a gym membership to fight my growing paunch and try to stay healthy. I asked Nancy if she wanted to join a gym with me.

"I'm not Carol."

"What does—"

"And I'm never going to look like Carol."

"Honey, you look fine," I said, but she was already out of the room.

Another time, I noticed Nancy's hair getting long and said: "Are you letting your hair grow out?"

"No, I just need a cut," she said.

"I always liked it longer. Maybe you should let it grow out."

The next day she came home with it shorter than ever. I think it indicated the start of her opting for non-descript, invisible clothing; wearing little or no makeup; and adopting a convenient, shake-and-go hair style.

* * *

I was back in my pumpkin patch when I noticed Carol taking a break with ice water, and stretching out in the sun, wearing her two-piece. Shoulder straps pulled down. Waistband rolled down to wee-bikini level. I worked the Baker-side of my pumpkin patch. It was hard not to look. Hard not to want to walk over. But I resisted. My stomach tightened. My mouth went dry. I focused on my pumpkins for a few minutes. I glanced over and saw her getting up, pulling the shoulder straps up, and rolling the waistband back into place. She pulled on a T-shirt and jean shorts.

I turned to focus on some weed pulling. I wondered: Was the pumpkin passion some sort of a transference of my desire for Carol? Or an attempt to "plant" myself in her interest as she tended her flower gardens–hose in hand–sometimes wearing those Lycra pants, or white shorts, or even in her two–piece bathing suit.

My reflex when I stepped out the back door was to look at the Baker house, to look for her; when entering my study, my path circled past the window for a glimpse at their pool and backyard before reaching my desk. Often she was there, fussing over her flowers. (I tried not to take offense she seldom watered the pumpkins. She left that duty to her girls.) From the window of my study, I watched for her to lounge by the pool; though, she seldom came to rest. Carol was a body in motion.

One day, not long before noon, while she puttered around her garden, I imagined myself touching her muscular calf. And then a more rational thought dawned–I'd never even had a private conversation with Carol. Other than the Deacons Dinner at the Bradstreets' and planting the pumpkin seeds, nothing more substantial than a "Hello, how are the kids?" or "lovely weather" had ever passed between us. Hardly titillating conversation.

So the next step, the first step, was to hold a real conversation with Carol. Find some excuse to actually talk. It came to me while sitting on my beach chair among my pumpkins. Brilliant. Obvious. A shared passion for plants. Carol and her flowers, me and my gargantuan gourds. In blue jean shorts, green T-shirt knotted under her breasts like a '40s pin–up girl, white tennis shoes, Carol watered her garden. When she noticed me looking, she waved again.

Crazy as a male beagle, my imagination went nuts. Was it possible Carol wanted me? What if we ran away together? Started a simpler life out west—in California. Became National Park rangers among the giant redwoods. Maybe work at Big Sur State Park and sell T-shirts, serve omelets to tourists from Ohio and Nebraska, and surf in the afternoons. Survive on nature's beauty, granola, and passion. Become hippie yogis and live to be a hundred.

Completely nuts.

To get back on track and prepare my next sermon, I flipped open my Bible randomly and began reading. I don't recall what because my concentration meandered.

"Hi, John."

The sprightly burst of energy caught me by surprise. Carol. Right here!

Shielding my eyes from the sun, "Hi," I said.

From my beach chair, her narrow waist tapered, belly button exposed below the knot of her shirt, right below my eye level.

"What're you doing?" she asked. "Hanging out with your best friends?"

Were they, these pumpkins, my best friends?

"That's how I think of my flowers, you know," Carol admitted. "They're always there for me. They brighten my day. They appreciate what I give them, and they give back even more. If that doesn't sound like a good friend, I don't know what does," she said. "Think I sound crazy?"

What amazed me was she didn't. Not even peculiar. (Though I knew she ought to.)

"Not at all," I grunted as I struggled to stand. Damn beach chairs—comfortable, but no graceful way out of one, especially when you fold my height in thirds. I lost my balance, and a firm grip caught my forearm and centered me. I looked down at the moist hand, fingers overlapping the bracelet on my wrist, her thin but muscular arm, with a cluster of freckles just below the elbow, her shoulder, her blonde hair pulled back, up to her lovely blue eyes. I knew those blue eyes read me and my thoughts. Her hand released my arm, but her eyes held me a moment longer. Meaning what? I wondered.

A breeze freed a wisp of blonde hair to blow across her face, interrupting our connection. Her finger lifted it as she turned her chin to the wind and tucked the wild strands back into the taut ponytail.

I wanted to ask Carol out on a date right then. Or at least to lunch. Was Nancy home? No, she slogged away at the daycare. Kids off to day camp. Matt harangued in some courtroom. But I could not force the question.

"John," she said, pausing as if a coquette, "can we talk?"

"Yes, of course."

"Good," she said. "How about lunch?"

Chapter Eleven

Lunch with Carol

Carol and I agreed to meet for lunch in an hour. I nearly ran to shower for a second time that day. While in the shower I thought about Carol, about her dip in the pool, about her in the shower next door. And the mystery of size responded. Hold on, fella. Lunch, focus on lunch.

I put on a striped tie and then boldly tossed it aside. Did you need a tie with a woman whose best friends were flowers? Such a woman would understand my zeal for Schwartz–that's the name I'd given my largest pumpkin, named after a relic of an Old Testament professor from seminary.

Before heading for the Bakers' house, I made a quick stop at my desk to mark this lunch in my calendar C+. Then I headed out, ducking under a tree branch crossing into their lawn, and there stood Carol. She wore tight–fitting white slacks, red sandals, a red sleeveless cotton sweater, and her aunt's oversized gold jewelry, as well as a cross at her neck. Gucci purse in hand. The outfit again embodied stodgy–sophistication beyond her years, like something my mother would wear to a club luncheon. Or like a trophy wife who'd married a man her father's age and had been sucked into his orbit of the country club set and throttling–back professional associates.

We climbed aboard Carol's Ford Explorer. "Where to?" she asked.

"Anywhere but Concord," I spoke before thinking.

"I hear *that*," she said and backed out of the drive.

* * *

Immediately, I fantasized she and I were married, childless, and free. Or not married! Lovers living together–once again dreaming of the California coast. Snorkeling in wetsuits among the kelp and frolicking with the otters. Frolicking *like* the otters!

Carol drove deliberately, speeding down Route 2 East.

"Where are we going?" I asked.

"Cambridge," she said. "Harvard Square."

Into the bohemian belly of metro Boston, she was a wolf in suburban clothing.

But would it remind her of Matt and his glory days at Harvard Law?

After circling the crowded square three times looking for a parking space, one opened. Trying to parallel park the SUV hog, Carol tapped the car behind and we heard the sound of broken glass. "Shit. Fuck. Crap. Damn," Carol said, pounding the steering wheel.

I jumped out to check the damage. Her high bumper had broken the headlight out of a rusty, old Toyota Corolla. Thinking fast, I pulled a twenty–dollar bill from my wallet, stuffed it inside the ragged glass opening, and told Carol to find a parking garage.

Harvard Square swarmed with summer tourists, milling about the gates of Harvard Yard, awed by thoughts of a nineteen–year–old Teddy Roosevelt, T.S. Eliot, Jack Kennedy, Henry David Thoreau, and dozens of other famous folk who passed through those gates. Parents wondering if their kids might merit such an education. And a number of kids hanging around pretending to be a Harvard student the way I once did late in high school, but I already knew back then I wouldn't follow my father through those hallowed gates. Like so many others, I marveled at the mystique of Harvard. As a freshman across the river at Boston University, I peeked in dorm windows of the anointed, and instead of marble busts of Shakespeare and Einstein and great philosophers, I was dismayed to see the same posters for the same rock bands from my BU dorm.

For seminary, Harvard rejected me. I thought I'd get in because of my father, but no. It pains me to admit it, but while in seminary at Gordon Conwell, thirty miles north of Boston, I hung out in Cambridge and posed as a Harvard Divinity student more than once, a pathetic attempt to improve myself in the eyes of strangers by brushing up against greatness. Why, I can't explain. I wanted to join the chosen. I looked in their eyes, searching for something special there, something I didn't have but might acquire. I also liked the gestalt of Harvard Square back then, the funky bars and bookstores, restaurants and coffee shops.

Now, walking those same streets with Carol, twenty-five years later, the changes were dramatic. And disheartening. It had become like a suburban shopping mall: Gap, Starbucks, Barnes & Noble, Uno's Pizza. Gone were the independent bookstores, the singular restaurants and bars–pushed out by soaring real estate prices.

* * *

Carol and I went to the Border Café. The quirky Tex–Mex joint tried a little too hard to be kitschy and clever in the Sou'West style, but the food was good and cheap. At the entrance, I held the door for Carol and put my hand on her back as she entered. My fingers tingled at the touch of her bra strap under the red sweater and the firmness of her back. I glanced back down Church Street to make sure no one had seen us. Anyone with my imagined intentions would know the need for stealth, but when you tower over the crowd, it's hard to hide.

I saw no one and ducked under the door only to whack my head on an old, dried-out piñata, a yellow-and-purple donkey, hanging from the ceiling. The string holding it broke, and the piñata crashed to the floor in a cloud of dust and cracked open. Desiccated candy scattered everywhere. The whole restaurant turned to see what had happened. Kids descended, materializing from nowhere, four or five urchins, scrambling around on the dirty floor, scrounging up the stale candy like puppies after spilled kibble. Then grownups swept in. Mothers scooped up kids. Waitresses and hostesses snatched up candy in competition with the urchins. Above the pandemonium towered the cause, me, not knowing whether to enter the fray or to back out the door. And then I turned to Carol, fearing a look of horror at being with the big clod, the freak, the weirdo with the Eraserhead hair. But no. She was laughing–not in horror or shame, not laughing at me–just reacting freely to the incident. Another gaffe by the giraffe. Carol's laugh, though not distinctive, not infectious or robust, lit up her lovely face and made me want to bend and kiss her. What's more, her laughter lifted me out of my embarrassment and bestowed humor on the situation, so I could laugh too.

Once the ruckus subsided, we were escorted to a table. One right in the middle of things. No quiet, romantic booth for us. We sat in flat, crude chairs *a la* Old Mexico, and the hostess handed us each a menu. Then we faced the awkward stretch when people sit down for a lunch. Do we talk first and then look at the menu after a prodding or two from the waitress? Or do we study the menu, discuss our choices, place an order, and then turn to the business of visiting? A small thing perhaps, but for some reason meaningful to me.

And then Carol said: "Are you one of those people who sits down and digs right into the menu? No talking until you've arrived at a decision? Or are you the type to talk until the waitress wants to scream?"

"Well, I don't have an official position on the subject, but I admit I try to play off whomever I'm with." A self-conscious blip arose for using "whomever" correctly only to end the sentence with a preposition and wonder if she'd think me uncultured. Oy.

"Me too," she said, "so I figured I'd just ask."

"The act of asking sort of implies you have a preference, though, don't you think?"

"Have we opened an existential dilemma?" Carol said, her eyes wide in mock horror.

An interruption: "Can I get you something to drink?" Pen poised, the waitress didn't even look at us.

"Any specials?" Carol asked.

"They're right inside the menu," the girl snipped.

Carol ordered a Diet Coke, and I ordered an iced tea.

After the waitress walked away, "Let's talk first," Carol said, "just for her."

We ran the course of talking about our kids and summer camps, etc.

Then, interrupted by the abrupt return of the waitress, we made her stand while we quickly scanned the menu and placed orders for burritos, mine chicken, hers beef (which surprised me a bit).

Then talk turned to plants, the way the whole lunch date started. Carol talked about her variety of plants and how tending them gave her a sense of peace, and she asked if I'd ever been interested in gardening, because she couldn't remember me doing it before the pumpkins. I confessed my newfound passion surprised me as much as anyone.

"Sometimes Matt gets so annoyed about my love of plants."

"Well, Nancy said to me, 'For God's sake, John, they're just pumpkins.' Then she accused me of caring more about the giant pumpkins than her or the kids."

I expected a laugh from Carol, but it didn't come.

"What did you say to her?" she asked.

"I told her it was nonsense." I paused a second and something gave way, a dam breaking. "But in truth, I do love Schwartz. That's what I call my biggest one, named after an old seminary professor. What Nancy doesn't understand, and I think maybe you, as a plant lover, might, is how Schwartz did not produce himself." She nodded, and I rolled on. "You see, I believe every person possesses God-given potential for greatness if only he, or she, can find a calling. No easy feat in this world, finding your calling. But this summer, I might have discovered mine in pumpkin growing. There's something kind of spiritual about it." Again I paused to see if she was with me before I went on. She was. So I let it all out, saying, "I think I could come to rank among the world's foremost pumpkin growers. And this"–previously vague thoughts rushed forth, taking shape on my lips, but I let the truth run–"this is the only first-class, even world–class, thing I've ever done. In school, I was a lousy athlete despite my height, unlike Matt, and just a B student. As a minister, I muddle along in my father's shadow, blocked in my efforts to bring change. And financially I feel left behind in our affluent town. But with Schwartz, it's different. Thousands of people at the Topsfield Fair will stand in awe of something I created. Let the cynics like Nancy call it mere pumpkin growing–with Schwartz I have a shot at a type of greatness. It's an opportunity that exists nowhere else in my life."

What I didn't say, what I left her to see for herself, was in becoming a pumpkin kingfish, I left Matt (who was but one of thousands of Boston lawyers), and even my distinguished father, far behind.

"Does this make sense to you?" I asked Carol.

"No," she said.

Oh my God, I thought, I totally exposed myself, pouring out my pain, my idiotic dream to a neighbor, but more, to a parishioner. Some of this I would hold back even from Dennis Cliff. Then I practically call myself a genius—the genius of giant gourds—and she sees right through it. I'm still the ugly nerd, the stork is a dork, who can't open his stupid locker, and Carol Baker poses nearby, the pretty cheerleader laughing at me.

Then she reached across the table to pat my forearm. "John, I'm kidding. You should've seen your face. I'm sorry. That was a little mean. Of course, I understand. I envy your passion to strive for something because I'm searching for a passion myself." She sighed and added, "I don't think I'm capable of greatness anywhere in my life."

I wanted to say, "Just look at you: you're the picture of greatness," but I held my tongue. I understood how beauty, like any God-given talent, guarantees no sense of satisfaction, no assurance of a passion. Someone with perfect pitch may not like music. Someone seven-foot tall may not like basketball.

"At the risk of cliché, Carol," I said, "life is a journey and as long as you're moving ahead, you are more likely to find your calling, your passion." I felt my face go a bit red at using the word "passion" before her, a loaded word. I paused.

She looked at her huge Diet Coke cup, took a drink and continued, "When I stop to think about it, when I'm honest with myself, I see my life passing me by." She glanced up to my eyes and back down to her drink. That's when she said, "I never finished school at North Dakota State—"

"North Dakota State?" I'd expected Wellesley, Smith, or Bowdoin.

"Didn't you know I'm from North Dakota?" she said.
I shook my head.

"Mostly from North Dakota. My father was a military nurse, so we moved around a lot. Mom was a nurse too, civilian side. After Dad left the Army, when I was twelve, my folks went to work for the Chippewa Tribe to help run a medical clinic at Turtle Mountain Indian Reservation on the northern edge of North Dakota."

North Dakota? Indian reservation? Military brat? Daughter of two nurses? I couldn't believe it. Then I imagined, her first kiss with an Indian boy behind an elementary school on a frigid Friday afternoon in February. My mouth gaped, "How'd ...?"

"How'd I get to New England? Matt," she said. "But it's a long story."

"I've got time if you have."

She smiled, nodded, and began: "We both had summer jobs at Grand Tetons National Park. Matt had just graduated in Amherst and was about to start law school."

"At Harvard," I nodded.

"No, he went to Suffolk Law at night while working as a Whirlpool sales rep during the day," she said. "But that's getting ahead in the story." I drifted totally unmoored in this sea of news. "Anyway, we fell in love among the Grand Teton mountains. I went back to school for my junior year, but at the semester break I dropped out and moved to Boston, figuring I'd finish college once I got here. But I never did."

"Why not?"

"Well, John." She looked up at the ceiling. "Life got in the way." She laughed and shook her head and continued before I had to ask. Her eyes moved to the tabletop now. "I got pregnant. We'd decided by then we wanted to get married–after Matt finished law school, so this accelerated things a couple of years. We got married and had a baby, a boy, but he died the next day from heart complications."

"I'm sorry," I said.

She paused and looked up at me. "You know, it's so long ago it seems like another life." Her eyes suddenly brimming, she added, "At least that's what I tell myself. But I think about my baby boy most days. I try to imagine what our lives would be like with him. He'd be fourteen years old now. Hard to believe. How would the girls be different?" Carol glanced around as if to make sure no one was within ear shot. "I wonder if Matt would be more connected to me and the girls. If he'd be different, happier."

"Seems like Matt has plenty to be happy about," I said.

"You'd think."

"But he's not?"

"I don't know." She paused again. "I know some things and some I don't."

I was about to ask what she meant, but I sensed she just needed to circle the thought before taking it up. I drank from my tea, crunched a chip with salsa, wiped my mouth, another sip of tea.

"He's jealous of your life, John," she said.

In a bad movie or TV show, I would have done a spit-take right there, spraying the table and lovely Carol with tea. Instead, I swallowed hard. "What?"

"He is. He envies your conviction, your calling to do God's work, the opportunity to help people, to be a key figure in the community, all of it."

How could it be a man who appeared to have everything could possibly want what I had? The handsome man with the gorgeous wife? The man with the power job and its whopping salary, the stylish suits, the SUV with leather seats, the fine home? And did he really think what I did was God's work? Did I? I had once. Back in Worthington I did. Back when "Reverend Crackstone" didn't have an ironic sting to it.

Carol must have read the disbelief in my eyes because she went on: "He really does, John. He greatly admires you."

Now this I flatly refused to believe. It was one thing to covet my position, my role. Even though I never fulfilled it to my own satisfaction, let alone my father's. From the outside, I understood how my career might look deeply satisfying and meaningful to someone. To a fool. But Matt Baker was no fool. Men of Matt's type and status simply did not admire me. So either Carol was flattering me, or Matt didn't know me. Either way, something inside me cooled to her words.

Then Carol said, "We both admire you," and I went warm and mushy again.

Why would you admire me? I wanted to ask, but I was afraid to shatter whatever status I held with her. Her hand rested on the table (it was heavily veined for a woman her age), and I wanted to rest my hand atop hers. Did I dare? No.

In a moment of silence, she looked deeply into my eyes, searching for something as her gaze shifted from one of my eyes to the other. I was afraid what she might find there in my oversized face. Perhaps a smudge of salsa. She had crow's feet, just fine lines. No doubt the result of sunbathing–or of the harsh North Dakota weather with frigid winters, blistering summers, and winds that left the northwest sides of trees barren. Or could there be something else?

"John?" Her eyes went down to her plate and back up, "Can I talk to you?"

We'd talked a great deal, I thought, and I'd learned more about her and Matt in the last few minutes than I'd known in ten years of living next door. Why stop now?

"I don't have anyone to talk to, to confide in," she said. "And it's very hard."

"Of course," I replied with the drawn resonance of a reverend. Although, the aplomb of my voice belied my fear. Many times I'd experienced a permanent separation from a parishioner following an outpouring of emotion or painful confession. They withdrew because I knew too much. A "dump–and–run" took me from confidante to threat; first they avoided me and then left the church: the man who admitted he'd been unfaithful to his wife with dozens of women; the woman who had maxed–out several credit cards secretly pushing her family beyond the brink of financial ruin and didn't know how to tell her husband; the man who admitted he'd gambled away his children's college fund; the woman junior executive who slept with the CEO to blackmail him for a promotion. It came with my job. But I did not want to lose Carol Baker now that she'd grown close–perhaps because I had no confidant myself and saw a potential one in her.

"My life sucks," she said.

I couldn't help but laugh from the jolt of this lovely woman, dressed like a Talbots model while speaking with coarse candor. A smile passed across her face and faded.

"Excuse my language, but it does," she said. "I am so isolated. Matt is completely disconnected from my life. He goes to work early, comes home late. He misses the girls' activities. Sometimes I think he's having an affair. But he seems too unhappy. Not to you probably, because he puts on a public face. But he's miserable at home. And so am I. Look at my life. If he's unhappy, I'm unhappy. What kind of life is that?"

Before I could answer, she rolled on.

"I have no friends, no family, no sense of community or connection, nothing. Every time I try to get involved with something in Concord, I feel shunned. The 'old rich' with their upper–crust circle don't want an outsider like me interloping on the plant sale for The Grange. The 'new rich' are so busy acting rich and name dropping that they're a bunch of idiots, off to play golf, or compare interior decorators. They don't want a girl from North Dakota who never finished college. The real people don't trust me because they think I'm part of the new rich. Ugly women don't like me because I'm too pretty. Pretty women don't trust me because they feel competitive or threatened. And I don't know the code of the eastern schools. Men, they either see me as a sex object, or they give me a wide berth, allowing nothing but the most superficial connection to avoid accusations from their wives. It's crazy."

"Maybe you should get involved with the church."

"I can't."

"Why not?"

"I don't believe in God."

The frankness or her words struck me like a slap. I knew many parishioners didn't believe in God and attended church for a variety of other reasons from habit to appearances, but none had the courage to say it so bluntly to my face. I loved her for it. I blocked the urge to say, "I don't believe either," because it wasn't so. Was it? Or did I want so desperately to connect with Carol I might renounce my faith on a folly?

"Sorry," she added with a shrug.

"Nothing to be sorry about." Was that the right thing to say? What would my father have said? Who cared? Of course it was right. "Why do you go to church?" I asked.

"For Matt. He thinks it's important for the girls and important for his connection to the community—good for his career. Gotta keep a good, Christian face on things." Then she added, "That's an oversimplification."

"Does Matt believe?"

"Are you kidding? That's another reason I doubt he's having an affair. He's so committed to God, to 'Jesus Christ as his personal savior,' that I expect him to say he wants to become a missionary or seminary student any day now."

"Does Matt know you don't believe?"

"He does, but he thinks as long as I go to church, I'll catch on eventually. Practice, practice, practice. Or maybe catch it like an infection."

Though I recognized the elephant standing next to the table, our conversation avoided anything sexual about spouses. Carol said how Nancy and I seemed to have such a strong relationship. I accepted the comment with an angular nod intended to express ambivalence, and hedged, "All relationships have weaknesses. All have their vicissitudes." Before I had to elaborate, the waitress spared me by delivering the check which I moved to pay, but yielded to Carol and her Platinum Visa Card.

"I invited you," she said.

After we drove back, we parked in her driveway and lingered in her SUV. I turned to Carol. "I'm sorry we never got to finish talking about how your life sucks."

"Don't worry about it. Who really cares about the discontentment of an affluent, white, suburban housewife? First world problems! What could possibly be so terrible?" She paused, and I waited. "With what I saw growing up on an Indian reservation, you'd think I'd be thrilled to be where I am in life. And in many ways, I am. We don't worry about our next meal. Don't worry about health insurance, or education, or housing. What do I have to be upset about, right? Believe me, I know what I have." She paused briefly: "Problem is, I also know what I'm missing."

I held her eyes for a beat. "I'd like to talk about that," I said.

"Next time," she answered.

"When?" I replied, trying not to sound too anxious.

"Thursday?" She meant it.

I pulled out my smartphone and opened the calendar to Thursday. Booked solid. "Thursday it is," I said brightly. The Ladies Auxiliary could plan the Labor Day raffle without me. Or with Shelly Andersen. "How about coffee in the afternoon, 1:30? There's a Pete's in Lexington."

"You're on," she said. "And John, thank you. It's really good to have a friend to confide in. I haven't had one in a long, long time."

"Me either," I said. And those two little words hit me hard. Not only was it true, but for the first time I'd tossed off one of the pastoral tenets: Never entangle your problems with someone you're counseling.

"Thank you," she said and leaned across the seat and kissed me, a peck on the cheek. More than a peck, a kiss, a very real kiss, and the impact of it lingered, tingled with an intensity as though my Crackstone facial nerves rushed to the point and cheered with high-fives.

I wanted to turn my lips to hers, wanted to wrap my arms around her. But of course I didn't. It would have required too much courage for the occasion. I had gotten to this point–now, patience.

* * *

Back in the house I had the sudden urge to vacuum and got started. Thursday for coffee, and Pete's was close but boring. I had to come up with something better. I was vacuuming the last rug downstairs when Nancy walked in. I turned off the vacuum. She gave me a look.

"What?" I said palms raised.

"What is right," she answered. "What have you done?"

"Huh?"

"John, you only vacuum when you've done something wrong. Did you break something or track in a bunch of mud from the pumpkin patch or something? The kids are okay?"

"The kids are fine. Nothing got broken. I just noticed the rug in my study needed a vac, and I thought I should help out a little more around here, so I vacuumed the rest of the rugs on this floor. Gee whiz."

"Okay, thank you," she said. "But if you broke something, you better come clean."

"Coming clean is what this is all about, Nancy, clean rugs." That and putting aside thoughts of Carol.

Chapter Twelve

Coffee with Carol

On Thursday, Carol and I did not go to Lexington's Pete's Coffee, but to Somerville, to Java Jazz. I had surfed the Web to unearth a cool coffee shop in Davis Square in an effort to make me look more hip in Carol's eyes. Java Jazz, an independent joint, featured up-and-coming jazz groups, mostly students from the Berklee College of Music and Tufts University. Different groups rotated through playing from noon to midnight. To hell with Harvard Square. The bohemian heart of Boston now pounded next door in Somerville's Davis Square (once called Slummerville by us snobs)–and Java Jazz was its left ventricle.

The floor was concrete, painted mocha. Tables with mismatched chairs lined two walls; stools with seats not much larger than a paperback book pegged the coffee bar like giant nails. Above the bar dangled six wires with high-efficiency light bulbs, the type with small tubes swirling like a Dairy Queen ice cream cone. On the walls hung original art. One long, olive-green wall held four huge canvases, each as big as a sheet of plywood. Upon closer inspection, I discovered they *were* sheets of plywood. Another wall, painted mustard-yellow, was dotted with small paintings from four-inch squares up to the size of a legal pad. Four couches, picked up at Salvation Army or maybe a street corner, anchored the area around the small stage, frayed fabric, sagging cushions. Not particularly inviting, but Carol must have thought otherwise and headed for a couch, so I followed. We sat down at the same time and sank into the frame.

"Whoa," Carol gasped, falling into me.

"The couch of no return," I said, and Carol laughed. I struggled to extract myself from the sofa. Then I took Carol's hand to haul her out. We moved to a quiet corner table where we could talk and enjoy the kids playing mellow jazz from the safety of wooden chairs. For three hours we hung out talking about plants, kids, schools, spouses—the stuff of life. And it turned out Carol, lovely Carol, looking like the country club mom, hated Concord as much as I did.

"Then how did you come to live in Concord and why do you stay?" I asked.

She explained Matt Baker grew up on a working-class street in neighboring Waltham, and Concord represented the trophy. He loved Concord, loved the white houses with black shutters, loved the history, powerful neighbors, and living at the center of prosperity. It showed everyone from his hometown that Matt had made it. Another of my assumptions about the Bakers was wrong: Matt wasn't a quarterback, but an offensive guard at Waltham High on a lousy football team, never played a sport in college, and went to the University of Massachusetts, not a fancy private school. When she'd mentioned Amherst before, Carol didn't mean Amherst College, but the town of Amherst where U. Mass is located.

"Don't take offense," I said. She nodded for me to go ahead. "Why do you drive a gas-guzzling SUV?"

"You mean the pollution machine? The devil's car?" she said with a laugh, and I was afraid I'd hit a nerve. "I don't care what I drive as long as it starts in the morning. Unlike cars my family had when I was growing up. I prefer a car, but Matt said the Explorer was safer for me and the girls, and if it was, I figured I could live with the environmental impact. But that was before all the news about rollovers and bad braking performance for SUVs. So you'll see a car, an actual car, parked in our driveway pretty soon, probably a Volvo wagon or whatever Matt thinks is safe."

As I came to know her better, I believed I could ask about her style of dress without offending. I had to know why she was so different from what her Talbots–conservative clothes suggested. The messages spun very much at odds–nothing in her choice said down–to–earth, Army brat, and kid who grew up on a North Dakota Indian reservation, or North Dakota State University drop–out. Finally I got up the courage to ask, "Why do you dress like you do? Like the country club wife?"

"That's bold," she said, and my heart tumbled. "John, I wear what I like."

"Of course," I said, sensing I'd offended far more than I'd imagined.

We were quiet for a bit. Both of us turned to watch the jazz quartet, and I cursed myself for being stupid enough to blunder into such territory.

Then Carol picked it up: "Or at least"–she paused–"I like what I wear well enough. I'll admit my clothes are about fitting in and upholding Matt's values. My jewelry is from Matt, but I think his mother chooses. Most of my clothes come from two places: Talbots and Ralph Lauren. Safe, conservative, practical. The only one of those three words that fit with my personality is practical. My position on fashion is kind of like the car. I don't really care what I wear so much–as long as it starts in the morning."

Her timing was good with the joke, and I laughed even though her tone left little room for it.

Then she turned to the jazz players again.

"I didn't mean to offend," I said.

"I know," she answered without looking at me and blindly patted my forearm.

* * *

We watched the jazz like strangers sharing a table, a circle of gold-specked Formica between us. A lesbian couple necked openly on the couch-of-no-return–their half-dozen piercings (eyebrows, nose, lip, and ears) made me itch–and I wondered what Carol thought of them. The smaller of the two caught me looking at them twice and whispered something to her girlfriend, lover, comrade. Then the other turned to sneer at me and flipped me the bird.

"Did you see that?" Carol said. "She gave you the finger." She laughed. "What did you do?"

"Nothing."

"John ... What did you do? Were you staring at the girls?" And she laughed again.

We were quiet and watched the jazz players.

Carol finally broke the silence between us: "You know, you don't really dress the way you are either. Look at the conservative suits you wear on Sundays. You're not a suit guy. You're a sweatshirt or sweater–and–jeans guy. A tweed sport-coat person when dressed up, but there you stand, John, every Sunday up before your flock in a dark suit, white or blue button–down shirt, red tie. Black or cordovan wingtips. Wingtips, John! Wingtips for crying out loud–the size of sea kayaks. What's that about? What's the message? Who are you trying to be, John Crackstone?"

Her words hit me like a blackjack. Just who the hell *was* I trying to be? Dad? Dear old Dad? The *real* Reverend Crackstone? I had adopted my father's dress to the thread. Carol was completely right: my clothes suited me about as well as the Talbots and gaudy jewelry suited her. But how could I change? Sounds stupid, but despite how ill–fitting they were to my spirit, the thought of trashing my seven, beautifully tailored suits stymied my brain. All of my suits were handmade by the Polish tailor in Acton–"Fifty years, and 'dis is the longest suits I ever made. The longest!"–I still heard him.

Carol turned back to the jazz players.

I laughed.

She turned to me.

"Aren't we a pair?" I said. "We don't dress for success; we dress to deceive. Or to hide in plain sight. We dress how others expect us to dress." From there, I was just thinking out loud. "What does it say about us? You're right. Who am I trying to be? Who am I trying to please? It hurts to hear myself say it, and it hurts to ponder, but you know, I think I'm trying to be my father–at least with my clothes. But maybe in other ways too. And I never wanted to be like my father. So why do I wear clothes that look like they came right from his closet? There are ministers who don't wear the dark suit every Sunday. Why do I? It's Concord, I think. It's the way a minister is supposed to dress in Concord."

"You never wanted to be like your father?"

"No."

"You don't want to be a very successful minister, a widely regarded community leader? Come on, John," she said. "If you didn't want to be like him, why did you follow him into the ministry? And why did you take over his job and move into his house? For crying out loud, John, be honest with yourself. From where I sit, you're desperately trying to be your father. Did you have two kids just like your father? Did you marry someone just like your mother? Wasn't she a school teacher like Nancy?"

Whack, whack, whack–her verbal blackjack came down again and again. I was punch drunk, out on my feet.

"Hell, John, you probably went to the same schools."

"No ..." I said, "but only because I wasn't accepted into his."

"John, John, John–" she said, her head shaking.

"And by the way, Nancy is nothing like my mother. Not really. Or, at least she didn't used to be."

"What does that mean?" Carol asked, blackjack at the ready.

"It just means, oh hell, Carol, it just means I don't know who Nancy is any more. The last time we felt connected was who knows when? What's worse is neither of us exhibits much concern about it. Neither of us misses the other enough maybe. We clank along through our lives on autopilot. It's kind of sad. And as for my mother, you know what? In many ways, I never knew who my mother was either. She lived in the shadow of my father, largely invisible. Even to herself, I suspect. She was nonexistent except in service to her king." Oh my god, I thought, what a horrible thing to say about your mother, you shit, you big turd, you seven-foot turd. "That's a terrible thing to say," I added.

"It's a worse way to feel."

My eyes welled-up and my throat went tight. "Yes."

I watched the college kids butcher a lick of John Coltrane and looked up at the ceiling, coaxing the tears back into my eyes.

We were quiet for a minute.

"That's probably how Matt sees me," Carol said. "Probably how a lot of people see me. It's how my children will look back on me if I'm not careful."

"Not you," I said.

"Don't patronize me. And don't be an amicable idiot," Carol hammered. "That pisses me off."

I sat back. "Wow, Sorry."

"John ..." she said, wagging her finger in a warning. "It means, I know how men tend to see me. Just because I have a pretty face or am slender–damn foolishness. Look at my life. I'm invisible except in service to my kids and my king."

I hadn't meant to spark this fire, and I sure as hell didn't know how to put it out. Again, lack of skill as a lady's man, or as a minister–I don't know which. Maybe both. She turned to the jazz musicians, but her whole body was rigid with anger, her jaw set.

I sat back and waited to see if the jazz would cool off her anger.

Who was this woman, Carol Baker? Who was Nancy Crackstone? Who was my sister? Who was my mother? Why was it I never had any women who were true friends? When did I lose my sense of knowing Nancy and why?

All of this bugged me but none of it got to me more than the question of my mother. My mother, my mother, my mother–who was she? Who was Lillian McLarson Crackstone? The question began to burn a hole. Man, I couldn't begin to answer the question. If you can't answer that one, if you don't know who your mother is, can a man know another woman? Since childhood I'd been so focused on my father. The whole family had, and certainly my thinking about the family, had revolved around my father. Other than grilled cheese sandwiches, and mittens, rides to the movies, and a quiet presence in the corner of the congregation, the "be carefuls" and "goodnight dears," who was my mother? Right there, drowning in a quarter–inch of cold coffee at the bottom of my cup, I resolved I had to go see my mother in Arizona and find out who she was.

About then, Carol turned from the jazz quartet, anger burning in her blue eyes like a gas flame. She wasn't ready to let me get away just yet.

"So who *was* Nancy, and why don't you know who she is now?"

Like a high school kid who doesn't want to do his homework, I groaned, "I don't know, Carol."

"Well you better figure it out, bucko," she said, still ticked off at me, and turned back to watch the band.

"You're right," I said, "I need to figure out my life in relation to the women close to me: my wife, my mother, my sister." I very nearly added Carol to the list. "Okay, I have my homework assignment. But how about you? Do you know who Matt is?"

"Oh yes, I know Matt Baker. When someone is as focused on goals as Matt, they become less complex, more narrow, easier to understand. He's not narrow in the conventional sense, not like your average businessman who can talk about his business and sports and little else. Matt gobbles up all kinds of facts and tidbits. You've seen it. He loves knowing things, but all these scraps of knowledge are not about curiosity–they serve a purpose. They demonstrate his intelligence and allow him to connect with people on most any subject. Which helps him win clients on the sidelines of kids' soccer games, at the hardware store, or at church events."

This last comment sounded an alarm in me. Was Matt's service in the church disingenuous? Was his faith? Was the Congregational Church his recruiting ground or stepping-stone, like joining the Chamber of Commerce was to an accountant?

"The problem is," she said, "he doesn't know who I am. And he doesn't show much desire to know."

"I find that hard to believe."

"Why?" she said, with the same edge in her voice she'd had when I blundered into the fashion comment.

"It's just I can't imagine not wanting to know you."

"John, you don't know me. We've lived next door to each other for nearly a decade, and you learned more about me in two days than in all those years. And you're just now getting to know me. Not that I'm so mysterious or complex. What I'm telling you is it's not easy for me to get to know people, and most people, for some reason, don't want to get to know me. Including my husband."

"Carol, I still find it hard to believe. I'd think that men especially would want to get to know you, if only because you're so beautiful."

"Two things. First, it's not such a great gift to be beautiful because, like I said before, some people don't trust you, and others want to possess you the way they want to own fine art. As for Matt, he has not shown much interest in me for a long time. He has big ambitions and is focused on his career and his clients, and there's not much time left over. I'm an asset. When he's home–and you know he gets home late most nights–when he's home, he's often at work, sitting at his desk in the home office, tapping away at the computer, drafting a contract or brief or whatever. Even when he's with us, his mind is at the office." As she spoke, she turned her wedding ring around and around, pausing with the big diamond on the inside and clenched. I wondered if it hurt. "About three times a year," she said, "I find him packing for a business trip that he forgot to even mention. If he took less interest in the girls and me, if he were less connected, he wouldn't come home at all. When I even begin to complain, he reminds me that our lifestyle, the ease and comfort of my lifestyle, exists because of how hard he works." She paused for a fraction of a second before continuing. "And that's true. After growing up on Army bases and a reservation, it's easy to recognize and appreciate where I am. But I'd happily live a simpler life and work part time, especially if it meant I could feel more complete as a person, and if we could be partners in parenting–because I'm just not good enough at it to go it alone–and if we could recapture some of the hus-band-and-wife thing again."

Boy, if I didn't want to pursue what that meant–*recapture some of the husband-and-wife thing*. Was it a euphemism for sex? Had to be. I wanted to delve into the subject, to dive into it, but how could I in the middle of her emotional sharing? I had no idea how to connect the vague dots in such a quantum leap. Hell, I'd never even learned calculus.

"You mentioned you'd like to work," I said. "What would that look like for you?" And recognizing the minister psycho-babble I stumbled on: "What would you do if you had the choice?" To this line straight out of Pastoral Care 102, she replied:

"Oh, God, I don't know, Reverend Crackstone."

I smiled at this poke.

"Maybe, you should pursue a job, or some meaningful volunteer work. Find something that helps you grow and gives you a sense of connection and fulfillment."

"Maybe," she replied with the thud of a hammer on concrete. "Matt likes having me home when the girls get out of school and in summers. He also likes providing for all of us in a fine and comfortable style, living in Concord–it's all part of the prize for being a successful lawyer. It separates him from his working-class upbringing, powers him above it, like a pole-vaulter or something. In the same way he strives to be a great lawyer, driven to rise above his education at Suffolk Law to stand above the best of his partners educated at Harvard. The thing is, as you saw with your father, reaching for the pinnacle in any field comes at a cost. And it's the family that pays the price."

Thinking about my childhood, I had to agree. We all came after my father and his job, the calling as we called it, the tending of the flock. But it made me wonder about all of those people out there who never reach for the pinnacle and screw up their families anyway. Like me. I hadn't screwed up my family much, but I was rolling toward the precipice. Perhaps because I didn't strive hard enough for the pinnacle, failing to reach my father's summits. And the drip-drip-drip of disappointment began to fill the pail of regret in my soul.

Again, I thought out loud and unchecked: "What if you could align the family behind the pursuit of the pinnacle–whatever it represented for the family leader–couldn't it actually create a bond? Does it have to create emotional waves of neglect, loneliness, and resentment?"

"Sounds like bullshit to me, John," she said. "How can the family bond around Matt trying to be the next Oliver Wendell Holmes? Or you trying to be the next William Crackstone? Or even your attempt to become the world's greatest pumpkin grower?" She looked at me for a second. "They are all personal pursuits with only one star. Matt's the star. You're the star. Don't expect a family to get behind your mission one hundred percent or to avoid becoming the wreckage."

Her voice carried a subtle but razor-sharp edge of disdain.

"I'm hardly a star," I said.

"But you want to be, Big John. That's the rub."

And I went quiet at the recognition.

Yes, I wanted to achieve greatness in something besides height, and I had come to accept I would never match my father in the ministry. I could at best be a stand-in–and I hadn't done my best for a long time. In pumpkins lay my shot at greatness.

The changeover of jazz groups covered our need for conversation; must have been time for psychology class. The new group included a skinny little white girl, an anorexic looking thing who probably weighed all of ninety-seven pounds, but when she sang, wow. Somewhere in her waifish chest were real lungs with real power. Neither Carol nor I could believe our ears and eyes. Rather than ape Billy Holiday or Nina Simone, she took her own tact and belted out her own angle on jazz standards.

We listened to four or five songs before leaving. Time for Carol to pick up her girls. Time for me to feed the pumpkins.

The drive back to Concord was a little quiet, perhaps as we both thought about what was said and what lay ahead. I kept wondering what the silence meant.

Chapter Thirteen

A Visit from Jack

The next morning, I went out to check on my pumpkins. I pulled my beach chair into the shade and deliberately turned it away from the Bakers' house. The way things had ended with Carol the day before at Java Jazz, I thought she'd want some room. I did too. She was pretty tough on me, pretty confrontational, but I wanted to be among my "friends" as she called them. I had my little table and a TV tray set up.

Next I built a tent over Schwartz made of a blue tarp and PVC pipes. I'd learned the sun dries the outside, making giant pumpkins more prone to splitting, a common problem. If one splits, you can't enter it in a competition. For my other three large ones, I bent small PVC pipes in a hoop and protected them with painters' drop cloths. This providing and protecting satisfied me and gave me a sense of accomplishment the way looking at a Thanksgiving feast did.

I took my seat in the faded beach chair and made notes for my next sermon. I couldn't help but also run some numbers again for the pumpkin seeds:

If Schwartz exceeded 2,000 pounds,

If Schwartz yielded 500 seeds,

If I got $50 per seed, that produced $25,000.

It wasn't enough to launch a business, but it would set me up for the next year, and cover part of a used BMW or Lexus. I also had the other three giants which might be top-ten finishers at the Topsfield Fair weigh-in. They could pull in $15 to $20 per seed. At 500 seeds each, we'd rake in more than $22,000. And for the other three giants, I could probably bet $5 to $10, so that's another–

"Having a campout with your friends?" It was Carol, Red Sox T-shirt and blue jean cutoffs.

"Hi," I said. I didn't try to get up since I'd made a fool of myself before.

"Do you have a minute?"

"Sure."

"Look, I'm sorry I was such a jerk yesterday. I really overstepped my bounds. I don't know what got into me."

"It's okay."

"No, not so much," Carol said. "And I want to apologize."

"I accept your apology."

"They're amazing, your pumpkins. They must be almost twice the size of ours."

"I culled out the smaller ones, and I water them like mad." I laughed. "I don't know if Matt mentioned it, but I even got in a little trouble with the deacons for the excessive water usage."

She laughed. "Those tight-asses."

"Matt sent a plumber over to look for leaks in our pipes."

"What? He's a tight-ass too. What a doofus."

We both laughed.

"Seriously, John, I also wanted to say I really appreciate your friendship over the last week." She paused. Her voice rose a couple of octaves, and her eyes went watery. "It's meant more to me than you know."

She stepped forward, closing the gap between us and gave me a big hug around the neck. With me sitting in the low beach chair, we were about the same height, and I hugged her back.

"I appreciate our friendship too," I said.

Carol started to let go and then pulled me close again, pulling my head down near her breasts, into the Red Sox logo. "I'm so sorry I was a bitch to you yesterday."

"Carol," I said in a soothing tone, and she let go of me, "you were never 'a bitch' to me. Your candor got a little pointed, but not bitchy." We both smiled, and she lifted a tear from her eye. "Most of it felt more like two friends being honest, and expressing that honesty in the safety of friendship."

She stepped forward and hugged me a third time, and I patted her back. "Thank you. I was so afraid I'd ruined it."

I started to speak, but decided there was nothing left to say.

"All right. Thank you again, for everything," she said. She started to walk away, tight jean shorts, and turned back, "Up for another coffee or lunch soon?"

"Yes." I flipped the page of my seed calculation and held up my pad with a blank page. "Early next week, Monday or Tuesday. After I give this sermon. Which means, I'd better get going on this sermon."

"Right," she said, pointing at me with both index fingers. "One of us has a job." And she bounded out of the yard.

* * *

After Carol left, I went back to work on my sermon, trying to focus and make headway. I had my smartphone and a dumb pencil, scratching a few notes on the old–fashioned pad of paper. But I wasn't getting much done between stints of weeding and watching for Carol. I had pulled my "Potentials" folder before coming outside–stuffed with incomplete or failed sermon ideas I still held onto, a hodge-podge of promising sparks and fragments from dreams, showers, drives home, or random readings. I was sorting through this rubbish, mining for a gemstone, when my phone rang.

It was Jack Corbett, my rich friend and software entrepreneur from Texas.

"Hey, buddy," he yelled over a ragged cell phone connection straining at its limits.

"Jack? Where are you?"

"Somewhere in the Midwest. Indiana? Ohio? I'm driving up to Boston on business—and to visit you, I hope."

He drove, he said, because he hadn't driven that path since moving to Texas after we finished seminary over twenty years ago. And because he'd just bought a 1966 Porsche 356. "Owned by a little old lady who only drove it to church on Sundays," Jack said. "Of course she drove it 100 miles an hour. And John"—he paused before adding—"I'm driving it 100 miles an hour myself right now, top down, and she handles like a dream—fan-fucking-tastic German engineering. I must look like an indigo bullet to those cows I just passed."

That's when I realized the cell connection was fine, it was just the road and wind noise.

"Just don't kill yourself before you get here, Cowboy," I told him.

"Talk to you tomorrow, partner."

* * *

The next morning, when I walked out the back door to check on my pumpkins, someone stood over Schwartz. I started to yell, but then realized it was Jack. He'd driven all night.

"You look like hell," I said as I crossed the backyard.

"At least I have an excuse. What's yours?" he said, slapping away my outstretched hand and giving me a bear hug.

When you're a friend, you get all of Jack all the time. "No-holding-back Jack" as a seminary-school dean dubbed him, when Jack bristled at the suggestion he learn when to hold his tongue following a heated argument with good old Professor Schwartz.

Hugging him, I realized how much shorter Jack was than I'd remembered. At five-feet, ten-inches—he stood more than a full foot shorter than me. But because of his success, it seemed his physical stature should exceed mine. He was still fit, not skinny but compact and well-built, like a good middle-aged tennis player. His hair remained thick and dark (graying around the temples for distinction), parted on the side, like a grown-up Ken doll, like the picture most people would draw of a successful company president.

"Dude, you've got some monster pumpkins going here," Jack said. "I've never seen anything like it. Especially this one." And he thumped Schwartz with his sneaker.

I resisted pushing him back and said, "Easy Cowboy, they're more fragile than they look."

"Well it looks about as fragile as a Brahman bull."

I told him the biggest one was named Schwartz.

"Schwartz?" He howled. "It really is an old bull! It's about as lumpy and bumpy as that old fart too. Wonder if the old son-of-a-bitch is still alive."

"He died a few years ago."

The smile slid from his face for a second. Then it returned, and he asked what was up with the pumpkins.

"So what brings you up to New England?" I asked.

"We'll get to that," he said, "but first I want to know what's with this Schwartz, the Great Pumpkin."

Since he was interested, I told him about the Topsfield Fair; about the process of planting the pumpkins; about my special, secret fertilizer (sparing the details of human hair and such); about the culling down to these select giants; about the huge water bill and the wacky reaction of my deacons; and, finally, about how I saw these pumpkins, specifically Schwartz, as an opportunity to achieve a mark of greatness.

It was then I realized I'd gone too far somewhere down the track. His eyes did not so much glaze over as darken with concern for me and my new passion. Obsession?

"It's a little crazy, Man," he said with a little shake of his head. "But I love it."

Then he backhanded my shoulder and added: "You didn't come to bunt." This baseball analogy was something Jack liked to say about his attitude toward life: "I didn't come to bunt." No, Jack Corbett swung for the fence, or he wasn't in the game.

Walking back to the house, Jack's energy, his bounce, reminded me of Dennis Cliff. As the thought dawned on me, I saw Jack and Dennis were similar, but also very different, and I doubted they'd even like each other. Each of them stood for something. Dennis was dedicated to God and his community. Jack to his company, his sense of fun, and business success. They were fully realized. It made me wonder at myself. Why was it every role I played in my life was an imperfect fit: father, husband, man–of–God, pumpkin grower, would–be lover?

Jack wanted to show me the classic sports car. After a few minutes of small talk and teasing about the long drive in the little car, which looked to me more like a deep–blue scarab beetle than the bullet Jack imagined, we went in the back door.

There at the sink stood a middle–aged woman, wearing baggy, old-man pajamas, her short hair mussed in all directions. My wife. She held a plain–white coffee mug. In a flash, my imagination pictured Carol in her kitchen, wearing an ivory teddy perhaps, or maybe she'd already be in her shiny white Lycra shorts and sports bra, preparing to hit the gym, blonde hair pulled back in a ponytail. And I imagined how impressed my old friend would be if the lovely Carol Baker were my wife.

Nancy's sleepy eyes registered who stood next to me, and she lit up. "Jack Corbett!" she yelled, "What are you doing here at this hour?" She banged down her mug and rushed to hug him. "Don't tell me you drove all night, you crazy nut." Then her face flashed a self-consciousness. "I'm a total mess," she said smoothing down her hair and closing her pajama top up around her neck. "You two sit down and have some coffee. I'll go try to get a little more presentable."

* * *

I reopened the subject of his visit.

Jack kind of shook his head. "It probably won't amount to much, but I have a series of meetings with a software firm in Cambridge. They're looking for leadership help."

Nancy came back and offered to make Jack breakfast.

"When was the last time you offered to make me breakfast?" I joked, but truth was I couldn't recall. When the kids came downstairs, it was funny to watch their discomfort with Jack and his with them. I would've expected the whacky, fun uncle routine, but that's not how it went. Both parties looked only briefly into each other's faces. I'd noticed this odd dance of childless adults around their friends' kids many times. Years ago, I assumed Jack would have kids, especially because he married young, but following his divorce, he never remarried.

After breakfast, Jack announced he could use a nap and went upstairs to the guest room for a snooze.

I woke him up about five hours later for a late lunch. Last I heard, he owned a company, so I wanted to hear more about the reason for his visit, and I started to wonder if he was hiding something. Was it really for a job? We walked into town to eat at the Wayward Tavern, and en route Jack marveled at the details and charm of old

Concord. The Wayward Tavern stood at the edge of the village, an inn built in the 1750s, and I had to crouch worse than at the Bradstreet home, almost as bad as our basement, to avoid the old chamfered beams in the ceiling. The hostess led us to a table by a window with its small panes looking out through wavy-and-bubbled glass toward the town green. Sitting there, one easily imagined the whispering Revolutionaries huddled over pewter tankards of ale, plotting the downfall of British rule.

When Jack noticed I hadn't opened the menu, he asked what I was having.

"The Plowman's," I said, and my mouth watered at the thought of the large bowl of thick beef stew and crusty bread–with a side salad to suit today's palate.

"Sounds good," Jack said.

The waitress brought us waters and took Jack's order and turned to me, saying with a nod: "Plowman's also, Reverend Crackstone?"

"So you're a regular, Reverend," Jack said.

"Yeah, I'm just a regular reverend." We both smiled.

"Are you two brothers?" the waitress asked.

"With this giraffe? No way."

"Or with this knucklehead?" I added.

The girl laughed and walked away. "Brothers?" I said.

"Brothers-by-choice," Jack said and raised his water glass.

"To brothers-by-choice," I said and tapped his glass.

In the brief pause that followed, Jack scanned the room. The atmosphere of the place was as authentic as it gets, the worn pine floorboards eighteen or twenty inches wide, the walk-in brick fireplace, the ancient paneling. The tables and chairs, while reproductions, were probably a hundred years old and showed plenty of wear, a lovely patina as they said on *Antiques Roadshow*, and did nothing to dispel the deep resonance of history. "Nothing like this in Texas," Jack said. "Kinda makes me want to move back to New England."

"You haven't spent much time here since seminary, right?"

"Just a few business trips."

"And what inspired this trip?"

"Well, my latest company failed."

I made a face.

"Yeah, I got cocky, after building and selling four companies. With Mesa Tech I thought I had figured out a better way to run it." He shook his head. "It just goes to show, past success may be an indicator of future success, but it's no guarantee."

"Did you lose a lot?" I asked.

"Yeah, I got slaughtered. But I had plenty squirreled away." He tapped his fingers on the table. "So financially, I'm fine. My pride, my business reputation, well, those took a hit. It might be a good time to get out of Texas." He tapped his fingertips on the table a few more times. "If you're in the game, you're going to lose sometimes. This time I lost. And that's why I'm here. I have meetings scheduled with MaxStaff Software, a Cambridge software company. One co-founded by a woman who was our Chief Technology Officer at Mesa Tech. We're friends and there's a high level of trust. We'll see, I'm just looking at options. While it's not clear, I think they want a senior leader to help them grow. Or they may be looking for investment. Hell, I could even end up running it." He took a deep breath, and started to tap his fingertips on the table again and stopped himself.

He went on to explain that a bunch of tech cowboys Jack knew in Austin wanted him to help run a startup company called Blue Ox Drones. They built drones for agriculture to track livestock, check crop growth, reduce broad spraying of pesticides, and manage irrigation. "The founder keeps saying: 'Blue Ox Drones, it's gonna be HUGE,'" Jack said, arms wide and grinning.

He'd also been recruited by a California venture capital firm to guide investments in Texas. "But it's hard to pick a winning racehorse, and when the economy sags or the competition coughs, these VC cats start calling at noon every day to ask about the morning burn rate, and they call again before they go home to kick the dog. So I'm probably not doing that, but I'm not rushing." He chuckled. "Part of me wants to step out of tech all together and open a farm stand in Vermont or something."

Or maybe start a pumpkin farm, I thought.

Over a second post-lunch pint of ale at the Wayward Tavern, I asked, "When you say you have money squirreled away—"

"Enough," he said. Then whispered: "Confidentially, into eight figures."

It took me a few seconds to comprehend just what that meant: 100,000 was six figures; a million, seven figures. "You mean over ten million dollars?" I hissed. My eyebrows hiked up and my head jutted forward in shock.

"Into the tens, yes," he said.

"Don't tease me," I whispered. "Are we talking eleven million or ninety-nine million?"

"About twenty-five," Jack said.

"So you don't really need a job."

"Depends on how you look at it, John. I don't need money. But I'm forty-nine years old, have a ton of business knowledge, plenty of energy, and a lot of desire. I'm not looking to quit. I'm thinking about what's next. Entrepreneurs have a hard time coasting."

I was just listening. But I also calculated when to tell him about the potential pumpkin business. Maybe Jack would invest, and I could work at it full time. Maybe we could do it together.

Chapter Fourteen

What Gets Measured

"Let me explain how I see business and how I got there," Jack said.

This was the day after his meetings in Cambridge with MaxStaff Software, and we were sitting on a slab of granite amid a jumble of boulders at the ocean's edge north of Boston. We'd gone for a ride in his 1966 Porsche–top down and me squeezed into the seat, wearing an orange university of Texas baseball hat he loaned me. "Otherwise your forehead and hair will catch more bugs than the grille," Jack said. The stupid hat barely fit with the back opened all the way. We ended up in the North Shore town of Magnolia, a place we frequented when at Gordon Conwell Seminary.

"After my MBA, when I got started in tech, I followed my mentors and read all the startup books and magazines and chased the venture capital dollars, all that crap. Only I didn't know it was crap.

"I totally bought into the money scorecard–followed Peter Drucker's saying, 'What gets measured gets managed.' And the measure was money–how much you pulled in from investors, the sales figures, the profit margins, how much you made, the house and cars, the neighborhood, even the view from my office window. All of the trappings.

I got good at it, really good at it. Built and sold four companies in a row.

"Anyway, here's what I learned after my fourth company, and some of my critics say it's why I failed with my fifth, with Mesa Tech. Those idiots." He shook his head. "I'm ashamed I had to learn it the hard way. But what matters is not the money. What matters is the people. What matters is job creation. Sounds simple, but it flies in the face of what the venture capital fools tell you. They want you to hold off hiring anyone until it's dire, until staff members strain to the breaking point, and if there's the smallest bump in the road, they want you to fire people as fast as you can."

A gray seagull flew overhead and dropped a crab on a granite boulder with a crack, then landed and started picking it apart. Jack didn't even notice and continued his speech.

"Sure, people are expensive. But if a business is not built to create jobs and to create wealth for others, what the hell is the point? If it's just to make the rich cats at the VC more money, that's both stupid and immoral. They don't need money. Same for the executives and founders. Beyond a point, I don't need money.

"What drives me today is creating good jobs. Simple as that.

"John, you know about my dad. He couldn't hold a job. The poor guy fought alcoholism his whole life. Until alcohol won. And the family lost. That's why I turned to the church and Christianity in high school. People there offered love and stability and understanding. Except when I became a minister. Then it got lonely, and after my affair, the judgmental charlatans who somehow forgot the fundamental idea of 'forgive each other as Christ forgave you' were quick to kick my ass into the street. The sons-of-bitches.

"So I turned to tech, and money, and typical success measures. Until I realized all of it amounted to worshiping a false God."

Another seagull, black-and-white, dropped out of the vast blue sky, colliding with the gray one to drive it away from the crab. They squared off and squawked at each other for a few seconds, wings half-cocked, before the gray one flew away.

Jack, unfazed by the racket, rolled on. "Most of my critics say my failure was I hired as many people as I could at Mesa Tech. Too many people, too fast. I say we hired as many as we needed to run the company in an effective and humane way. Staff could get home for dinner with their families and coach little league soccer or help with homework. Maybe I did encourage my management team to hire a few extra people in advance of the growth curve. But you know what? People wanted to work for us, for me, and we were going great guns. Until ..."

This was the first time Jack Corbett paused since he started this rant. His hand pushed back his hair, and he scanned the shoreline, his eyes coming back to focus on the granite between us as if he were recounting the headlines in the business section.

"Okay," I said, to make sure I was tracking, "some of your critics say you grew too fast and hired too many people. I get that. But what do the others say?"

"Thanks for asking me to dig into my failure, Reverend Crackstone." He laughed. "Just kidding." He thought about it for a few seconds and said, "In the simplest terms, the other critics say I just wasn't able to lead a company with twenty-two hundred employees.

"Here's what I say to that. *Maybe.* Maybe I took my eye off the ball. Maybe we grew too fast and became slow-footed. Maybe we were complacent. Maybe I fulfilled the Peter Principle as CEO."

Again he paused. "But we were going strong. Until a better technology beat us. Everybody knows change happens fast in tech, and when Microsoft decided to invade our data-management niche and bought our strongest competitor and then heavily invested in our second-best competitor. They both blew past us like we were competing in the Tour de France on tricycles.

"So, yeah, we crashed and burned. I lost a lot of money and took a reputation hit, but worse, I had to lay off twenty-two hundred people, great people. All those jobs, gone. It was a much bigger and more public failure than getting booted from the ministry in a Texas cow town.

"Do I have something to prove, now?" Jack paused, looking at the gulls gathering near us.

I waited.

"Do I have something to prove? Depends on the day you ask me. Some days I want to build another company to kick ass and show the world it's okay to put people over profit. Not 'okay', it's *better*. Sometimes I want to get on the VC side and prove it with two dozen small companies. And sometimes I want to walk away from it all and run my little Vermont farm stand.

"No matter what, I know the next thing will be something more human than most of the tech industry. And smaller than Mesa Tech. I want to work with people I care about and do work with a direct and positive impact on people's lives. These management types talk about balancing their personal and professional lives, but the higher up they go, the less personal life they have. Married to their jobs. Not that I want to get married. My goal is to blur the lines of professional and personal until they're one and the same. In clear, tangible, and rewarding service to people. Minimize pressure and stress. Reduce guilt and FOMO. Make your life wholly one thing that grows into a rewarding and satisfying sum total. Then—"

He halted. He turned away to look out at the water, then at the two dozen or so gulls perched on the boulders in the sun, all facing the sea.

Jack interrupted himself, turning to me: "Wasn't it John Updike who said about seagulls, 'as if God made too many to make any one well'?"

I laughed. "I don't know. You were the English major." They were a motley crew, the gulls, in various shades of black and white and gray—most with some feather out of place or seaweed hanging from a beak or a bloody eye.

I was quiet, waiting for Jack to circle back to his thought.

He was still looking at the birds, so I decided to bring it back. "Let me challenge you a bit," I said. "On one hand you're talking about people having a personal life outside work, being the little league coach or whatever, and then you're talking about blending the personal and professional life into one. That sounds like Google with their campuses of housing, food, and endless work hours. Aren't those two ideas at odds?"

His blue-gray eyes came back. "Do they have to be?" He rubbed his jaw. "Can't they coexist? I was speaking of myself, of my own life, when I said I wanted to blur the personal and professional until they're one and the same. I hope to achieve that level of meaning in my life. I don't envision it for staff members. There's a reason many employees ..."—Jack emphasized "employees" with air quotes—"... buy bass boats to go fishing, or dream of a cabin in the woods—because they need to escape work. And they should. I support them. But in my own life, I want the fulfillment to blend across my waking hours. As it does for the best ministers, right?" He paused to solidify the idea. "Like it probably does for you, John. It's all work in a way; all in service of God, right? Even sitting in on a church beautification committee or some community service group, it's all work, but it's all fulfilling because it's in service of the greater mission."

Is it? I wondered. *Is it fulfilling? And is it in service of a greater mission?* There was no question it all felt like work. Even with the help of Shelly Andersen, if I was awake, I was working. Or that's how it felt. Until the pumpkins. Them, and Carol Baker.

Jack was talking again.

"—and then there's the other side of you—of *me*—that wants to kick ass and take the hill. I'm good at business, John. I get excited about a great idea, a challenge, and I'm all in. I like to rally others around it, and push it through execution."

He slapped his thighs. I waited, watching him machete through his thoughts. On the long drive from Texas, he'd had a lot of time to think. "Let's walk and talk, okay?"

We got up, my knees and hips a little stiff from sitting on granite. We climbed the beautiful boulders and walked along the sloped stretches of granite wary of deep cracks and staying clear of the dark, slippery algae near the water threatening a slide into the cold ocean with the promise of death by waves pummeling us against rock and unable to get a grip with the wet algae, and no way to pull your friend out. At a tide pool we paused to take it in. Not much bigger than a bath tub, it teemed with life–small crabs, snails, worms, insects, minnows, and plants in colors from green and rusty–red to maroon and yellow. A small world.

"I wonder if I could abdicate boardroom skirmishes to help hayseeds grow more hay or sell apples in Burlington," Jack said. "One minute yes, one minute no."

"Indecision is not usually your style."

"Usually not on the losing end," he replied, an edge rising in his voice. "Usually not given time to reflect on the morass of my life. Usually not faced with the question of what to do next."

"We haven't talked about how your meetings went yesterday," I said.

"It went well. It was fun. They've got a good technology, about 180 people, and I think I could help them grow and get better. No offer yet, but I think they will. My role would be as Chief Operating Officer with a plan to become CEO in a few years. There'd be stock and stock options as part of it."

"If they offer, do you think you'll take it?"

"I don't know yet. It would be easy to step into it, logical. But ..."

"But what?"

He looked at me for a second. "I've done it," he said. "It's kinda more of the same."

We walked on and started toward the car. My thoughts turned to the pumpkin business. We stopped before the wooded path back to the parking lot to absorb a final view of the ocean, waves crashing on the rocks.

"Okay, Jack, I have an idea," I said. "I'm just going to say it straight out. I've been thinking about turning my pumpkin hobby into a business. Maybe you should join me."

He could just barely keep from rolling his eyes. If I weren't a foot taller and fifty pounds heavier, and maybe just a little crazy, I think he would have rolled those eyes and scoffed. Instead, he looked straight at me, probably looking for laughter to rise, so we could both howl about it. But no, I was serious.

"Reverend Crackstone, it's a leap, a giant leap from a gardening hobby–even if you're really good at it–to building a business. I have to say it sounds pretty crazy."

He turned and started up the path through the trees toward the parking area, and I followed. After putting it out there, I wasn't going to just let discussion drop.

"That's why I need your help," I said. "You have the Midas touch, Jack, and I have a great idea." I explained about the trending hobby of growing giant pumpkins and the price of giant seeds. I rattled off the potential revenues–if the seeds were $10 each, $20 each, or $300 each, and by the time we got back to the car, Jack stopped laughing.

We got in his vintage Porsche and headed on up Route 127, cruising along with the top down.

"Okay," Jack said, "there's gold in them-thar seeds. But that's a lifestyle business, which means basically you're just creating a job for yourself so you don't have to work for 'The Man.' There's nothing wrong with that, and it sounds like you have a passion for it. But it's not really a business."

"I don't get it," I said, feeling a little annoyed and defensive because he took what I saw making me as rich as my neighbors and undercut it with his idea of *just creating a job for myself.*

"A true business can stand on its own. It can be replicated," he said. "One way to think about it is if you, as the owner, get hit by a bus, does the business die too, or can it continue?"

I nodded at this idea.

"This is all well explained in a book called *The E-Myth Revisited.* You should read it." Off the top of his head, Jack brought structure to the idea of building a business—an actual pumpkin seed business and not a money-making hobby or creating a job for myself. He said I could create a pumpkin-seed farm, then codify best practices for growing and delivery, then build a cooperative with other farmers. Next, I could centralize processing, packaging, and distribution of these valuable seeds.

"See," I said, "the Midas touch." He laughed, and I went on: "We'd make a great team Corbett and Crackstone—C & C Seeds. This meets your desire for a low-tech, human-scale business, working with people you like—you *do* like me, right?" I paused for a beat. "You'd get away from your high-pressure, high-tech world. Let's get back to the earth and build something that's interesting, fun, and meaningful."

He smiled. "I'll think about it. I'm not saying 'yes', but I'll think about it. I also have a second round of meetings with these tech weenies in Cambridge."

"Don't do it," I said.

He laughed, "What?"

"Don't go. It's not what you want," I said. "Just more of the same."

Chapter Fifteen

Pumpkin Possibilities

Jack took the second round of meetings with MaxStaff.

I had trouble sleeping the night before, thinking about what Jack had said about building a business instead of a job. Around 5:30 a.m. I got up, went downstairs, and turned on the coffee maker on my way out into the cool morning air to check my pumpkins. There sat Schwartz in the pre-dawn light. Something leaped in my heart every time I saw him. The other, nameless giants were wonderful in their own way, and I was happy to have them, but Schwartz took dominion. He owned his space. There was no questioning his authority. Don't mess with Schwartz.

The soaking hose oozed around the clock. I still gave Schwartz a taste of my magical fertilizer, but only twice a week. It was water he wanted now. Experts say pumpkins in this size range grow thirty pounds or more per day in late summer. By my estimate, using some measurements and calculations I found on the web, Schwartz looked close to world-record size. I imagined a picture of me with Schwartz in the *Boston Globe* and *Yankee Magazine* and pondered what I should wear. My butt tingled with the thought of a big check in my wallet for more than $30,000, and soon after gliding around Concord in a lightly-used BMW 5-Series.

I went back in for a Crackstone-sized mug of coffee as well as a pen and pad of paper.

* * *

"You're up early," Nancy said when I walked in the back door.

"Farmer John," I said, "tending my crops."

"They're pretty amazing, and what's next for the pumpkins after the Topsfield Fair?"

"I plan to sell seeds to make some money, more if I win, of course. But with the largest ones, I can sell seeds. And I'll save some for planting next year."

"Next year?" Nancy cocked an eyebrow. "I thought this was a one-year whim. Now you're thinking of it as an ongoing hobby?"

I pulled a big mug from the cabinet and started pouring coffee. "Bigger and better next year," I said. "I actually think it could become a side business."

"Oh, John, come on."

"Really. I researched it, and I've done the math. I think I'll make over $20,000 this year alone. It could easily get much bigger than just a hobby."

"Slow down, Farmer Brown. Don't forget you have a full-time job—and a family," she said. "Health insurance, housing, most of our income, retirement all of that is on you, big guy."

"As if it could ever slip my mind." I nodded at her and gave a fake grin. "Yes, giant pumpkins as a hobby. A hobby with a financial upside."

She cocked her eyebrow again. "As long as it doesn't—"

"Long as it doesn't cost me my job. I get it," I said and walked out the door with my coffee and pad of paper. *Unless. Unless. Unless,* I thought …

I sat down in my squat beach chair next to Schwartz, and turned my mind again to making a business of pumpkin growing. It could be huge if done right. One advantage of vegetable passion was its pace; you get time to ponder, which worked well for me because all of this took me far afield from twenty-plus years in the ministry. My thoughts vined along the ground, and my mind picked up momentum, pad and pencil in hand moving fast. Selling seeds, number one.

Why stop with seeds?

The next easy idea was selling big pumpkins for Halloween and giants for businesses and schools who'd want impressive pumpkin displays. Of course there was a market for seeds as a snack food as well as pumpkin pies. I dreamed of an ass-kicking assault on the flabby potato: mashed pumpkin instead of mashed potatoes, pumpkin French fries, pumpkin chips. All healthier than the sorry spud. And more: pumpkin pretzels, Budweiser pumpkin beer for the masses, factory production of pumpkin bread (for a better peanut butter and jelly sandwich!), pumpkin ice cream, pumpkin-flavored breakfast cereal, coffee-infused pumpkin fiber as Mother Nature's perfectly gentle and natural laxative which also reduces risks of colon cancer and lowers cholesterol (study pending), chocolate-covered pumpkin bars ...

I scrawled ideas as fast as I could, capitalizing on this ballooning brainstorm, this rare and evanescent flash of inspiration. A moment of brilliance. Of—dare I say it?—genius.

There at the hub of this spinning wheel of creativity, sat me, John Crackstone as pioneer of the whole unexplored world of pumpkin benefits beyond just food. This marked my territory—my milieu. Perhaps as a body lotion, suntan lotion, or a salve for sunburn (goodbye aloe vera), or as a beauty cream—for an organic, healthy hint of orange, for a natural glow—like our 45th president (perhaps he'd endorse it). As nature's own hair tonic and shampoo additive to give hair a natural bounce, and a wonderful smell that enhances the human libido (study pending), and it gives your hair a wonderful new sheen. (That's it! We'll call this miracle product NewSheen, may need to partner with Procter & Gamble for marketing and distribution–partnership pending.) Pumpkins to create plastics, replacing the lowly soy bean. Why not use the fibrous body or vines for paper-making? It saves trees, a more rapidly replaced natural resource, and we all get to enjoy a fresh smelling newspaper or a naturally golden-colored toilet paper! Gear up the engine of capitalism and marketing behind the mighty pumpkin, nature's perfect plant for food, pharmaceuticals, beauty, intestines, and industry. There was really no end.

I would benefit mankind. Improve the environment (study pending). Saving trees at least with the paper idea. How about pumpkins as a source for clean-burning ethanol to fuel cars and trucks?

This had to be a better service to man (and to God maybe?) than me standing in the pulpit week after week, reinforcing the opinions and beliefs of my monochromatic, narrow-minded flock. This pumpkin enterprise (empire?) would also be something Jack would love.

Several pages of scrawl filled my pad, and more ideas bubbled up in my silent, solo brainstorm–my brain hurricane. Later, I'd type all of this gold into my laptop, sort it out and prioritize it to share with Jack Corbett. But now I was on a roll.

* * *

Late morning, I was back in my beach chair drawing inspiration from my best friends. I donned the editor's hat to get serious and review the morning reverie, to prioritize, and to strike nutty ideas. The amazing thing was, most of the ideas stuck–they had merit (pending research) and carried the weight of what I'd heard business folks call "a strong value proposition." So I kept all the ideas, at least for now. Prioritizing proved difficult, and I was hacking away at the list when a voice popped the bubble of my concentration.

"What's up, Farmer John?" came Jack's voice. The voice of technology. I looked at my watch–he was back early.

Annoyance percolated toward Jack for him uprooting my hubris–my tuberous hubris? No, the pumpkin is no tuber; it's a huge and beautiful fruit. A seed bearing structure of a flowering plant–technically classified as a species in the genus Cucurbits of the family Cucurbitaceae.

Just Jack's tone of voice made me question the viability of even sharing my possibly brilliant, possibly loony ideas. That and his jaunty stance, rolling heel-to-toe and toe-to-heel with a smug grin–which, of course, came off as superior. Part of me wanted to crack Jack, bash him over the head for interrupting my reverie, for surely calling into question and shooting down my raft of brilliance. From my beach chair vantage point on my old friend–and for some reason my in-the-instant adversary–our relationship presented as oblique. Oblique because I'm 6'11" and he's 5'10". Something competitive or confrontational in his looming over me like an eagle over a rabbit. But I was no rabbit. As I struggled awkwardly to rise out of my beach chair, his talons closed on my forearm to help me up. Once on my hind legs, I rose to my full height, just inside his personal space, and his hot hand released my arm. Even as I leaned in, I was asking myself what the hell I was doing. Or was going to do.

He backed off a half step.

To spare me embarrassing myself, God granted a voice to drift in from across the backyard. Carol.

"John? Joohhnnnn?" She called my name with a softly stretched "O" and lingering over the "hn" like a hum. This tone had flowed from all my old girlfriends, a handful of flirts, my wife (when younger). And no one else. It was an unmistakable marker.

Could this tone come from Carol naively?

"Over here." My voice crisp. A bark in contrast to Carol's song. A subconscious signal to her perhaps? I don't know. Yes, I did, a signal for sure.

Jack and I watched Carol emerge at the edge of the yard, ducking under some branches between our yards. She wore a white polo shirt and red shorts, and I heard Jack whisper, "Oh my," at the sight of her. The hair on the back of my neck rose in a desire to protect Carol.

He rolled untethered to pursue the object of my infatuation, free from marriage, free from any rules of religion or society.

"Hi," she said to Jack, hand extended, "I'm Carol Baker, girl next door."

Jack laughed a bit too hard. "I'm Jack Corbett," he said and gently shook her hand a little too long.

"Carol's husband is one of the deacons of our church," I added, reaching for a scrap of order.

"The girl next door married the deacon," Jack said. "Sounds like the title of a play."

"A comedy, I assure you," Carol said.

"And a Broadway hit," Jack replied.

"Starring ..."

"George Clooney," Jack said, indicating himself. "And Britney Spears."

"Britney Spears!" Carol gasped. "No way. How about ... Kate Hepburn."

"Other than the fact that she died and was your age back in 1955, it's fine by me," Jack said.

This was getting too cute, too flirtatious.

"Are you over here to spy on my pumpkins?" I said to Carol, then turned to Jack. "We gave the Bakers some giant pumpkin seeds, and we've got a friendly wager going to see who will grow the largest pumpkin."

"I concede," she said and told Jack, "Besides, this guy has the gift, an orange thumb if ever there was one. I predict he will leave the ministry for farm life."

I shot Jack a look to say shut up, but I said with a jaunty tone: "It could happen."

"I believe it," Carol said. Then to Jack: "He's obsessed with these pumpkins. Or at least the big dude in the middle. If you ever need to find him, this is the first place to look."

"I'm not obsessed."

"You are!" Carol said. "I think John Crackstone has his sights on a world record."

Jack laughed.

"We'll see in October at the Topsfield Fair," I said. Shifting gears, while I sensed Jack's eyes roam over her, I added, "Carol, we still on for lunch?"

"Yeah. I was leaving for the club to play tennis and wondered if we could meet afterward."

"Sure. How about the Japanese place in Lexington."

"I was thinking about that barbecue place in Somerville, Redbones," Carol said.

"Texas beef ribs?" Jack said.

"Oh, yeah!" Carol said, like an Army brat. "Second only to the Memphis dry rub pork ribs."

"Memphis dry rub?" Jack said. "Sounds like a crime against pork."

"A sin against porcine? Hardly," she said, the vowels in her voice getting harder. "You from Texas?"

"Yep, sure am." Jack twanged it up.

"That explains it," Carol said.

"Trust me," I said, "it explains a great many things."

"Let me tell you something, my Lone Star friend," Carol said. "There's wrong and there's dead wrong. About Memphis dry rub, you're dead wrong."

"Well, you all mind if I join you for lunch to give this dry rub a run?" Jack asked.

"Sure, why not?" Carol said before I could come up with some reason to derail the idea. "Long as you don't mind discussing the strategic plan for the Women's Auxiliary."

"How could I bear to miss it?" Jack said. "Actually, strategy is one of my strong suits."

Oh brother, I wanted to howl, *One of his strong suits, one of so very many*. But I let it go.

"Nice to meet you, Jack," Carol said, shaking hands again.

"The pleasure was all mine," Jack gushed.

Then Carol turned to me and said, "Can I speak with you a second?" She started toward her house. I jogged a couple of steps to pick up at her shoulder, leaning forward to hear her.

"Good friend of yours?"

"Well, yeah," I said sensing her falling for him with his clever banter. "Old college buddy. He's not always so clever and cute."

"I guess you could call it clever and cute," she whispered.

Wanting to change the subject, I asked, "When did you join the Women's Auxiliary?"

"I didn't. I was trying to find an out. No offense, but I couldn't get through a whole lunch with your friend's flirty chit-chat. I need to talk with you, and I didn't want to be rude to your friend."

A giddiness flickered in me. "I'll take care of it," I said.

"Good. Sorry to put you in that position." Her hand alighted briefly on my forearm. "Thanks, John."

Back with Jack, he said to me, "Wow, she is one hot Betty–and with a name like Baker–give me a break. What's cooking in the oven, Mrs. Baker? How the hell do you get any work done with her bouncing around next door? She's a little ditzy, but you can't have everything."

I wanted to say, *She's not ditzy at all, you moron*. But why encourage him?

"About lunch," Jack said, "I think I'll pass. Discussing the

Women's Auxiliary is about as gripping as making little log cabins out of popsicle sticks."

"I'll break it to her gently," I said.

* * *

Jack and I turned back from Carol and looked at the pumpkins. That's when I recalled to him Carol's mention of the pumpkin profession and asked Jack if he thought such a thing possible.

"I don't know," he said. "Not here in your backyard."

"No. I figured as much. But do you think it's possible?"

"Don't know. There are a lot of factors and a lot of questions. Off the top of my head." And he switched into business advisor mode and gushed a tsunami of tough questions: "How much land would you need? Where would you get it? What is the cost of entry? What are the capital costs, for equipment, supplies, labor? Could you raise the money privately, or seek investors? Would you staff up or subcontract with current farmers? Would you become the farmer and buy equipment? Buy land? Lease land? Is there a supply of labor for harvest? Do you have a high-profit niche that will deliver a rapid break-even? If your plan requires processing pumpkins–into pie filling, for example–how and where will you do it? Do it yourself or partner with a large food company? Which one? How do you ship raw materials? What about product distribution? What about marketing? Have you written a business plan? Have you done any ROI modeling?"

He took a breath. "And most important, is there really a market for any of it? You can't be the first clodhopper to think of expanding the pumpkin market. Who are you selling to and who is buying? Why are they buying? Why should they care? Have you tested any products you've dreamed up? What's your go-to-market strategy? Why hasn't it been done?"

My brain was swamped with the questions.

He'd stopped talking–finally–and I hadn't even noticed.

"Jack," I said, "I don't know about any of that stuff." My toe tapped my smallest pumpkin–probably weighed in at about three hundred pounds, but it had great shape and color–and I looked at my friend. "But I've got ideas. A ton of ideas." That's when I held out my pages of scribbled notes. His eyebrows went up.

He didn't have to say it. I knew spinning out ideas was the easy part, the fun part, but success hid in mastering the mountain of details and surrounding yourself with a team of people who shared the vision, ready to execute with excellence. "Execute with excellence," sounded like jargon from one of my executive deacons. I'm sure I picked it up from the business pages of the Sunday *New York Times*. Beyond Jack's lifting the lid, I knew the can brimmed with a thousand more questions.

"I'm no businessman," I said. "That's your line. My hope is that I can tell you my ideas, and you can help me figure out the business questions. Money's a problem, no question. But you can help there too. You have the means to make it happen, and you have business contacts who can help if we need it."

Both of us were quiet for a minute or so. Seemed a lot longer. I took up the slack.

"Look, you're out of work right now, Jack. You're sick of the high–tech rat race. Speaking of that, how'd your meetings go today?"

"Hard to say," he answered. "Not bad, but not as well as yesterday." He paused as if he'd been trying to puzzle it out. "We ended early, which is usually not a good sign. But yesterday went so well, I thought they might make an offer this morning."

"Forget those guys," I said. "You mentioned consulting with Vermont farmers. Why not with me? I'm not inspired to preach anymore." I stopped and glanced around, realizing

I'd said it right out loud in my backyard, the backyard of the parsonage. I went on at a whisper: "Going through the motions is what I do. I don't respect the congregation, and I don't think they respect me either. But these pumpkins captured my imagination. I have dozens of ideas, but I need help."

"I'll say you need help," my friend said, laughing.

Maybe I did need mental help, but I was driven to tell him my vision and see if he might fund it. I told him we needed to sit down over paper and think through it. We walked to Concord Coffee where we sat in a quiet, corner booth, and I uncorked all the business dreams bottled up in me. I let it all hang out. With enthusiasm. But at hushed levels, so no one from town might overhear. With abandon I laid out before Jack my passion for pumpkins. My vision. With a long-winded ramble, I went through all the commercial possibilities I had imagined.

Dutifully, my friend listened, took a few notes.

When I finally finished, he said, "I don't think I've ever seen you like this. And honestly, I don't know if I should be happy or worried." He sat back in his chair and polished off the last of his cold coffee. "You have as much passion as any entrepreneur I've ever seen. That's great. And terrible. It takes passion and commitment to launch a new business and make it succeed, sustained passion to get through the hard times, the dips. But passion can also blind you to the many obstacles and realities," he said. "All these dreams you talk about, are you prepared to work like a dog and sacrifice to make them real? Because it takes big sacrifice. Do you grasp the possible price? Not in money–well, that too sometimes–but in terms of your family and social standing and your future? And we still haven't talked about a customer. Without a customer, a repeat buyer, you don't have a business."

"Something has to change in my life. I can't go on as a charlatan."

"You're no charlatan," he said.

"I am. Or at least I'm bordering on one, and I'm beginning to loathe myself."

"I thought self-loathing was a rite of passage for ministers," he said. When I smirked, he followed up: "*Isn't* it? Have you sought counseling about this? It's a booming industry, you know, pastoral counseling for pastors."

It was the first time someone suggested I seek counseling.

"Maybe you need to leave this church and not the ministry," Jack said. "Maybe it's the Concord Congregational Church you loathe–"

"No kidding," I interrupted.

"–but I think you loathe yourself only as minister of this one church," he said.

"I've considered the point. But I'm not sure I can leave my father's church."

"Do you mean our Father, who art in heaven? Or do you mean your dad?"

I laughed.

"I mean it, John," he said. "They're different things, you know. Don't confuse them."

Jack's words marked the first time the Father (capital "F") and the father (small "f") confusion had been put to me, forced on me, in such an open, straight-ahead, no-ducking, Jack-Corbett way. I'm sure–I mean, I know–this point of confusion had needled me before. But only since I was about six years old.

I played back a historical reel of my life through the lens of Jack's question regarding my potential confusion of Father in heaven and father in his study. My dad led his flock (by the nose, some might say), and he certainly led me, shaping all of my early knowledge of the Bible, my faith in God, and my understanding of God and Christ. He shaped me with the confidence of a master sculptor. Dare I say, of a supreme being? A superior being? Or a psychological bully? That might be too much. He was not a bully. At least, not most of the time. Though everyone knew, when he forged an opinion, he stood tough and intelligent enough and authoritative enough to crush opposition, twisting one to his position on most anything.

As a malleable boy, I stood no chance of opposing him. My best option to grow–psychologically speaking, because I had no problem growing physically–was to nibble at the edges of a narrow band of acceptable behavior and to relax in the knowledge my father's greatest attention focused on his work, on leading his flock, and the spotlight of his in-tellectual, spiritual, psychological power with all of its heat seldom shined on me as long as I steered within that nar-row band of acceptable behavior. At some age, probably late in high school, it dawned on me what he found accept-able was only defined by how it might reflect on him–in other words, only my visible, public behavior.

For example, he never rooted out my *Penthouse* mag-azines at the bottom of my sock drawer, never spoke to me about drugs or alcohol, but I got a stern talking to for yucking it up with a couple of buddies and doing standing leapfrogs over each other on Monument Square to impress a couple of high school girls. I remember reminding him Jesus Christ had long hair and a beard, during an argument about me growing a beard and long hair during college. It so outraged him, he practically smote me for it.

"Still with me, Mr. Wizard?" Jack said. "Thought I'd lost you behind the curtain for a minute."

"I was just thinking about your 'father' observation. Interesting question to ponder, but right now, I don't want to talk about dear old Dad. I want to talk about our pump-kin business."

"I want to talk about your father."

"Oh, man," I said, whining like a five-year-old (or like a high-school kid). "My father and all of that is hard. Too hard to tease out here in this coffee shop."

"The pumpkin business is hard too. A lot harder than you think—and too hard to tease out here in the coffee shop." He paused. "I know you think there's a huge potential in pumpkins. Every entrepreneur thinks they have a billion-dollar idea. I hear you, but there are some very real and big barriers to entry. Let me tell you something else, John, when you ask a venture capitalist to back your idea, you talk about what the VC wants to talk about. So, as both your friend and your prospective investor, we're going to talk about you and your father."

After we talked, Jack insisted I seek resolution with my father (and my Father who art in Heaven, if necessary). He even insisted on paying for my flight to Arizona to meet with Dad. He put it like this: "John, before you make any career-ending, life-altering decisions, you really need to deal with your father."

Jack said while I was in Arizona he planned to research the market, business challenges, and some of the opportunities, so we could focus our efforts. "Most businesses fail because the partners can't work together. They fight over how work is shared, priorities, money, where to focus their efforts, even why they went into business. I've been there. And never again. So we need to resolve some stuff to build a solid partnership." He paused before saying the next thing: "And both partners need to be invested, in terms of time, effort, and money. If we go forward, I will be the major financial backer, but you'll need to put in some cash. I'd say $60,000 to get started." He must have seen fear in my face. "Not right now. But soon, so figure out where you can get some money. Maybe talk to your dad." He also said he'd take care of my backyard pumpkins like a partner and get to know the product.

"I'll also ask Carol to help with the pumpkins," I said. "Which reminds me, I'm supposed to meet her for lunch."

Chapter Sixteen

The Trouble with Jack

We were walking to her SUV when Carol's hand gripped my forearm to stop me. Her touch sent a jolt of electricity through my chest. "My keys," she said and turned on her heel and bounded up to the house. Taking two steps at a time up to the back door, she looked weightless–a quick, effortless athleticism. Thin and lovely in black tights and a teal T-shirt, her blonde ponytail bounced in rhythm. When she reappeared, she wore Matt's red-and-black plaid shirt hanging down to mid-thigh.

"Ready Reverend?" she said jangling keys on her way to her SUV.

Once buckled in the soft, leather seats, she rolled down the driveway. "I noticed your bracelet again," she said as she pulled out on the quiet street. "You said Nancy gave it to you. Does it have any special meaning?"

I told her all about it, how Nancy had designed it and the meaning of each bead and the leather and the silver thread.

"And here I just thought it was cool looking," Carol said. "She gave you a very thoughtful gift, John. I wish Matt would wear something like that, a reminder of his family and his values."

"It's missing one thing," I said.

"What?"

"A big honking orange bead in the middle!"

She just laughed and shook her head.

On the road to Redbones, the barbecue spot in Davis Square, we didn't talk much. Not until: "So John, what's the story with your friend Jack?"

I sensed her attraction to him. That off-putting first impression had flipped. "Well ..." I hesitated. "Jack is one of my best friends." I started to say "my brother-by-choice," but held up. "He's complicated with a complicated past." She said nothing, so I continued. "We met at seminary."

"Really?"

"Yeah, but a lot has changed." I told her about Jack's marriage falling apart and being thrown out of his church, a low point in his life, and his ascendant business career. I told about his record of spotting opportunities early and getting out before the downturn, making him very successful. Carol Baker was impressed, and so was I in the retelling.

"And why is he here now?"

Why now indeed? Was it my grace moment? My trial moment? Did his visit exist outside faith? What did Jack's arrival bring for me and my family? For Carol? For the pumpkin business?

"He's here to explore a business opportunity," I said, and decided to say no more. But I did say this: "Jack thinks I should go visit my parents in Arizona, and he even offered to pay for the flight."

When Carol asked why, I glossed over Jack's opinion that I had unresolved issues with my father. I also withheld the need to ask my old man for a pile of money to start a business.

"John, your father is getting old, you know? Like, if not now, when? And if your rich friend offered to pay for your trip, why not do it? I know you worry about money."

How did she know I worried about money? I hadn't mentioned it. Had I? Besides, I didn't really worry about it. I thought about money. I pined for it maybe. Was angry and anxious about money, but I said, "In the words of, Alfred E. Neuman, 'What? Me worry?'"

She granted a polite laugh. "Who's Alfred E. Neuman?"

"He was a great American philosopher and political pundit from the 1950s to the 2010s." Then I laughed.

"C'mon, who is he?"

"He was the main cartoon character, and cover boy, for the humor rag called *MAD*."

"I remember seeing that magazine, but I never read it."

"Well that explains everything," I said.

We rode in silence for a while.

Carol turned on the radio, to NPR, and we listened to Terry Gross on *Fresh Air* interview a reporter about her experiences as a war correspondent. She'd observed civil war in Syria and the war Russia started with Ukraine, and a couple of other armed conflicts. When the reporter described the random violence of bombing and the example of a girl who'd been wounded during an attack, Carol clicked off the radio. "Why does the world feel so crazy right now? Wars and school shootings and domestic violence. Why? And how can we stop it? How can people like you and me, sitting in our comfortable Concord homes, stop the insanity?" When I failed to answer, she went on: "Like, how do you reconcile this with your faith in Christianity?"

"How do any of us?" My fingers turned the beads on my right wrist.

"No, how do *you*, John? As a religious leader, you stand for something. How do you stand your ground?"

"Wow, 'stand your ground' makes me sound like one of those gun nuts."

"Seriously, how do you make sense of Christian faith, or any faith, in the face of this cruel, crazy world?"

"This is a timeless question, an unanswerable question," I said. "I wish I had the answer. Evil exists. I do think with all of today's news coverage, we hear about more of the cruel and crazy all over the globe like never before. But in the face of all the bad news, there's a Harvard professor, Steven Pinker, who wrote a book claiming there's less violence today than in the past. There's more opportunity for the world's poor to rise up. More respect and education for women. So as bad as the news makes us feel, the world really is a better place today."

"Bullshit," she said.

Always a fast driver, Carol was flying now, on the edge of reckless.

"Okay, can you slow down? Please," I said. She glanced down and saw she was speeding and slowed. "I know it doesn't sound like a safer, more sane world from the news. But the data says—"

"Data," she scoffed. "There's always data."

Speeding again, she caught herself and slowed. Carol went on: "What's the saying? 'Lies, damned lies, and statistics.' Data, statistics, same shit."

"You're right," I said. "People bend and select data to make their point."

"So what can you believe? Isn't that one of the big issues today? Fake news, alternative facts, truthiness, and so on. It's gotten to the point where people can't agree on the so-called facts." She paused. "It's part of the crazy in our country. A lot of people only believe their opinions. Facts, science, truth be damned. Or they manipulate data to support their opinions."

We were quiet for a bit.

Then I spoke: "Standing with faith is a challenge. Always has been."

No response. At least the SUV didn't gain speed.

I went on: "For me, faith has to do with hope, active hope, taking action against all that is wrong with the world."

"It's a beautiful thing to say here in a car," she said. "But you don't preach it on Sundays, John."

No, I didn't.

* * *

After our drive, part of me didn't want to have lunch with Carol. I had imagined kissing her, wrapping my very long arms around the small body of this North Dakota girl off the Indian reservation and just holding her there, allowing our hungry souls to intertwine each other until joy filled us up. But then we ruined the chance by talking about the blurring of facts, and war, and faith, and how I had failed to connect faith and hope (active hope) for the congregation. Now, I just wanted to go home and take a nap.

Another part of me wanted to fight with her, hammer her a little on a few points, and share back some of the pain she'd inflicted.

At Redbones, we settled in a booth, and studied the menu without saying a word. Very unlike our first lunch together. We ordered. The waitress took the menus and left us facing each other.

We looked into each other's eyes. Was it love?

"I'm sorry I keep attacking you or your positions," she said.

I felt myself forgiving her. Mostly. "It's okay. Comes with the territory."

An uncomfortable silence ballooned.

"I like the art in here," Carol said looking around.

A stilted conversation followed about the paintings on the walls, all by one artist, using bold black outlines with vibrant colors and rough, layered paint. They were funny images of fish (the one over our table had a fish with a human arm extending from its mouth holding a bone), pigs, and cows, some with people. They carried a child-like grasp of reality with an adult's sense of humor.

"Like cave paintings by a comedian," Carol said.

The waitress rushed back with our food and clunked down the heavy plates like she was in a hurry and vanished without a word.

Carol, wide-eyed, said, "Didn't even have time to ask for an extra napkin."

I kind of wished the waitress had pulled up a chair to hang out with us.

We ate for a few minutes in silence. Then Carol sat up straight and said, "No, John, it's not okay to attack you like that. I need to figure out what's driving it."

This was my chance to hit back—at least a little. "So let me ask you something."

Her hands went to the edge of the table as if to brace herself, and her eyes narrowed slightly, but I blundered ahead: "What do you stand for, or what do you want to stand for, Carol? What do you believe in?"

Her eyes immediately began to fill, and it wasn't from the hot barbecue sauce. "I thought I just needed a friend. But now I think it's more."

Was she about to say she'd fallen for me or wanted me?

She went on. "What I think I need is a sense of *purpose*. Two days ago, when it rained all day, I watched an old movie on TV, and there was this scene where a beautiful, wealthy debutant had climbed up on a bridge railing. She is about to commit suicide when along walks Spencer Tracy and he talks to the despondent girl. He says, 'Miss, do you have a job?' She says no. And he goes, 'You need to get a job. Because it's hard to be sad and useful at the same time.' That makes sense to me, John. Matt isn't sad, and his job gives him a sense of purpose. Your job, your calling, gives you a sense of purpose."

Even as her words entered my ears, I doubted it.

"But I don't have a job, don't have a sense of purpose beyond taking care of the girls—and I love my girls—but I need something more. I need to feel useful."

I didn't know what to say. For years, I'd seen a similar malaise on people searching for meaning, for purpose. Often it was a woman trapped in a job when she wanted to be home taking care of kids. But almost as common was Carol's desire to do more than care for kids, usually with guilt from society insisting taking care of your kids should be enough. Sometimes in my endless march of sessions with congregants, I wondered if anyone was happy. That's the plague of the pastoral: We seldom spend time with the happy and content.

Then I paused and stepped out of my head and empathized from my heart for Carol Baker.

Here a woman in pain sat across from me.

Both of us eating barbecue, coleslaw, and cornbread.

It didn't matter she was beautiful and sexy.

Or that she lived in an elegant house in a prosperous town.

Or that she had two lovely daughters.

Or that her husband was a successful lawyer.

What mattered was how could I help.

How could I–the big oaf, the stork is a dork, another gaffe by the giraffe–find grace and clarity in my mental–emotional food processor to guide my sometimes–congregant and friend (and unlikely lover)?

"I hear you," I said. "And I understand your search for purpose." I wanted to add, "Probably better than you would imagine," but enough grace filled me to see this wasn't about me. I said, "Your thought about finding a job to feel useful and to find purpose makes sense. Often our path to fulfillment is multi-faceted, and the journey is seldom straight-forward."

Reflecting on my own words as I spoke, I thought of my pumpkin business. How I still hungered for it. How might my talents and my ministerial–skills help it fly? My own meandering journey now required me to go see my parents, my father.

I hadn't asked for a dime since college and now this: a request for $60,000 from Dad.

* * *

When I got home, crossing under the branches into the back yard, there sat Jack in my beach chair by Schwartz. I thought he was asleep. No, he was looking at his phone.

"Welcome home, Big John." Then he started singing a weird folk song: "I'm Long-John, I'm a long time gone, boy, like a turkey through the corn, boy, with my long clothes on." Then he stopped singing, "Johnny Crackstone. You know, Johnny Crackstone is a good name for a baseball player." He went into an announcer voice: "Johnny Crackstone, rounding third and heading for home." And laughed. "Yes, to the question you're about to ask. I've had a little to drink, but I'm not drunk, just goofing."

I walked over to the back deck, took a lawn chair and carried it back, put it close to him, and sat down. "What's up Jack?"

"MaxStaff called to say they were going in a different direction. They passed. My old CTO, the co-founder, she had to call and tell me."

I just sat there for a few seconds. "Well, it clears the path for C & C Seeds. Take door number two."

"I need to come clean about something," Jack said, his hand rising to push his hair back. "I lied to you, John. I'm not a millionaire. Well, I am and I'm not." He sighed.

"What does this double-talk mean?" I asked.

"At Mesa Tech, one of my partners, the Chief Financial Officer, hid employee tax withholding. He tried to make the numbers look better, and it sure did. We probably hired another two hundred people based on those fudged numbers. Eventually the IRS woke up to news of our growth and hiring spree, and looked into the tax numbers. The

CFO's tax fraud ran into millions of dollars. He went to jail, four years, but all of the partners–especially me as the CEO–were slapped with huge fines. I narrowly avoided going to jail myself." He held up a finger and thumb about a quarter-inch apart: "That close. Maybe closer."

I nearly interrupted to ask if he *should* have gone to jail.

"Tax evasion was the final nail in the coffin for Mesa Tech. The IRS took half my personal nest egg, $25 million off the top. And left me with a bill for $25 million more."

"So you're broke?!" I bellowed.

"Hold on," he said. "Not really."

"More double-talk–"

"Listen, John," he said. "My attorneys worked out a deal. The IRS is taking six hundred grand a year, $50,000 a month. If I do that consistently for twelve years, over and above my other taxes, they'll forgive the rest of the debt." He paused.

He could probably see my head swimming in the numbers. Twenty-five million gone, $50,000 a month? For a dozen years? This was crazy money.

"Do you want me to explain the rest?" he asked, and I shrugged. "So I owe the government $7.2 million more, which is a lot–"

"Ya think?"

"–which is a lot," he continued, his hand up to slow me down. "They have a claim on the whole $25 million I have left, so I can't spend the principal. I'm living on interest from the conservative investments the IRS allowed. Which is enough. I sold my big house in Dallas, renting a condo, so that's a separate nest egg."

"So when this is over, you'll be–"

"Sixty-two years old," Jack said.

"Man ..." I mumbled, but it made me question if I could trust him. Did he really not know about the tax evasion?

"Yeah ..." After a few seconds, he added, "I thought the MaxStaff job would turn it around for me, cover all the costs. But it ain't happening. So let's go big on the pumpkin thing—assuming the validation process works out."

We were quiet for a minute.

Then for another minute.

Chapter Seventeen

Visiting AZ

Nancy insisted I arrive at the airport two hours before departure despite my attempts to explain that Arizona was not an international flight, requiring customs, and I hadn't missed a flight since my early 30s. Nancy wanted time to park (even though she simply dropped me off at the departures curb), and she didn't want me to risk ticketing lines (despite my e-ticket in hand). Her final point was with my height, I'd probably get pulled aside by security. In reality, the only hassle came when the screener marveled at the size of my shoes and an excitable security guard ran to her aid, hand on his pistol.

I bought two magazines in the terminal, *Inc.* and *Fast Company*, to prep for my days as an entrepreneur. I settled in to read but was distracted by the soaring, graceful terminal. Overhead the metal structure's silver beams arched across to a tremendous glass wall which flooded the area with natural light, compelling you to look up into the clouds to watch planes circle the airport or climb skyward from take-off. The space radiated peace and purpose, like a modern Grand Central Station, or like the vaulted ceiling of an old cathedral, a monument to the jet age.

This was the kind of place Jack knew well. He flew all over the country, probably hung out in the Elite Flyer

Lounge. What was he doing today? Slipping over to see Carol Baker? Was she interested in Jack? Rich, well dressed and coiffed, and with the stupid sports car, he was dashing. Me? I was none of those things–the stork is a dork. Why would Carol find me interesting or worthy of her attentions when she could have Jack at the snap of her slender fingers? He was more fun–his stupid sports car again, and a vintage one to boot, as if the attention of a new Porsche was so pedestrian. Meanwhile I clanked around in my old Ford Taurus wagon. The rounded fenders and headlights of his Porsche 356, sculpted just so, evoked the sensual shape of perfect breasts. That was no accident of form. It was functional enough to be a car, yes, but the shape was seductive, subliminally so for those lacking self-reflection. The rear of the car, like the rear of Carol, also sculpted: small, rounded, athletic (even aerodynamic?). Oh, yes, Jack would offer her a ride in his car. Stealing away to the North Shore, to visit Rocky Neck art galleries, to find some sun-warmed stone to recline upon, to smell the sea, and listen to the waves, basking in nature's beauty and human beauty. Every sense engaged. Even perhaps the sense of taste?

I had to stop, to quiet this thinking, this worry, this fretful daydream.

To distract myself, I pulled out my fine, glossy magazines, and flipped through stories about successful businesses, tales of rags–to–riches entrepreneurs (even a couple of rags–to–riches–and–back–to–rags), with advice on funding your startup, with insights on technology, with ways to avoid the pitfalls of small business (including a "Why You Should Never Hire Your Spouse" tidbit, which I took to heart). With every page, I grew more excited. I could do this. They could interview me one day. They'd love the story of a wild–haired giraffe who pioneered an industry of growing pumpkins, the former minister who discovered his soul, his true calling, in a backyard pumpkin patch.

Something moved next to me, a little English sparrow perched on the arm of the next chair, turning its head to look up into my eyes as if to say, "Got some bread, Bub?" Then two of his little friends flitted down to the blue carpet around my feet. Each eyed me with anticipation. "I got nothing, guys," I said. After a little more hopping around, they flew over to a man with a newspaper and muffin. Two boys, brothers, one probably ten, Gordon's age, the other maybe eight, like Megan, tried to sneak up on the sparrows, new Red Sox hats in hand to net them. The birds took off, just as the older boy pounced, throwing his hat at them. Missed by a mile.

"Careful, boys," I said, "those are attack sparrows."

"Really?" the younger brother said.

The older brother backhanded him in the chest, and they both smirked and ran back to their parents.

It made me miss my kids. Made me wonder when I'd last had a light-hearted chuckle with them or had taken time to just goof off with them. I couldn't remember it. Over the previous year, maybe two years, certainly before the pumpkins, I'd been a dour soul around home. Unhappy in my work–and as a minister, your work is your life really–so I was unhappy and preoccupied in my life. I was afraid, okay, terrified, of what my unhappiness meant. It might force a major change, a career move, a move to another place–or I might get fired for subpar fundraising. And I had no idea what I'd do next. I clung to the job like a life raft. While also aching to escape. Of course, clinging to the raft kept me in the rapids. Maybe I needed to get out of the water, dry off, and then decide if I wanted back in, right?

* * *

When they finally called for my plane to board, I left the spacious, Zen-like waiting area to go into a narrow, semi-lit tunnel leading to the gates where a crowd waited. The air smelled stale. The ease I'd enjoyed in the large waiting area squeezed out of me in the pinched corridor like toothpaste out of a tube, a very big tube, and I suppressed a growing claustrophobia. Plane seating is never easy when you're seven-foot, and waiting in line it occurred to me I hadn't requested the exit row. Glancing at my e-ticket, I saw the nightmare. Center seat, back in the tail of the plane.

When I arrived to the very last row, the two passengers groaned when they saw me. They'd already spread out a virtual picnic over my narrow, cramped little seat: books, magazine, newspaper, a muffin in a white bag. Then there was the matter of my modest carry-on bag—no room left in the overhead.

"You'll have to put it under the seat in front of you, sir," the attendant said with all the humanity of a robot.

"Hello, I'm seven-feet tall," I said. "There's no way I can put this bag under the seat. I'm not sure my size-seventeen shoes will fit."

She stepped back to look at my feet. "Those aren't shoes, they're canoes!" she proclaimed. Her audience tittered at the stand-up comic. "Follow me," she said and snatched my bag.

I followed her to the exit row. There, a high school kid, or maybe college-aged, sat on the aisle. She leaned close to him, putting a hand on his shoulder. He pulled the headphones off his ears. I didn't get it all, but her message went something like this: "I've got a former basketball star here who can't fit into his seat. I wondered if you'd mind switching for him? The Celtics would appreciate it." The kid whirled in his seat, fully expecting Larry Bird, Bill Russell, or Kevin Garnett. Instead, just another oversized, white stiff. The attendant continued, "In appreciation, you may have the beverage of your choice, including a beer."

"Can I have it now?" he asked. Never mind it was not yet 9:00 in the morning.

"Of course," she said rising. "You are twenty-one, I assume."

Not a chance.

"Oh, yeah. Of course." The kid was already moving to the back of the plane.

Kismet was on my side for once, and I settled in for a smooth flight. A few hours later, we landed softly in Phoenix, right on time.

* * *

At baggage claim, my bag, identified by the little yellow ribbon Megan had tied on a zipper to help me find it, flopped onto the carousel unharmed along with the others. This always surprises me, though I've only had my luggage damaged once, exposing my giant, not-quite-white undies for all the world to marvel over. All was right with the world. Except I couldn't find my parents. We'd agreed to meet at baggage claim.

I called my folks. No answer. Mom's voice on the answering machine. My father had sworn off answering machines after being tethered to one in Concord. In a funny reversal, my mother, after years of resenting how my father came into the house and checked the answering machine first thing, now insisted on having one. Mom collected messages from members of The Arizona Gray Hairs—the name her women's group gave themselves, a clutch of old snow birds who shared an interest in history and got together for tea and occasionally fluttered around historic sites near Phoenix. Lil-Big-un (my mom's high school nickname because Lillian McLarson stood six-feet tall—or five-twelve as she joked) was also a member of "The Sexy Six," a splinter group with a penchant for antiquing and laughter.

Anyway, my old man refused to touch the answering machine in his retirement, so it fell to Mom to jot down messages for him, which mostly covered tee times with the old codgers at the golf course.

To see if they were parked by the curb, I stepped outside into the oven of Arizona in August. My breath was sucked out of me by the utter, absolute absence of humidity and the intensity of the heat, even in the shade. My mouth dried as parched as toilet paper in seconds. AZ's arid heat pressed in on me, making me want to retreat into the air-conditioned terminal. But then the shock of it passed. There was something curiously refreshing in the heat too. In the sheer intensity of it. The very difference of it. *You're not in Concord, Massachusetts any more, Johnny Crackstone,* I thought. And I liked it for that if nothing else.

I stepped out of the shade, lugging my bags (I still resist those very-practical rolling bags because they were designed for people at least a foot shorter than me and I ended up carrying them anyway) and crossed the street, asphalt soft as a rubber mat, to a traffic island. Wow, the sun pounded down and the heat simmered up from the pavement, scorching at least another ten degrees hotter than by the door. Overhead stretched the classic, cloudless desert blue sky. There's no other sky quite like it, in depth and crispness, especially when it lies in contrast to the rust-colored Navaho sandstone or the pale greens of desert flora. It was too hot on the traffic island, and there was no sign of my folks, so I crossed back by the doors. I thought, *So this is Arizona in summer,* when some old jackass in a brown Buick honked at me. He waited until I crossed right in front of his car to honk. Jesus! Pissed me off.

I looked up. It was Dad.

I tried to toss off my annoyance. He probably didn't want to open the window and let the precious air conditioning out. In an instant my mother emerged from the car. I registered how she had aged since I'd seen her last—about a year ago. I hugged her, and she felt small. Frail. And slightly stooped, making her shorter than her normal, or former, 5'12" height. She hugged me and let go, then hugged me again as if I might escape if she didn't recapture me.

I heard the "thunk" of the trunk unlocking. I let go of Mom and loaded my bags into the trunk, answered her questions about the smooth plane ride, and waved off her apology for the sauna–like heat. She insisted I sit in the front for the leg room, just as it had been since I was fourteen, when I was as tall as my 6'4" father. Mom and Sue in the back, then Mom alone back there, me and the old man up front. He really was an old man now: eighty–eight years old. Should he be driving? He looked remarkably fit, sitting rod–straight, a full head of white hair, skin bronzed.

"Son," he said, hand extended for a handshake as he checked his rearview mirror and prepared to pull away from the curb. My fingers went to the beads on my bracelet.

From the back seat, Mom reported temperatures had exceeded 100 degrees every afternoon in the last week. But my father had managed to play nine holes of golf each day, either at dawn or at dusk.

During small talk of Gordon's baseball and Megan's softball, of tennis lessons, and Nancy's preschool work, I watched the colors of Arizona summer pass the window. Wherever man pressed his hand in this desert place, colors glared unnatural: cars, buildings, signs, lights, asphalt or concrete, and stretches of bright green grass around buildings and houses. Strange how we humans harbor a need to push back the desert. Why?

* * *

That evening, Dad and I went out to play a round of golf. The old man insisted I tee off first. Now, I'm no golfer, and I reminded him of this fact as I set up and proceeded to hook a low drive dribbling up the fairway and into the rough.

"Raised your head," he said and stepped past me to set up his first tee shot. Old William Crackstone used the driver as a cane to stand back up. But then, so had I when it was my turn, and I was 40 years younger. Dad took a couple of stiff-looking practice swings, stepped up, and clocked the ball. An impressive drive, straight and high, the white sphere floated like a satellite against the blue desert sky, and rolled down the center of the bright green fairway about 200 yards out and well beyond my ball.

"Well played, sir," I said.

He didn't reply.

As he drove our cart, I was jolted again by the boldness of the green color, especially where the carpet of the fairway extended into the lush rough and the rough met the rock and sand of the desert.

I'd made visits to the desert before and was always struck by two things: the brilliant blue sky, as I said, but also the subtle colors of the earth. The ranges of browns and pale greens as if the sun baked most chlorophyll out of the few plants struggling to survive. So when you saw a small desert flower, it delighted the eye like a joyous defiance of the harsh climate, as splendid as a Russian folk dance blooming in the face of the Soviet's repressive regime.

But out on the golf course, a thick, plush carpet of grass gleamed like a Myrtle Beach country club or like the outfield at Fenway Park. Like nothing else in Arizona. It was the anti-desert. As I thought of the prodigious volume of water it took to keep the course so green in this heat, the tremendous waste of water it took–this was no place to grow pumpkins. In a place where water was precious, this excessive irrigation offended my sense of right and wrong.

Though part of me knew I was lighting a fuse, I said to my father as we walked to our golf balls, "I can't believe how green the grass is."

"Beautiful, isn't it?" he said, his voice flush with admiration.

"Yes, and no," I answered. "Looks great, but when you think about the price. The vast amounts of water, such a precious resource here in the Southwest, wasted for green grass."

"Not wasted," he shot back.

"God didn't intend this to be a lush green space, Dad. It's a desert."

"I know it's a desert. God gave us a brain and volition to change things. Why is this any more wasteful than silver used in the film or movie business?"

"I wasn't talking about silv–"

"These Arizona golf courses entertain thousands of people every day. They employ hundreds of people in this area. They attract tourists from across America. They are a prize of ingenuity and a reflection of man's determination to improve his world."

"There are other ways to–"

"Would you have these hundreds of people lose their jobs?"

"No, but–"

"Do you think entertainment and physical exercise are bad?"

"Dad, that's not wha–"

"I'm sick of simple-minded environmentalists who think everything is bad if nature didn't plan it that way. Meanwhile they drive cars, wear clothes with nylon and polyester–made in China by the way and shipped thousands of miles over here–and they use electricity. I am sick and tired of these simple-minded arguments. Do I think we have a right to destroy the planet? Hell no. But can you imagine life without oil? Can you?"

"Dad, calm down." His face was red, veins on his neck popping, and I imagined a heart attack on the fairway of the first hole on my first afternoon in town. Son as assassin.

"I asked you a simple question, John," he demanded. "Can you imagine a world where oil was never discovered?" He glared at me. "You just think about it for a minute while you go hit your ball."

I did. And I couldn't. Everything around me was made of oil or petrochemicals. The rubber grip on the four–iron. The metal shaft. The rubber on the ball and in it. The ink on the ball. The soles of my sneakers. The acrylic blend of my socks. The processing of the cotton in my shorts. My watchband and watch. The tires on the cart. Dad's pace-maker. The soaking–hose endlessly watering my giant pumpkins back home. The jet I rode in to get here, the runway for take–off and landing, the computer that pro-cessed my ticket, the wires that carried the electricity to the computer, the power plant generating the electricity. The trucks that sent my clothes to the store, that sent my lunch to the restaurant. No, I couldn't imagine the world without massive consumption of oil.

Then it hit me. I'd been beaten by the old master again. Why was I thinking about oil when I started with water? Water to oil, oil and water. This was my father to a T. The old master turned and twisted the argument, until you were ensnared in something altogether different.

I set up over my ball and took a massive swing, chop-ping it out of the rough and dribbling across the fairway into the rough on the other side.

"Raised your head again," the old man called.

"No I didn't," I shot back.

"Raised your shoulders then."

"Dad, I'm six–foot, eleven inches tall, and I'm using clubs designed for a guy five–nine. Of course my swing is off."

"Do you expect the clubhouse to stock rental clubs for guys your size?"

What I wanted to say was: *Dad, please don't make me kill you on the first hole.*

I imagined charging him with my four iron held high like a warrior of the Dark Ages and cleaving the old chief's head. But I didn't say a word. Didn't move. Instead, I just looked at him and let the hazardous waste of fury leach back into the contaminated soil of my brain. Then I decided to go back to the clubhouse, no conversation about it, and call it a day to try to enjoy a beer or two at The 19th Hole and wait for Dad. It was pretty stinking hot out there anyway, and getting hotter by the second.

"Tell you what," Dad said, "you take my clubs. They'll be too short for you too, but better than those stupid things."

I didn't want his prized Ping clubs. It was a nice offer, but I didn't want them. With my luck, I'd break one somehow. Besides, I was no golfer. I didn't even like golf. He did. He loved it. He tracked his performance, keeping his handicap with religious zeal. Probably had insisted I come play with him just to trounce me, the old father–still–able–to–better–his–boy routine. I pledged never to do that to Gordon or Megan. Golf was another tool Dad had used to stay close to the leaders of Concord. My job came with a full membership to the Concord Country Club, but we seldom used it. I went once a year to hack one round of golf in a benefit for Boston Children's Hospital.

Finally, I spoke. "No, Dad. You go ahead and play. I'll meet you back at the clubhouse."

He stomped and insisted I finish the round.

"No, Dad. I'm no golfer," I said. "You go ahead. It's fine. For me, it's just a frustration. I'll have a coffee or a beer and read the paper or a magazine. Enjoy your round."

He even gave it the "What kind of man begins a game and doesn't finish it? I didn't raise a quitter."

His demands gave me a new sense of power and calm. "Dad, go ahead and play. I'm no golfer–which I just proved. It's your game. I'll see you back to the clubhouse."

I started walking back.

"Goddammit, John," he growled, knowing his rare swearing always jolted his family. But not this time. "If you don't play, I won't either."

"That's entirely up to you," I said. With that, I shouldered the bag of rented clubs and walked back. Left my ball in the rough, which I'm sure galled him yet further. I heard him curse me under his breath as I walked away from his game.

It felt great. Like I was a real adult, standing up to my father in a reasonable, calm, and honest way. I just hoped I hadn't spoiled the big ask of $60K.

The clubhouse rose out of the desert like something from the Black Forest in Germany. Heavy, dark beams with scrollwork carved into the ends, gray stone, huge fireplace (perfect for the 100-degree weather), slate floors. Kind of weird. You'd expect some sort of adobe architecture, or something out of the American rustic. At least they had a good newsstand, and I bought something I'd never seen before, an issue of *Launch*–"A Magazine for the Inspired Entrepreneur"–and ordered an iced tea.

While I sat there, I thought about Dad at age eighty-eight, about how vigorous and sharp (as well as sharp-tongued) he remained. I knew at my size I'd probably never live that long. I'd read the research. For a human of my size, the heart has to work too hard, the lungs, the veins. We just wear out earlier. I told myself I'd start working out when I turned fifty, in two years, with the simple goal of healthy to eighty. Though even eighty would be a stretch–no pun intended.

Chapter Eighteen

Deep with Dad

I saw Dad approaching the clubhouse with two of his golf-ing buddies, and I turned my beads for good luck. He'd caught up with them on the course and finished nine. When they came in, one man—a big guy with the swagger and bulk of a former college linebacker who had a hell of a schnoz and deep lines on his face, which suggested a life-long curmudgeon—charged straight into the Pro Shop. Dad paused between the Pro Shop and The 19th Hole, and we both listened to his golf buddy raise hell. "There's a god-damn Indian sleeping under a tree by the seventh green," a thick index finger jabbing at the golf pro a few inches from his chest. "That's the third time this month I've seen one of these drunks, sleeping it off on our course. Found one in a bunker last Tuesday morning and had half a mind to take a sand wedge to him. This has got to end. And I mean now!" His fist hammered the counter. "What are you going to do about it?"

The pro apologized and with real concern (genuine?), thanked the old badger for reporting the trespass, and promptly called security. After thanking the member again for his help, the pro said they were checking the course twice a day for trespassers, but he'd step it up to three times and post more "private property–no trespassing signs" immediately. He smoothed the ruffled fir, working it like an old pro, slick as an old pastor.

Dad came into the bar with a grin and said to me, "Let's get a drink."

I ordered a beer. He had scotch on the rocks–three fingers. After a couple quiet sips, I asked what he thought of the scene back a few minutes ago.

"Chris is a good guy in many ways, but he can be a bull in the china shop, and there's a bit of black in his heart. We're friendly, but he's not a friend."

"And ..."

"You mean, what did I think of Chris's anger about the Indian, the Native American? Did I agree with him? Do I hate drunks sleeping it off on the golf course? Do I hate Indians? Am I a racist?" He gave me a level look as he summed up my line of questions.

"Sure, yeah, all of that," I answered.

He took a long drink of scotch.

"Well, first of all, I'm not sure he was even a Native American, might have been a Latin American, or a white man. We didn't go over and ask. You heard Chris's assumption. But I don't want people sleeping on the golf course. For one thing, they could get hurt. For another, I play golf to escape worries of the world. Out there, it's me and the ball and a club and the sky and the sun." He paused as he pictured all of it. "For years, I've used golf to avoid fighting or stressing over what I can't change, or don't have the energy to change, or don't have the courage to change. After the 9/11 terrorist attack, I went out and played eighteen holes, ate a late lunch, and played another eighteen. I couldn't help those people except to pray for them and ask why–which I did on every fairway. I felt hopeless and helpless. But when I got to the ball, it was me and the ball and the club again. At least for those few seconds, I found peace," he said.

"I don't like invasions of my meaningless, little escape. But maybe that's what God wants. Despite the fact that I feel I've done my duty to Him. Which answers part one."

He took a quick sip of scotch. I waited.

"Do I care if the man was a Native American? Yes and no. No, because anyone in his condition makes me sad, the homeless in Boston or Phoenix, regardless of race. Selfishly, I find it hard to laugh and be happy. Hard to celebrate sinking a 20-foot putt, too."

He took another drink, a longer one. Then pressed his palms, spread out, on the bar, the way I'd seen him do a thousand times at the pulpit.

"On to the biggest and most interesting question you wanted to ask, or implied: am I a racist? I don't think so. But I suffer from implicit bias, like everyone else. I see it in myself more clearly than I did at your age. Back then, I thought I understood the world better than I did, better than I do now.

"I don't know, John, it's hard work to be present in the world, to keep learning when your mind wants to check the box and move on. You're probably better at it than I am. My default now is to slow down and listen. Around political stuff, I ask myself what's the higher level of personal freedom? Take gay marriage. I would have opposed it when I was young, but I support it now. What right do I have to restrict someone else's freedom or their joy? At times these things challenge my religion—not so much my faith—but I learned to set the constructs of religion aside and think about what's best for the society. Or I try to. I'm getting better."

"Wow," I said.

"Wow?" he replied.

All of this surprised me. When I was a kid, if my dad was a superhero, he'd be *Dogma Man—able to quell doubt with a single decree!* But here, Dogma Man sounded transformed into someone just home from a Mindfulness retreat. Like a Buddhist monk down from the mountain.

I didn't say any of that.

What I said was: "Dad, I'm impressed you're so open-minded about these things. I think it's great."

He swirled his glass, the ice nearly melted, and lifted it to his mouth.

He wiped his lips. "The world is more complicated than I knew, and society is changing faster than ever now. It's a lot easier for me, without the responsibility of a church and congregation. I imagine it's hard for you. Concord is not exactly quick to embrace change. I'm sure *that* hasn't changed."

"No it hasn't," I said. "Especially the deacons."

"Especially the deacons," he said, nodding.

I wanted to ask for his guidance with them but feared admitting incompetence. Clearly he'd figured out how to thrive in Concord.

"John, there is so much we don't know about each other," he said. "And there are things we can never know. Even if we spent a lifetime in the same room. That's just how it is between fathers and sons." He smiled and added, "Which helps one focus on the putting game."

He finished his drink and paused, collecting his thoughts before he spoke again, and the look in his eye when he turned to me told me something of a portent was coming. He took a breath, being careful now, knowing, sensing, whatever came next would linger with me for a lifetime. He looked up as if displaying his handsome profile–maybe looking God in the eye–before speaking.

"Son, I know the job in Concord is a challenge. And I know it probably came easier to me, to my nature, than it does for you. But I hope you appreciate it. I poured everything I had into building Concord Congregational into the peerless institution it is. It's the pinnacle. It's a great position providing a solid financial foundation for your family. Being able to install you in that position and to save you from that little New Hampshire backwater stands as one of my proudest achievements, my final achievement as a minister, and as a father in a way."

Dogma Man was swinging into action.

"I do appreciate it, Dad," I said. Though I did not.

"Good, because you just can't leave that position." He paused again to tip the empty glass to his lips, and I waited. "No matter how hard it can get, stick with it. It is worth striving to get better at for a lifetime–those challenges drive personal and spiritual growth."

While my father paused yet again, straining the power of the dramatic pause, I pondered how debates with deacons over bills for water or lawn fertilizer brought me closer to my fellow man or to God. But I remained quiet.

He smoothed back his white hair which was thinner than I remembered it. "I don't know what I'd do if you left what I built, what I built for you."

Really? You built it for me? I wanted to say. I don't think so. Your ego, Dogma Man played a pretty significant role.

I realized I could never confess I'd felt forced into the Concord job; that it *was* a burden; that I *did* want out, that I resented him and the oversized shoes he left behind, which my size–seventeen feet would never adequately fill.

But also, in the gravity of the situation, I realized the emotions I held.

You bastard, Daddy. Why couldn't you have been a failure so I could succeed? Or have been a carpenter like your father? Then others would marvel at my humble beginnings and see me as a great success too, as an overachiever.

Weighed apart from Dad, my accomplishments were considerable. But then, could anyone–especially me–consider my accomplishments apart from him? And always then, Reverend William Crackstone would outshine me.

Could I help but hate him? Could I help but blame him? Could I help but want to escape Concord?

And yet, in the face of all the opportunities, could I help but thank him?

Chapter Nineteen

With Mom and Dad

While my father and I sat at The 19th Hole clubhouse bar, another long quiet swelled between us like an inflating balloon, like a rapidly growing pumpkin. We each gulped our drinks. Checked the muted TV.

I glanced at my watch.

Then looked at it again to see what time it was.

It struck me that the quiet between us would have to end with nothing less than a Piper Cub crashing through the roof, or the gas stove exploding in the kitchen, or a SWAT team bursting in and slamming a wicked waitress to the floor, or at least an old geezer in the throes of a massive heart attack jumping his golf cart across the putting green and slamming through the picture window. Something monumental had to pop our expanding bulge of silence.

Mercifully, the bartender switched the television to a Diamondbacks baseball game. We each ordered another drink and talked about the Red Sox and how, despite past World Series wins, they had returned to their annual tease with a stumbling run for the pennant. Dad admitted he reluctantly rooted for the Diamondbacks even though they were a new team and in part because they were. "No decades of lament, no Curse of the Bambino, no cold spring games, no decades of unfilled longing or flogging at the hands of the Yankees." With the Diamondbacks, a World Series championship came in their fourth year and fun in the sun with the boys of summer.

Just drunk enough by this point to open up, I stepped out on the glass roof of the greenhouse.

"You know ..." I said and wished I had a nickname for him because father and son got in the way, and calling him Will or William was impossible. If only I could call him "Colonel" or "Captain" or "Skipper," something that recognized his status but not as a pastor or father. Maybe even "Comrade" or "Confidante" or "Advisor." Instead: "... Dad," dumbled out of my mouth just as it did when I was a teenager looking for the right words because conversation swerved toward danger when I shared the jumble of my mind's confusion with this man who seemed to have his whole life and every action fixed as straight and strong and rigid (and as warm) as an I-beam—as straight as his posture, as perfect as his hair.

I said to him, "To your point about the ministry perhaps not being my calling ... I've been thinking." That hitch knotted my throat. "I've been thinking about leaving." For all my daydreams, I hadn't uttered these words aloud. A dizzying rush overtook me, and I gripped the bar, glad to be sitting.

He turned to look at me squarely, "What? No. After what I just said about not leaving Concord? You've got to be kidding. Are you thinking about leaving Concord or the ministry?"

"The ministry, Concord, both," I choked out. "Maybe." The catch in my throat again. "Maybe both. Maybe neither. I'm not sure." How I wished I could say it with power and conviction. Or wished I could take it all back until certain.

"Somehow I'm not surprised," my old man said.

Not surprised I considered leaving? Or not surprised I was unsure? Not surprised I failed to appreciate the prize he had handed me?

"Have you suffered a crisis of faith?" he asked. "Have you lost your way? Or is it you no longer feel the calling? Maybe you never felt the calling, and that's why you struggled."

This started to resemble an exit interview. Alarm bells reminded me that most of my deacons had been Dad's and were still friends with him, still spoke to him frequently. I'd be a fool to assume his allegiance was stronger to me than to his former flock. Previously, I'd kept this in mind and kept the vicissitudes of my anger or annoyance to myself. I hadn't fully made up my mind about leaving the job, let alone the ministry. I had no place to go as yet. And I didn't want to just walk away, nor could I afford to. So this whole subject was way too premature to bring up with my father. Had I imagined a Dennis Cliff type of discussion?

"So, what are you thinking?" he asked again. "Or have you already found a new job and are here to inform me?"

"No, no, I'm not close to a decision yet. I'm just thinking."

"Thinking what? What's your leaning?"

I took a long draw off my beer and let him sit in silence while I decided whether or not to answer. Whether or not this was the time to ask him for $60,000 to start a business. Not.

My turn to wield the dramatic pause.

Then, almost without thinking, I decided to drop my guard entirely and said straight out: "Right now, Dad, I'm thinking about becoming a pumpkin farmer, growing giant pumpkins."

My Dad nearly spit out his drink. He laughed out loud and slapped the bar three times, laughed like I hadn't heard him laugh since ... since ever, like I'd never seen. His laugh rolled into a hacking cough, and he had to spit into a handkerchief pulled from his hip pocket. Tears flowed from his eyes by the time he was ready to speak again.

"Oh, you got me there, John," he said. "I'd forgotten how funny you can be."

When I told him I wasn't kidding, he didn't think it so funny and suggested I check myself into McLean Hospital or into The Logan Center in the Adirondacks for "mentally-exhausted" ministers.

I told him about my giant pumpkins in the backyard and how they'd unleashed something in me I'd never known, and how the new passion was real and more deeply satisfying than anything I'd ever experienced. And I was going to hold onto it if I could. During this pontification, my mind flashed images of Carol Baker in those tight, white shorts, muscular legs tapering so nicely into white tennis shoes.

Dad reminded me the world was full of passionate hobbyists who traveled the world to play golf, fish for bass, or dress up at *Star Trek* conventions–but they don't trash a great and meaningful career for it. Certainly not when they'd achieved a level like Concord Congregationalist Church.

I rejoined with a long-winded blather about the beauty of tending life and seeing measurable results from my efforts as the pumpkins took hold under my care, about the honor and grace and truth of farming, about pursuing passion in life and how it had meaning all its own.

When I finally ran out of gas, the old man let me sit in the quiet for a minute.

Then he said: "Who is she?"

"What?" I bolted in mock astonishment.

"You heard me plain enough," he said. "Who the hell is she? I've been around long enough to know this kind of madness has a woman mixed up in it. That's your passion. So tell me who she is."

"I don't have to tell you anything," I said, my voice whining like a high school kid's. But of course I did tell him about Carol Baker. Making clear there had been no touching, no untoward words even. However, I did leave out my occasional, randy dreams. What I told him was I had deep feelings for Carol. (I was just a breath short of saying I'd fallen in love with her.) And with pumpkins.

What I saw on his face I thought to be a length of compassion, but just enough for me to hang myself. After polishing off his drink and taking a deep sigh, the old man finally spoke: "Son, you've got a defective compass."

* * *

My father and I didn't talk until we were back in his Buick, halfway back to his and my mother's condo. Like a heavyweight, he knew he'd landed the knockout punch and left me flat on the canvas my head spinning while he settled the bar tab.

Finally, I'd regrouped enough to say, "A defective compass? How can you say that? I have not acted on my desire for Carol."

"God knows what's in your heart. And so do you."

"Yeah, well, there's still enough goodness and direction in me to keep me from straying off the path."

"Really?" he said. "You want me to tell you the strongest indicator of your malfunctioning compass?" He glared at me with the eyes of an angry sage unwilling to suffer fools. "It's your kids."

"My kids are fine!" I hammered, fighting back the defensiveness in my tone. "This is not about my kids. Keep my kids out of this."

"That's the problem. It's not about your kids. And it should be. It's about the fact you haven't mentioned your wife or kids the whole time you've been here except when your mother asked how they were and you tossed off, 'Oh they're fine, doing great.' You've kept your kids out of it all right, not a thought about your kids. Or your wife. You've just got your eye on a sweet piece of ass."

No kidding, those were my old man's exact words, "A sweet piece of ass." I'd never heard him use such coarse language.

He continued: "It's got your head turned around to the point where you're obsessed with growing giant pumpkins. Good God, boy! Yes, your moral compass is spinning, out of control."

I saw the $60,000 slip down the drain in that instant.

* * *

After going out to dinner with my folks at the local MCL (I hadn't had liver and onions with sides of mashed potatoes and gravy as well as macaroni and cheese for a long, long time), I told them I needed to walk off dinner and take in the cooler night air.

I hadn't gone far when thoughts of Carol Baker intruded. Was she skinny-dipping tonight? Was she having sex with Matt? Was Jack making a play for her?

I kept walking, trying to just take in the neighborhood. It was like all typical American suburbs, could be from Maryland or Iowa or California (scaled down for empty nesters). Here and there a dash of adobe. The air was dry, cooler, comfortable, but desert dry. I wandered to the edge of the golf course where Dad and I'd had such a lovely time. I walked a cart path, pausing to take in the stars. More stars appeared the farther I went from my parents' neighborhood. So I kept walking.

At the farthest point of the golf course and the cart path, at the outermost green and tee at the top of a hill where lush grass collided with rock and sand and desiccated scrub, I looked up, and the Milky Way spilled out overhead, a dusting of countless stars across the desert sky.

I wished I were there with Carol Baker. I pulled out my phone to call her, doing it fast, before I got scared and stopped.

"Hello?" came a sleepy voice, and I realized it was two hours later in Concord.

I glanced at my phone, midnight back home. "Carol, hello. I'm sorry to call so late. I didn't think about the time difference."

"Reverend Crackstone?"

"Yes, it's me, John."

"Aren't you in Arizona visiting your parents?"

"Yes," I said. Now why the hell did I call her? I'm sure I woke up Matt too. What would I say? "You know, I went for an evening walk, and the stars out here are amazing. It made me think about when you lived on the reservation in North Dakota the night skies were probably like this."

"Yes, I remember amazing stars there. But I'm tired and should get back to bed." I heard someone speak in the background, Matt wanting to know why I called. I heard her whisper something back. "I need to get back to sleep. Goodnight, Reverend."

"Sorry to wake you, Carol. Goodnight."

I sat on a bench next to the ball washer like an idiot. Why had I called? Just to hear her voice? Why hadn't it dawned on me to share the starry night with Nancy or Gordon or Megan? My dad was right, I'd lost my way. I had fallen for Carol, taking a right turn off the road of friendship right into a ditch. I looked up again. Overhead stars amazed, but I couldn't remember how to recognize the North Star. Didn't even know which way was north.

I looked out over the golf course and saw a long-legged dog running across the fairway, then two more after him, and another three. They vanished into the desert brush. Seconds later an ungodly yipping-howling rose from the desert. The dogs were coyotes. Chilling. Frighteningly close.

It made me wonder if a pack of hungry coyotes would attack a man, a seven-foot man. I gave the beads on my
bracelet a spin and headed back, short-cutting across the
fairway rather than taking the cart path. With images of a
hungry pack of coyotes descending from the desert wilderness, I walked fast, running a little and keeping watch over
my shoulder and listening. As I neared the final fairway
toward the suburbs, the sprinkler system kicked on. Huge
jets of water plumed in all directions, pumping thousands
of gallons per minute of the desert's most precious resource
high in the air across the lush green grass. And soaking me
in the process. There was no way to avoid those sweeping
geysers.

I walked the rest of the way cold and wet. Mom and
Dad got a good laugh at the sight of me. When I told them
about the coyotes, they weren't surprised. Lots of neighbors
had lost cats and dogs to them.

Wet and cold, I claimed jet lag and went to bed.

Laying on a pillow smelling faintly of rose essence, I
pondered the sting of my father's words. What could be
worse than a minister with a faulty compass? How could I
"lead the flock," in the arrogant parlance of my training, if I
could not find my own way? And was it true I was lost in
the wilderness?

Or had I instead begun to make my own way in this
world, finally, and without the convenient compass of any
church doctrine or morality or my father's pointing arm?
My slow growth, less vegetable, more geologic in its agility,
had guided me to reconsider the fallacy of "the calling" and
awaken to the possibility and the necessity to step away
from my church, from my father's church, from any church,
from any set of defined givens and rules, to explore the
world openly with a freshness and innocence of being that
let the facts of existence and nature and life; the facts of
rock and earth and sky and water; the facts of family and

blood and bone and love; as well as the whim of serendip-
ity and luck and happenstance–not to mention the entire
spectrum of spirituality–letting all of these things shape
how I saw the world, and how I led my life.

This thinking began to blend with the imaginary as the
tectonic plates of consciousness and slumber slid one over
another, and my psychological pluck soon remade me as
a cowboy riding fast through the desert of a 1940s black-
and-white Western, with my gray-and-white dappled
Appaloosa horse leaping over sagebrush and cacti as if we
were about to be gunned down until, stopping in a swirl
of dust, I came upon a brilliant green golf course. Then
I heard a gunshot and at the last instant, saw the white
sphere of a golf ball shooting through the gray light until
it struck the head of my horse, and as it crumpled beneath
me, I leapt from the saddle–and damn–near fell out of bed.

* * *

The next morning I'd planned breakfast with Mom, just a
quick good luck to Dad on his way out for an early round of
golf. Mom hadn't made an appearance yet, so I poured another cup of coffee and wandered around the condo. When
I went into the den, I noticed a historical document framed
on the wall. It was a Land Warrant for the Indiana Territory,
awarding five sections to an Isaac Crackstone in 1807, and it
was signed by none other than Thomas Jefferson. I'd never
seen it before, and I'd never heard of an Isaac Crackstone.

A noise and I turned to see Lil–Big–un shuffle in from
the kitchen, wearing her fuzzy pink slippers, and carrying
a mug of coffee. She looked tall as ever, but tired. She was
old now, my mom, eighty-four years old.

When I said good morning, she sprang to life.

"Oh, Honey." Her hands smoothing her hair. "I overslept.
I'm so sorry. I've had trouble sleeping recently, and then

around five in the morning I fall back asleep like a stone and can hardly wake up."

I wondered if I should worry about this.

I asked her about the Land Grant on the wall and Isaac, but she knew little of it. Except this, which she tossed over her shoulder as she shuffled back to the kitchen for a second cup of coffee like it was old news: "All I know is we still have a small farm somewhere in Indiana. I've never seen it, and I don't think your father's been there since he was in grade school."

"But this Land Grant says five sections. How much land is that?" I said, following her into the kitchen.

"I don't know," she said. "The family sold most of it, and I don't know why we kept this last plot. We rent it out to a farmer. I thought you knew about this." She took my mug and poured me another coffee. "There's some connection to the Revolutionary War, and then Indian battles on the western frontier. You'll have to ask your father."

She was already retreating down the hall. "Let me get dressed, and we can make breakfast."

I'd never heard about a family farm, but now I might have something much bigger than the $60,000 to bring to the C & C Pumpkin Partnership–the CCPP.

When Mom came back, she was more herself, with an energetic bounce in her step. We ended up making breakfast there at home and ate on the back patio, scrambled eggs, toast, berries, and more coffee. Even in the shade, the day was warming up fast in the morning sun.

Although Mom found the desert interesting and enjoyed the winters, she missed New England summers. The summer heat in Arizona was "like living in an oven," she said. If she had her way, they'd spend half the year on Cape Cod or the North Shore, for daily walks on the beach and cooling breezes–not to mention regular visits with grandkids and old friends. But she said my father didn't think they could afford it. This struck me as odd because I'd never heard my father express money concerns. (It also dampened my hope for the $60,000.) Dad had moved among the most wealthy of Concord, with his aristocratic airs, but of course he wasn't rich. His salary probably never exceeded mine. They'd done well to end up in a nice 55-plus community, with a two-bedroom condo (plus den) a half mile from the golf course. But not *on* the golf course.

As Mom and I plodded through small talk of mother and adult son, I began to think, *Who is this woman?* What I knew of her would fill a cup, not a bucket: devoted wife, dedicated mother to my sister and me—but did she love her teaching career? Did she love her role in the family or as a minister's wife?

My mother's family, the McLarsons, washed ashore with the 1840s crush of Irish immigrants escaping the potato famine. They raced from New York to Northeastern Ohio to join the Industrial Revolution. A mostly quiet, bright girl, my mother, Lillian McLarson, grew up in Cleveland and went to Wellesley College in Massachusetts. Though she aimed to be a librarian, Mom left school before graduating to marry my father when he finished at Harvard Divinity. She went back to college later and became an elementary school teacher.

My parents, arm-in-arm, can still own a room—but other than being tall and elegant, Mom resembles my father in few ways. She focused on my sister and me, then her students, steering clear of my father's work for the most part and absolutely avoiding politics. Except when the Governor asked my father to run for Lieutenant Governor. It marked the only time I recall my mother putting her foot down against Dad, and Reverend William Crackstone stuck to the pulpit.

I noticed Mom sure didn't love her garden. Everything desiccated to the color of toast, grass baked brown and bleaching white under the unforgiving sun. Her boxwoods curled yellow and brown like gnarled muffins. Two small-ish trees about my height held a handful of pale-green leaves weakly fluttering in the non-breeze.

"So, Mom, what's the story of your yard and garden? What's the eulogy?"

"John, we live in a desert now, and there's a terrible drought," she said. "It's unnatural, and wasteful to water a Connecticut garden." Here she held up air-quotation marks. "That's what our real estate agent called it when she showed us the condo. Whoever heard of such nonsense, a Connecticut garden in the middle of Arizona?"

"I didn't know you were an environmentalist," I said.

"From where I sit, it's about what is right. God didn't create these plants for this environment. Water is both scarce and expensive. Besides, the state is helping to pay for desert landscapes to replace this folly."

After a beat of silence, Mom said, "John, your father told me about your career conversation last night." Oh, boy, I thought now Lil-Big-un is going to weigh in and some-how straighten it out. Or straighten me out. Hell, maybe I should ask her to loan me the $60,000.

"Yeah, Dad laughed so hard, he just about passed an ice cube through his nose," I said.

She smiled. "I can understand how you'd want to do something different. It's hard to live in someone's shadow. I know. I lived in your father's shadow too. It was different of course. But–"

This was like riding a bicycle too fast downhill. Front wheel wobbling, wanting it to stop or slow down so badly you may just bail out.

What if I had never taken the Concord job? What then?

"–I don't know if pumpkin farming is the answer," she said. "Maybe it is. You need to go slow and listen to your heart. Consider your God-given talents." Then she pointed at me. "And your God–given family." And I knew Dad had told her about Carol. "Then ask yourself if you've discovered a hobby or a career."

Did she think I was a little kid? Did she think this high-school counseling was helpful? Did she think I hadn't pondered these things?

"What does Nancy think of this pumpkin business?"

What did Nancy think of it? I hadn't shared the larger vision yet. I didn't want to scare her. "Nancy and I have talked about it some, but the vision has grown," I said. "I plan to partner with my friend Jack, who's a very successful businessman. We're planning it now, and then I'll share the details with Nancy."

"Sounds like you need to include her. Nancy's smart. You've always been a team, so this concerns me a little."

"Mom, I know you're trying to be helpful, but I've thought–"

"John," she said sharply, "focus on your talents and your family. It's like your team and height in basketball."

Great, a sports analogy?

"Mom, you liked basketball and wanted me to play. I didn't like it, and it's a shame I was born tall, because I wasted it. A God–given talent wasted. How many millions of people would've killed for my height, for what I have and never wanted. What a disappointment I must have been to you all these years."

"John, John, John, slow down. Just listen a minute. Here's what I'm saying, what I'm saying badly, so let me try again. If you had a world–class singing voice and perfect pitch, I would have made you take voice lessons. I would have dreamt of you on stage singing to the world."

"I get it, Mom." A person can express disappointment a million ways.

"You know it's not as simple as me wanting you to make the most of your talents." She cleared her voice twice, before continuing. "Sure, that was part of it. But I also know special talents get unlocked with hard work and a dose of success. That requires some pushing from the parent. I've always struggled with how much to push and when to step back and let you and Susan wander forward to find your own way. I probably pushed basketball too hard early, but I backed off. You must have struggled to balance these things for your own kids."

I hadn't really, or maybe Nancy managed the balance for me. I figured the kids would find their own way. If they fell into soccer or trumpet or painting, great. If not, well they'd sort it out like the rest of us.

"Some people, not everyone," Mom said, still trying to make herself understood, "have a special talent you can't teach. But most of us have to piece together our talents and interests–what everyone calls 'passions' now, which may be too strong a word–and begin to build matching skills. Much of this happens without conscious effort or reflection. You take a job, find a good boss or mentor, fall in with a few likable colleagues and move through life as a productive citizen and a generally happy person. That's fine, and fine is fine for most people. Maybe your passion becomes rooting for the Bruins or Red Sox, I don't know."

"Mom–"

Her index finger came up stopping my interruption.

She continued: "Step down a level and the job is convenient and pays the mortgage, keeps the kids in shoes, that sort of thing. This person plods ahead. Not happy, not miserable. Another step down and you have folks who pursued a profession and trained for it and achieved a position, and now they feel trapped by it. Lots of lawyers, teachers, and dentists on that step. Ministers too. Lots of ministers feel trapped."

She looked around her dead garden. "Thing is, all of this can change fast. A new manager or colleague comes in, or you move to a new company, and everything changes for better or worse. So it may not be the career, it may be the job, or the people around the job, that's killing someone a little bit every day."

"Mom—"

"Let me finish. Almost finished. When I taught in the Belmont schools, life was great until we got a new principal, and he ruined it. So I moved to Acton schools and stayed for twenty years." She paused. "All I'm saying is a person can step away from a difficult situation without leaving a whole career or risking a family."

Now I started to hear her. This was Mom's way of granting permission for me to make a change, to leave Concord, or suggesting I leave for another minister position. While protecting my family. Without taking on the risks of becoming an entrepreneur. And without me asking her for the $60,000.

* * *

I still had to ask Dad for the money before I left that day, and now I also wanted to ask about the Indiana farmland. I'd come to resolve some things, and I had. Some of them. My old man had surprised me with his take on race as well as with his declaration of my defective compass. His advice and his view of his gift of Concord was clear, and I myself was more clear, more at peace, about how I viewed his gift. Even though I hadn't articulated it to him. My father's gift sat there like the unwanted wedding gift you can't return.

Certainly Mom's understanding and generosity had smoothed the way to leave Concord—at least if there were another church.

When Dad got back from golf, I asked if he'd go for a short walk before I had to catch my flight. Already hot, and he'd been out on the course, but he agreed. We walked a block from the house with small talk about his golf game and neighbors. We walked slowly, again reminding me of his age.

"Dad, I have a few things to say before I leave. So please just listen for a minute.

"First, I love you and Mom.

"I respect you and your accomplishments.

"I admire your drive and sense of purpose.

"I ask that you accept our differences, and the things that worked for you may not work for me. I know it's hard for you, but Concord has not been great for me, and I need a change. This pumpkin passion surprised me. I'm partnering with my old friend Jack Corbett, who has become a very successful businessman. We plan a big future in the business, from processing and selling seeds for giant pumpkins to making pumpkin a more popular food choice and even some non-food uses. It's a real business opportunity."

"May I speak now?" he asked, and I motioned for him to go ahead.

"First, I love you too. I hope that doesn't surprise you. I'm aware I don't show it very well. But I do. And thank you for the respect and admiration, though I sometimes think I get more credit than I deserve." He paused as we took a few strides in our walk. "As for the last point about us being different. Yes, I see it. I've always seen it, John. While my efforts may be faulty, I do try to be of help. I've tried to be of help to you and your family."

We walked on. I heard the yips of coyotes in the distance.

"Here's the thing," he said. "If you really want to pursue this pumpkin business, I'm not going to try to stop you. You're a grown man. Just be sure it's a good opportunity. And put your family first in these decisions. This neighbor infatuation will pass, but your family, you've got to protect it, Son."

He sounded tired.

"I will, Dad. I have two last things to talk to you about for my part of starting the business. The first is to ask about the farm in Indiana. Is there anyway Jack and I can rent some land? I didn't even know about the farm or Isaac Crackstone until this morning."

"I guess I never told you. A warrant of land, essentially a land grant, came his way in the early 1800s for military back pay and as a reward. Isaac was a soldier under George Rogers Clark in the Revolutionary War, and stayed with Clark when he went to fight Indians in the Indiana Territory. I don't remember all the details, but Isaac was given five sections of land. A section is 640 acres."

"Wow," I said, "that's a lot of land."

"It was," he said. "There's just one section left with four hundred tillable-acres. The rest is woods along the Wabash River. No buildings, just land. I've thought about selling it, but my father asked me to keep it, and I like the connection to old Isaac Crackstone. In a family of New England ministers and merchants, he must've been a black sheep: Revolutionary War soldier, frontiersman, and a farmer who never returned."

I was trying to be respectful, but time was running low, and this history lesson was running long. "Dad, do you think Jack and I could rent some of the land?"

"The land is yours, Son. Or it will be when I die," he said. "Susan gets the condo. You get the farm."

Holy crap, I thought, it was my destiny to be a farmer.

"But for now," I asked tentatively, "can I rent some of the land for next spring?"

"We have a contract with the farmer, but we can work something out," he said. "First, you'll need to let me know how much land you'll need."

"That's great," I said. "Dad, I have one last thing for my part of starting the business, I need $60,000."

He laughed in an ah-ha way. "There it is." He slapped his thigh. "There's the reason you came out to visit."

"I won't lie to you, the money was part of it, yes. Can you help? I'll pay it back with interest. You'd be an investor," I said, though I hadn't thought that through. "But I also came to visit you and Mom."

"And to ask for $60,000. Don't forget the small detail of $60,000."

"I have another option for some of it," I said. "There's a pumpkin contest, and if I win, it's $30,000. But that's not until fall."

"Well, how soon do you need the money? When is this pumpkin business supposed to start? And are you going to quit your job at the church first? That sounds risky."

"I'm not sure how soon I'd need the money. But soon. As for the job, I don't plan to quit right away. Jack and I are each putting in $60,000 to start, and Jack has investments he can borrow against." I didn't want to get into Jack's tax evasion case and how the government locked up most of his wealth. "Over time, Jack will be the lead investor from money he made selling his software business. Right now, most of his money is tied up."

"Sounds like he's rich. With his money, why do you need mine? My $60,000 is nothing compared to what he probably has. I said I'd help you get land from the farm," he said. "But $60,000, it's a lot of money to me. And to you, I'd guess."

Dad was agitated now. First tired and now agitated. I worried about him and saw a park up ahead, a green space with shade trees and a little fountain. Like something out of Connecticut, Mom would say.

"Let's sit down up here, Dad."

There was a drinking fountain at the park and Dad went directly there for a long drink. Then he joined me on the bench.

"You okay?" I said.

"Me? Sure," he said in a gruff voice. "I'm fine. Fine."

I imagined him falling over dead as he said those words. We sat quietly.

I saw Dad thinking. The heft of $60,000 and possibly losing it. The weight of a son's request. The fear of being old and cash–poor. That scared me too. It would kill me to blow it and leave Mom and Dad old and penniless.

"Look, Dad, I know $60,000 is a lot of money. If you don't have it or can't risk it, I understand."

"But where else can you get it?"

"I don't know. You're the first person I asked. Maybe I can borrow it from multiple people."

My father took a deep breath, rubbing both knees, "I'll have to talk to your mother about it. We've always made major decisions like this together. I couldn't write a check today anyway. Money's locked up in retirement accounts."

Maybe they really didn't have much money. Mom had said she wished she could spend summers in New England, but Dad told her they couldn't afford it.

"Dad, if you and Mom decide it's too risky, I'll understand," I said.

At that point, I wished I'd never asked. There was a chance Schwartz could win the Topsfield weigh–in, or finish as one of the nation's largest pumpkins. Then I could raise money selling seeds. It would delay us–or me. Perhaps Jack would let me put the money in later. Or maybe this was Jack's test of my resolve and resourcefulness.

"But I do need the money soon," I said, the urgency rising in my voice unchecked.

"Let me talk to your mother first, but I don't want to get your hopes up, John." He sounded annoyed and stood up. "I hear you walking away from an unparalleled position in Concord during what smacks of a mid–life crisis. To support all of that, I'd like to start by seeing a business plan for this pumpkin idea." He sighed. "Now you've got a plane to catch."

I wondered if I'd have to lose my father to take up the pumpkin business. Would he come around if I was successful?

Chapter Twenty

Living the Dream

Back in Concord, over coffee at the Wayward Tavern (following a reminder from my smartphone calendar marked JC, which most people might think a meeting with Jesus Christ, but stood for Jack Corbett, could also stand for John Crackstone, BTW), I looked across our village green, known as Monument Square, while waiting for Jack, who was late as usual. We planned to advance the pumpkin-enterprise dream. I looked forward to announcing the prospects of the Indiana farm ground if not the procurement of $60,000. Through the front window, with its small panes of ancient, wavy glass, I appreciated the verdant, New England morning, mid-morning now, and warm, but nothing like Arizona. Tourists coursed around the village. Kids climbed on the base of the granite obelisk. Parents paused for a few seconds to try and tease out the meaning of "Faithful unto Death" carved into the monument base. Rental cars already clogged the road out to the Old North Bridge. Locals complained about tourists, but they are as much a part of Concord as white houses with black shutters. For all its foibles, it was a beautiful village, a touch Disney perhaps, with the ordinances restricting building colors and materials as well as signage, but it did preserve the character. A lovely veneer.

Before thoughts of my hometown turned ugly, Jack arrived. A waitress zipped right over, bringing him coffee. A favorite with waitresses for his Texas-sized tips, he got better service than I'd earned over a dozen years as a regular. Corbett's very un-Yankee-like tips left me looking a little cheap.

Jack took a sip of coffee and looked up at me. "Did you get the $60,000 from your dad?"

Pow, a punch in the gut. Now he tested me, and I'd failed. "He and my mom are thinking about it, and he'd like to see a business plan."

"That's smart," Jack said, and my blood pressure eased a little. "The streamlined business plan is almost ready. I worked on it while you were gone, so I'll finish it up."

"But he's not real supportive of me leaving the pinnacle of the Congregational universe."

"What's your plan B? Gotta have a plan B in business. Gotta be ready to pivot."

"Thinking about it," I said.

"Think fast." He took a drink of coffee. "How about your meetings with your dad?"

We talked about how it went, and Jack thought it sounded good.

Then our talk turned to business, and I told him about the family farm and prospects to rent some of the four-hundred tillable acres.

"Fantastic," Jack said, hand up for a high-five. "You came back with a huge score." Then he said he'd figure out how many acres we should rent in the first three years. He was especially excited about it being near the river which would reduce irrigation costs assuming we could get a permit to tap into the river.

Just as American Colonial leaders had met in this very room of the Wayward Tavern plotting to rise up against the Crown nearly two hundred and fifty years earlier, Jack and I schemed to topple the established snack–food kings behind the rise of a pumpkin enterprise, with pumpkin seeds, toasted and flavored for all, perhaps pumpkin chips, chipotle–pumpkin chips.

Fields of orange orbs getting huge under sunlight and sprinklers filled my imagination, and me in a red pickup truck–like a latter-day Isaac Crackstone–rolling out to check my fields, maybe getting a black Labrador to ride along with me, his big, square head hanging out the window. Then bubbled up an image of me steering a green–and–yellow John Deere tractor in the Indiana fields and teaching Gordon and Megan to drive it too.

"Yo, Big John, you with me?" Jack said shattering my daydream.

He went on, quick to point out how this break on the Indiana farm meant he could revise the business plan which had included the crazy price of land in New England, especially near Boston. Jack thought two hundred acres would be plenty for the first few years, and we could expand into the full four hundred acres later and rent even more in the future. Using the agri–business model Jack recommended– to contract with independent farmers and have them raise pumpkins to our specifications and sell to us at pre-set prices–would help us manage cost of goods.

It all sounded good to me, until he said: "Of course they can't all be giant pumpkins."

"Hold on, Cowboy," I said. "That's the brand. We Be Giant Pumpkins. It's what we're about."

"John, I didn't step up to the plate to bunt," he said. "I think we can own pumpkins, not just giant pumpkins, the way Orville Redenbacher owned popcorn. Think about it." Jack made the case that growing giant pumpkins took huge amounts of water, excessive amounts, which drove costs up and profits down–even if the water was free, the pumps were still expensive energy hogs. Also the water requirements of giant pumpkins limited our ability to scale the business. Finally, they tended to split in the sun, and we couldn't babysit fields of Schwartz-sized monsters, setting up little tents for each one.

"I like the Orville Redenbacher analogy," I said, "and you're probably right about not doing only giant pumpkins, but we have to do some. To be the kings of pumpkins, we need to be giants in the business." I paused and rubbed my chin before going on. "I have a plan for making giant pumpkins popular for businesses, schools, homes, and it wouldn't take much land to grow a few thousand giants—or even a few hundred. And selling seeds for giants is wildly profitable."

He didn't argue, but he didn't agree. I waited for him to reply, and he took his time.

Then he leaned forward on his elbows. "We're talking a big, big business, John. Not a novelty."

Novelty.

* * *

By the end of our meeting, which rolled past coffee into a working lunch over a couple of The Plowman's, we had bulldozed through several fundamental business items. For example, Jack insisted if he put in the money to start the company, beyond our initial $60K each, he needed to own sixty percent of it. I got thirty percent, and ten percent would be held in common stock to offer future key employees and to create a stock-option program. I admit I understood little of this and was giddy at the idea of owning a big chunk of a real corporation, even if its value calculated as worthless right then.

Before we created a company, Jack said, we still needed to conduct deeper "due diligence" to build a full business plan, including a "proforma" with costs and profit projections for the first three and five years. That in turn meant research on production costs, land costs, farmer contract rates, as well as processing, manufacturing, packaging, distribution, marketing, sales, and more. Then the product pricing side and what the profits might be. And we needed competitive research and market research. I nodded along, my brain agog with all the work to do that rocketed way past any of my experience. Jack explained he already had a couple of his contacts back in Texas conducting research and due diligence while I traveled to Arizona. It was too early to get excited, but the preliminary work showed promise.

What else had he done while I was in Arizona? Had he made a move toward Carol? Had she made a move toward him?

While I listened for hints of an interest in Carol, I told myself to focus on the business, on this conversation.

"So," I said, "what's in the streamlined business plan?"

"A lot of guesses and assumptions," Jack said and laughed. "It's not all bullshit, but there's not a lot of real meat on the bones."

I just hoped my father's business acumen and education floated on the same plane as mine.

Then Jack washed away my concern by sliding a sheet of paper across the table to me, dropping what he thought our salaries should be for the first two years, the next two years—with and without performance bonuses—and then, if all went as planned, "which it never does," what we might make in years five and six.

"Can you live on that?" he asked with a grin.

I thought it was a joke at first. It was a lot of money, much more than I ever dreamed of making. These numbers made my seed calculations look like paper-route money. My head swam with the details—it was more than a little daunting—and I wondered how I could contribute enough to justify the executive-sized salary. A salary my deacons would lust for. I also marveled at how Jack had transformed himself from an average seminary student into a highly successful businessman. All of his playful goofiness vanished in this meeting, and he screwed-down intense focus on what steps led to victory. All of this process, these details and considerations were at his fingertips. I trusted him to take the lead.

When I confessed concern about my ability to contribute enough value to the company other than as cheerleader and dreamer, Jack replied, "Mr. Crackstone, if you can be an effective cheerleader and dreamer with the right people, in the right way, at the right time—you'll earn every penny."

What would I do with the extra money?

Feather the college funds?

Buy a brand new BMW and roll like the executive I hoped to become?

Then it hit me—of course—Carol Baker.

I could offer her a job. Carol wanted to work, to find a sense of purpose beyond her role as a mother. Now I could be her source of purpose. And passion? Working side-by-side, shoulder-to-shoulder, hip-to-hip ...

Like Jack said, we wouldn't do this alone, we'd need staff. Why not start with Carol? She was smart. I knew and trusted her. Might need to keep an eye on Jack and his potential interest in Carol, but we might even escape Concord together. Move to Indiana, following in the footsteps of Isaac Crackstone, to run the pumpkin business—emotional pioneers—and never return. There was no reason to run the business from Concord or New England. Costs were lower in the Midwest, closer to farmers and other food processors: Kellogg, General Mills, General Foods, and dozens of others large and small.

Even if we half-realized Jack's projections, we'd be rich. Especially in Indiana where the money went farther. I didn't need to impress my deacons. Let those losers find out about my accomplishments in the church flyer or the Concord High alumni email–or in the business pages.

* * *

When Jack and I finished, I went straight to Carol Baker's house and knocked on the back door–with courage and confidence this time. A little sweat ran down the side of my face, armpits damp. Not especially attractive, but I had an attractive offer. She came around the house, garden hose in hand.

We sat on their back deck, under an umbrella with iced tea. The cold tea was refreshing, and it gave me the courage to dive in. "Carol, I'm here because–well, first I have to ask you to keep this in complete confidence, you can't even tell Matt, especially not Matt." Did I notice her eyebrows rise a little? "Nancy doesn't know about it either, or not much." Her eyebrows rose again, and her eyes focused on her drink.

"Did you kill one of the deacons, John?"

I laughed. "No, not today. Tomorrow, who knows?" I smiled at her bright laugh, "It's a big idea, a big orange idea." I proceeded to outline the vision for the pumpkin enterprise–minus the beauty products, paper, and laxative. She listened. Her expression inscrutable. Inscrutable as a pumpkin.

"The last part, the real reason I'm here," I said, "is this: I want to offer you a job." She smiled and looked at the table. I went on: "You said you were looking for a purpose. Well, this might be it. We're just starting. There are so many things you could do to help us grow the business." I paused to drink from the tea and let the job offer sink in.

She was quiet, her finger tracing the sweat beading up on the cold glass in front of her.

"What do you think?" I asked.

"You sound pretty serious about this pumpkin business."

"We are. Jack has worked up a preliminary business plan, and we think it could be huge." I held off mentioning the potential move to Indiana. One thing at a time.

"Well, it's interesting, and I really appreciate you thinking of me. But I'll need to think about it. And at some point–when it's okay with you–I'll have to discuss it with Matt."

I realized I hadn't thought that part through. Yes, she'd have to talk to Matt. For some reason, I imagined she might just jump in to try it. But telling Matt would probably end my Reverend job. Still, I could navigate it for a while. And some dark corner of my brain thought, *Hey, Stupid, you just committed career suicide with this conversation, an accidental suicide (death knell pending).*

"Does this mean you'll leave the church?" Carol asked. For a second, I wondered if she saw it as a way to break free from Matt and Concord. To join me.

"If all of it works out, yes. But not right away. Spring at the earliest," I said. "Probably spring." Although this was another detail I hadn't sorted out. And that dark corner spoke up again: *Stop talking. Just please stop talking.*

"Sounds like you have a lot to work out yet," she said.

"Yeah, it's a startup, you know. And you could get in on the ground floor."

* * *

Two days later, Jack emailed me the preliminary business plan. I didn't even open it. I just forwarded it to Mom and Dad.

* * *

"Dr. Mike, it's Jack Corbett and John Crackstone calling from Massachusetts." Jack hunched over my kitchen table practically yelling into his smartphone on speaker mode. The

216

table was one my parents had left for us, one I'd known all my life. "Good to meet you."

"Hi, guys," Mike said, "I hear you clearly, no need to yell."

"Oh," Jack said and slid back in his seat.

Mike was an agronomy professor from Purdue University, a connection through one of Jack's friends. Jack had sent Dr. Mike information about the Indiana farm ground, which was in Tippecanoe County, the same as Purdue with its renowned agriculture program. Now Dr. Mike held forth in full professor mode, his voice poured over the little speaker rich and full like a PBS documentary narrator, instructing about the soil type and drainage and so forth, all geared-up and geeked-out about the US Geological Survey database, enabling him to accomplish in a few hours what years ago would require months of work.

"Here's the good news," Dr. Mike said. "Several areas here in Indiana match the soil profile where the largest pumpkins grow in Oregon and New England. Most track the river valleys here in Northern Indiana–featuring a combination of glacier deposits and loamy river deposits–and your land there outside the town of Battle Ground, along the Wabash River matches that profile."

When I heard those words, I had to stifle a giggle and a Hallelujah. The Lord had provided! The US Government had provided! My ancestors had provided! Even dear old Dad had provided! And a heavenly abundance in the form of splendid, orange orbs–yes, pumpkins by the millions, growing huge under Hoosier skies and bathed in the hallowed waters of the Wabash. All of it to fulfill the blessed gift of God and Nature and big white glaciers. All of it had come together in such a way to assure greatness–and prosperity! In that instant my heart pounded like a Pentecostal minister's mid-sermon.

Mike was still talking: "It's pretty country," he said.

Who cares? I thought.

"The hills and bluffs over the river and woolly country roads make it more like southern New Hampshire than the big, flat fields you see between here and Chicago," Mike said.

Another 'Hallelujah' and two 'who cares?' Happy bonuses.

Mike said it was easy to get permits to pump water directly from the river for irrigation or from irrigation ponds fed by the river. Either way, no need for a commercial well to supply water for pumpkins. That alone would save many thousands of dollars, he said.

More blessings and another suppressed Hallelujah.

Jack wrote down all the info from Mike, and after the call, we Googled the location, checking out the satellite and street views. It was indeed pretty country. Jack wanted to hop on a jet and check it out.

I had to re-jigger my schedule with Shelly Andersen and re-balance Nancy's expectations too. But yes, of course I had to go with him to visit the future farm for our pumpkin empire and the one-time home of Isaac Crackstone—my future farm ground. And the fulfillment of family destiny.

* * *

I had flown over America before—I have to admit I'd only stopped in the flyover-states twice, for conferences in Chicago and Cincinnati—but this time, I sat in the exit row looking out the little portal window at the patchwork of fields, especially as we neared the Indianapolis Airport. Descending, it looked so flat, I thought I could discern the curvature of the earth. Maybe I could.

Jack and I picked up a rental car, a mid-sized Chevrolet, and headed north toward Lafayette and Purdue to pick up Dr. Mike. Spoiled by expensive European cars, Jack muttered in disgust about the car, wondering out loud if the American automotive industry existed merely to supply rental cars. Mike was ready when we arrived, waiting outside a classroom building. After quick intros, he jumped in the back, and in a few minutes, we slipped the city into the countryside with wide, flat roads and a deep ditch on each side. Jack sped past vast fields of corn and soybeans, and Mike directed the way from right behind him. I noticed Mike's remarkable voice; a deep, rich voice perfect for an NPR radio announcer or PBS narrator had he not become a professor.

Nearing the town of Battle Ground, Mike slipped into historian mode, his orotund timbre brought to life the story of the Battle of Tippecanoe like a documentary. In 1811, a Shawnee Indian village sat on a bluff above the Wabash River, near the confluence with the Tippecanoe River. Tecumseh, the Shawnee leader, was amassing a force to fight the Americans over a treaty he considered unjust and illegal in the Indiana Territory. Future US president William Henry Harrison led a band of about a thousand soldiers against eight hundred Shawnee warriors. Mike had us take a slight detour over to Prophetstown State Park where the Indians had camped. Both sides lost about sixty-five men, and the American soldiers drove the Indians out, stole the spoils, and burned their village.

While none of this history had anything to do with our mission, it touched me, making me wonder about Isaac Crackstone and his farm. The land warrant, or land grant, had come his way before the Battle of Tippecanoe, and his five sections surely included this hallowed ground. Did he support the Indians? Did he want them out?

Mike directed us to Pretty Prairie Road and my family farm. It was pretty country as Mike and the name of the road suggested. We got out and walked part of the land. It included broad fields, mostly flat but with some contour. The rest of the acreage traced the Wabash River, with big, beautiful sycamores and cottonwoods. These bottom grounds, Mike explained, featured a combination of sand for rapid drainage as well as the rich loam from river deposits, ideal for pumpkin growing. I felt that excitement tingle again. Then Mike pulled out a topographic map to show where we might install irrigation ponds and how they would work, being fed from higher upriver. Finally, Mike suggested we take a flyover in a private plane to see the entire farm. Jack was all over it and couldn't wait for a ride. But there was not time to book a private plane before we had to return to Boston. Next trip.

We headed back to Indianapolis where we shared a room with two queen beds (part of bootstrapping startup mode, Jack said) in a remade hotel downtown, and we ate the best steak dinner of my life at a place called St. Elmo's. Over dinner, I nearly broached the subject of Jack's attraction to Carol, but chickened out. If there were something to tell, he'd tell me. Right? Right, I told myself and let it pass. It was a beautiful summer night, and after the meal we walked around the one-time rustbelt city which now gleamed in renaissance with a mix of new buildings and old buildings made new. The next morning, we caught a cab to the airport and zipped back to Boston.

* * *

Once home, I found an envelope Nancy had set aside for me. The address was typed on an old Smith Corona (with a flying "d" in Concord). Return address: Arizona. Inside was a check for $60,000 written in my mother's shaky hand. There was a brief note: "Follow your dreams, John. We love you, Mom and Dad."

"What'd your mom send?" Nancy asked.

"A check for $60,000."

Nancy laughed out loud. "Oh, sure."

I thought about leaving it at that but decided to tell her the whole story. "Well, first let me tell you, I have a plan to cover our health insurance and housing."

Nancy's smile vanished.

Then I told her about how Jack and I had planned to start the pumpkin business and how there were still details to work out, but it looked very promising. With more details, I hoped she'd get excited about the idea.

It didn't quite unfold that way.

"You two are idiots," she said. "What do you know about starting a pumpkin business? Either of you? A software company for ministers and churches, maybe. But pumpkins? Come on, Mr. Crackstone. I also think it's a bad idea to take that much money from your parents. Can they afford it?"

I pulled the check out of my pocket and held it out. "After they reviewed the preliminary business plan, they *invested* $60,000. It's an investment. They're not stupid."

"Present evidence is not in their favor," she said and walked out of the room, saying she couldn't talk to me right now.

I looked at the check in my hand. Maybe my father had a change of heart, and I wouldn't lose him after all. Or Jack's business plan had convinced him.

Chapter Twenty-One

Pumpkin Contest

Over the next ten days, Jack and I met with Nancy three times.

"Look," Jack said while we worked on a PowerPoint presentation for her, "we will have to convince a lot of skeptics. Let's start with your wife. After all, Nancy will legally be a partner. If you get divorced, she'll own half your shares. You die, she's my new partner. Besides, I've seen what happens when a partner's spouse is not on board. We need Nancy."

In the first meeting, we walked her through the business plan, showing her the numbers: estimated consumer market size and growth, cost of entry and investment curve, as well as the income projections for the Chief Cheerleader.

She, sitting with arms crossed, was a tough audience. First, she threw shade on our numbers. Then she questioned the costs. Finally, she slashed away at our category competence. "In short," Nancy said, "I love you both, but I don't think you guys know what you're doing."

In the second meeting, Jack showed Nancy his business track record (which I found impressive, Nancy less so) and shared his financial situation, including the tax problems. He also showed how he would personally invest in the company while seeking additional investors along the way to lower his risks and accelerate the company. Nancy asked if he was willing to create a set-aside account to assure this level of funding for the company. Jack tried to negotiate something similar and at a lower amount. Nancy just looked at him in silence, uncomfortable silence. Finally, Jack said okay. Nancy nodded and said she wanted to see the legal agreement as well as monthly account statements. Jack conceded. That helped.

By our third presentation to Nancy, we backed off the grand plans–less "pie-in-the-sky" as Nancy once called it–and went deep on the first year, with a nod to projections in year two and three. She softened, but no embrace yet.

"Okay, Nancy," Jack said. "Here's what I propose." He turned the laptop toward himself to open a new file. Then, before he turned the laptop back toward Nancy, he said, "This is not negotiable." He shared a presentation I hadn't seen. He pledged to pay my salary out of his pocket for the first year of the company no matter what. "And if it all goes to hell," he said, advancing to the next slide, "I'll pay your current, combined income for two more years." He looked at her with a grin like he expected a hug. Nancy looked at him, her expression and body language sphinx-like, her silence lingering. "This assures you and your kids some security."

Nancy let the silence grow uncomfortable.

"Nanc–" I started, but her index finger shot up to cut me off without breaking her fix on Jack's eyes, and she kept her finger up. My fingers went to the beads on my bracelet, turning the Nancy bead over and over.

Jack laughed, and shook his head. "Plus $1,200 per month for health benefits for the family across all three years. Okay?"

"Okay," Nancy said. "Now add it to your slide, and more importantly, add it to the list of legal papers for your lawyer to write up in plain English." Now she lowered her finger.

"Okay," he said and turned the computer and typed in the addition and turned it back to her. She nodded. "But

Nancy, you know, there's risk in any business, especially a startup. You have to be willing to take a risk."

"Jack," she said, and I didn't like her tone, "don't talk to me about risk like I'm an idiot. There's risk all over this deal. I'm taking a lot of risk here. I have a family that includes two young kids. We have to give up the home we've enjoyed for twelve years, which was part of our compensation and was not included in the agreement we just made. Until about sixty seconds ago, we would have lost health care. What happens in year four? Assuming we get to year four. Trust me, there's still plenty of risk left over for some sleepless nights." She took a breath, and her tone softened a little. "As the mother, and co-head of this family, my first responsibility is to mitigate risks to my kids, and if that means seeking assurances from a multi-millionaire partner, I'll reach for it. So, yeah, I recognize the risks."

With that, Nancy was on board.

And I could return my attention to the pumpkins.

* * *

In late summer and early September, the pace of pumpkin growth stunned me. Even though I'd read about it, and anticipated it, the bulking up still amazed me. To measure Schwartz and see his girth expand six inches–each day–up to forty inches a week was exhilarating, intoxicating. The literature said giant pumpkins gained up to thirty pounds daily–over two hundred pounds a week! It took tons of water to fuel that growth, and I kept it flowing.

I rested my hand on Schwartz, almost able to feel the cells dividing and dividing again under my fingers. There had to be a sound, trillions of units of life bringing billions more to life. I put my ear to the cool, moist skin and held my breath.

The thing I heard was this: "Does he have a heartbeat?"

I pulled back. Carol Baker smiled and then laughed. "Caught you," she said. "At least you weren't kissing it."

I chuckled, and did not admit I had kissed Schwartz, the smooth cool skin against my lips. "With him growing so fast," I said, "I thought there had to be some sound."

Carol laughed. Time to change the subject, so I said, "Hey, have you had a chance to think about the job offer to work on the pumpkin business?"

"Not really." Her tone was flat, like a rejection. "That's why I came over. Just wanted you to know I don't have an answer."

"Is there a problem? A problem with Jack? Or with me?" Could it be me? Is she rejecting me? Does she want Jack?

"No, nothing like–well," she said. "No problem with you at all. With Jack, well, I don't know him. I'd want to get to know him before signing up." Then she wagged her finger like a mom to her child. "Besides, you guys still have a lot to figure out before it's real. I'll be patient."

No problem with me. That was good. Wanted to get to know Jack better–that could mean several things.

I patted Schwartz. "Things can change fast, you know."

Carol laughed again. "Well, I've got to get back to my own garden. I'll let you know if my petunias start whispering." And she sashayed away, looking lovely as always.

* * *

In early October, the Wednesday before the Topsfield Fair, I walked home from a meeting of the Women's Auxiliary, finally free of the lingering old ladies (OCMs all) and their rose essence as well as their marathon remembrances of my wonderful father. As I walked up the driveway, I saw Matt Baker standing over Schwartz. I suppressed my instinct to protect Schwartz, to order Matt back, back, back like a yapping poodle or an old woman shooing a goat from the garden.

"You win the pumpkin growing competition, John," Matt announced as I approached. The lawyer fished a hundred-dollar bill out of his tri-fold wallet (Father, Son, and the Holy Ghost), leaving more bills behind (more hundreds?). The last time someone had handed me a hundred-dollar bill was when I graduated from seminary. Dad gave me a crisp one, a reward for going into the family business. The C-note from Matt had been around the block. Not tattered, but certainly passed. It held the two folds from Matt's wallet, but showed a memory for a bi-fold it had known. I thanked him, folded it in half and rammed it into my pocket like a grocery receipt.

"You know," Matt said, "I've been thinking about how to lift these giants into a trailer for the fair."

For weeks I'd worried about moving Schwartz without a Humpty Dumpty scene.

Friday we went to U-Haul and rented an open-air trailer, then drove to the hardware store to buy a pair of heavy-duty tarps for a sling. Matt insisted on paying for it all because I'd provided the seeds. I accepted. On the way back, I recruited some strong young men from church to heft the practice pumpkin. Then came Matt's stroke of genius. Raiding Carol's stocking drawer, we plundered a dozen pairs of pantyhose: sheer, black, navy, red, white, tan. We stretched the legs of the pantyhose around the pumpkin, knotting them at the ankles to extend them and give the pumpkin support, using as many pairs from as many angles as possible. During the process, I imagined Carol's shapely legs filling out these nylons and noted the little cotton crotch.

The plan worked. I took pleasure in the straining necks of the men who lifted Matt's tremendous pumpkin into the trailer. But it was the smallest of the four we planned to take, and everyone agreed we couldn't lift Schwartz ourselves. I'd checked the internet for details on past world champions, and based on dimensions, I grew confident Schwartz might contend for a world record, which weighed 2,145 pounds–nearly as much as a Mini Cooper, and not much smaller. So there was no way our small group could lift him.

I called the Concord City Garage (sometimes it's nice to be a community leader), and in three minutes a city tractor with a front-end loader and four workmen showed up. I'm sure those guys thought I was a nut, the way I hovered around and orchestrated every move, like an old woman overseeing the fire department fetching her cat from a tree. But I have to say, they had fun and were patient, even enthusiastic–if for no other reason than for a story to tell back at the garage of another Concord wacko. Those guys wrapped and lifted my second and third giant for practice before tackling Schwartz. I had waited as long as possible for the final act in the pumpkin patch–I had to cut the vine feeding Schwartz. I knew the growing time was over, still I hesitated with the hand-saw, wondering if one more hour, one more second might be the difference in stretching the world record. The group waited, and I had to cut the cord. I did it fast, leaving a regulation-sized stem of two inches. Every cut of the saw reminded me of cutting the umbilical cord when Gordon and Megan were born. Yes, I cut the cord then (I did not do it for the congregant whose hand I held as she gave birth), and I cut the cord now for mighty Schwartz. I stepped back from the deed half expecting my hands to be covered in blood, but no. The stem was mostly dry.

Then, as if hefting a giant egg, the Concord City workers gently raised my gargantuan gourd, eased across the lawn, and lowered him onto the nest of straw in the trailer. They even stayed to help pack straw around each pumpkin and offered to tag along the next day.

There in the trailer, among Matt's pumpkins, Schwartz ruled.

* * *

Morning brought a fall day from the cover of an L.L. Bean catalog, foliage in screaming colors, a snap to the air but warm sunshine. The air smelled fresh, tinged with the dank scent of fallen leaves. The glory of the morning foreshadowed my crown as the world's greatest pumpkin grower. If I won, it would be a boon to launch the business. ("The world's greatest pumpkin grower brings you the world's greatest pumpkin seeds.") Jack roared up in his vintage Porsche, top down, with two boxes of doughnuts and two boxes of coffee and put them on the hood of Matt's Grand Cherokee. Carol pranced out in a burnt-orange crew-neck sweater and jeans like a college sorority girl on game day with coffee mugs for the gang. Nancy brought out cream and sugar. Matt threw a Nerf football for the kids, the old football player remembering game days like this one.

I paced back and forth from the doughnuts on the hood of the SUV to the trailer where I could admire Schwartz. I ate three doughnuts and pondered a fourth before I knew it. Brushing some dirt off my massive pumpkin, I remembered a ploy I'd considered: taking a large syringe and needle to pump water or gel into Schwartz to add weight. But I didn't for fear of splitting and because I couldn't imagine a pumpkin more colossal—easily five times the size of a bean-bag chair. A grown man could sit inside, a normal-sized man.

I barked at the kids for climbing on the trailer to retrieve the football when it nearly hit Schwartz, and Carol chirped, "Oh, John, they won't hurt your baby."

That shut me up. But it didn't keep me from taking a fourth doughnut—or was it a fifth?—and leaning up against the trailer to stand guard.

* * *

At the Topsfield Fairgrounds, we pulled into the barn where the great pumpkins were weighed. "Let's see what ya got there. Ain't them dandies?" said the scale supervisor. In his newish bib overalls, plaid flannel shirt, and clean baseball cap, the guy had to be an insurance agent or a local bank vice president in costume. "Boy, that one there's a monster. Looks like we got us a contender." Then he clucked for the "fellas" to come over to hoist the pumpkins out of the trailer.

The front-end loader set Schwartz on the scales, and Mr. Bib Overalls slid the weights to 1,500 pounds and the needle didn't budge. Ha.

At 2,000, the needle floated, and my heart dipped. I wanted to thumb the scale, wished I hadn't rubbed off that bit of dirt this morning. My heart thumped in my chest, and I held my breath.

The scale's ten-pound-slide kept going, 2,050, 2,100, 2,150, and it didn't stop until it hovered at 2,317 pounds—a new world record by over 100 pounds!

It made me lightheaded.

Everyone sent up a cheer, and I couldn't help but beam and laugh. Hugs and high-fives all around. Strangers patting me on the back. A tear or two flowed before I could draw down my composure.

I'd done it.

In a single growing season, I, John Crackstone, by the grace of God, gumption, and a whole lot of water, became the greatest pumpkin grower in history.

We stayed to watch other pumpkins weighed, but none were even close. I lingered in the spotlight with Schwartz, people taking pictures with me and Schwartz while I calculated my winnings: $5,000 first prize, plus another $5,000 for the world record, then $10 per pound for each of the 2,317 pounds adding $23,170. It totaled $33,170. Not a bad payday.

"Dude," Jack reached up high to put his arm around my shoulder and pulled me close and whispered, "This is a big PR coup for us. A springboard to launch the company. You've got to think about what to tell the press, about our new company." Once again, he clapped me on the back and extended his arm for a fist bump.

I started to imagine a photo of me on the front page of the *Boston Globe* and the story of our new company.

Then a gleaming red flatbed truck pulled in, and the crowd got noisy. I pushed in, leaning over the shorter men for a look, and my knees went weak at the sight. Nestled in a bed of straw with carbuncle-like warts sat a blotchy, wretched mountain of a gourd that looked like it might bite, Jabba the Hutt in vegetable form. It was gigantic, monstrous.

The idiot in bib overalls did his best Green Acres imitation: "Woo-wee, I do believe that big fella there's gonna break the scale."

With a greater interest than anyone else in the crowd, I watched the men work with the sling to lift the beast. Maybe they'll drop it, I thought, or it will split open under the stress of the sling and be disqualified. Yes, God, please cleave this vile specimen, I prayed. With all the earnestness and urgency of a monk straining to stop an oncoming Visigoth warrior with a heavenly cry, I beseeched the heavens.

But the giant held. The hoist gently lowered it onto the scales.

Slowly the cartoon in bib overalls slid the large counter weights. "Ladies and gentlemen," he crowed, "we reached 2,000 pounds, one ton, and the scale's zero pointer has not budged."

He moved to the hundred pound slide. "Two-thousand, one-hundred–"

The zero pointer refused to float.

"Two-thousand, two-hundred—" He stopped to look at the crowd, and so did I. It had swelled to more than twice the size, maybe four hundred people. "Ladies and gentlemen, that right there would have won last year. But not this year. This year, we have already broken the world record." He pointed at me before he turned back to the scale and slid the hundred pound weight.

"Two-thousand, three-hundred—"

At this weight, the zero pointer had floated with Schwartz. My heart sank, when the pointer failed to budge.

"Two-thousand, four-hundred—" Now he turned to the crowd to say what I already knew. "Ladies and gentlemen, we have a new world record!" The crowd roared. Nancy's arm wrapped around my waist and Jack's hand reached up on my shoulder. "This day marks the first time in history that a new world record was set and then broken in the same day."

He turned back to the scale: "Two-thousand, five-hundred—"

And finally the damn zero pointer floated.

The monster weighed 2,522 pounds—204 pounds more than mighty Schwartz. It was grown by the pumpkin wizard out of southern New Hampshire, a mailman, who'd set a world record six years before.

I fought back disappointment in my chest. Gone in an instant, vanished, that sense of being the greatest in the world at something. Gone was my self-righteousness from an accomplishment to silence any critic (including Nancy) by flipping my absurd, backyard obsession into world-class achievement. And, of course, gone was the satisfaction of a $33,000 payday. The win–win–win was now a loss–loss–loss.

* * *

A new contest followed, one I didn't know about. Students from Montserrat College of Art in Beverly carved the top-ten pumpkins into giant jack-o-lanterns. I started to withdraw Schwartz, but Nancy put her foot down.

"It's part of the event, and you're not going to spoil it," she said.

Feeling defeated, I wanted to leave, but Gordon and Megan wanted to see the giant jack-o-lanterns. So our group milled around the fair. First we went to the livestock barn to visit the pigs the size of hippos, steers big as trucks, sheep you could saddle. Soon I mindlessly followed the pack, imagining some college kid with an eyebrow ring and a pierced tongue taking a chain saw and hatchet to Schwartz. The midway should have been fun, watching the kids on the hokey, rattle-trap rides, but the kids sensed danger. At the carnival games, Matt demonstrated his athletic prowess by shooting a basketball into an impossibly small hoop to win a big pink teddy bear for one daughter and a purple one for the other girl. Eventually we headed back toward the pumpkins and passed through the garden barn: zucchinis as big as your thigh, strawberries the size of tennis balls, cabbages larger than your head. The whole fair I realized—Schwartz included—was a freak show. Not a celebration of nature but a celebration of man's ability to twist nature into something perverse.

* * *

The big, world-record PR balloon had popped. All my dreams and schemes reduced to a silly lark. No one else in our Concord crew carried that weight as they enjoyed the fair. I smiled along as I watched Jack defeat Matt at dart throwing to win a stuffed dog, which he flirtingly gave to Carol and which she accepted with laughter and a one-armed half-hug. There beside them, grinning at the playfulness stood the giant, the giant failure. Yes, of course, I had briefly, very briefly, held a world record, and I had grown the *second-largest* pumpkin in history. But there at the midway of the fair, in that moment next to the dart game, in that window of my life, I stood ridiculous. To grow a pumpkin, I had neglected my duties as a minister, and thus had put my family at risk. What a fool. I'd neglected my duties as a father and husband as well. My crazy dreams of Carol wanting to have an affair with me. What did I know about pulling off a steamy affair? What did I know about business? All the meetings with Jack about what we needed to do, the magnitude of complexity required to form and build a corporation grew daunting, terrifying. I lost sleep over it.

I would be found out for the fraud I was.

How long before the fool was unveiled?

In my defeat and failure, a pumpkin empire sounded not only impossible, it sounded insane.

* * *

The jack–o–lantern contest was set up on a makeshift stage in the Arena Barn, curtain drawn. As we sat and waited, maudlin memories overtook me. The first blossoms. How the base of each flower had swelled, slowly forming infant pumpkins, green ping-pong balls. When I had to cut away the weaker ones. And how they'd grown through the summer under my care (leaving an immense water bill for the deacons to mutter about), getting huge. Becoming Schwartz.

Okay, I didn't win, but I had grown the world's sec-ond–largest pumpkin in history–and I set the world record, if only briefly. Despite the disappointment of not winning first prize, it was a huge accomplishment. I had to give myself that. After only my first try, only one pumpkin in history grew larger than Schwartz, and that from a man who'd been at it for many years. The market for my seeds would bring in some serious money, depending on how many seeds. Some of these giants had very few seeds, some about a thousand.

Finally a professor from the art college, a man dressed in black and too old for his shoulder-length ponytail, came out to emcee the show. He talked about the giant jack-o-lanterns we were about to see. He even blathered to the audience about me having a genetic advantage for growing things oversized.

In the midst of the noise and anticipation, there I sat in a kind of stillness and quiet, waiting for another wave of emotion, of joy or sadness, to overtake me—like another wave curling to crash on the beach.

When the curtain opened, people actually cheered.

Front and center, complete with horns, tremendous nose, ears, and a tuft of crazy hair atop, sat Schwartz with a vile smirk, carved into the devil. "John, it looks like you," Carol shouted, laughing. I heard Jack and Nancy agree.

The resemblance was evident. Then I saw why. Otto, my hair-cutting friend from Concord, little Joanne Nuratto, my supplier of human hair for my magic growing potion, stood on stage with the other artists. She pointed at me when we made eye contact.

I looked at Schwartz. What did it mean, a devil? Or did it mean nothing more than Halloween fun? Sometimes a cigar is just a cigar. There were other demons among ten giant jack-o-lanterns. And a couple of clowns.

Before I could over-think it, I heard cutting through the crowd applause and cheer, a piercing full-bore laugh, an infectious guffaw that registered both familiar and bygone. It was Nancy. How long had it been since I'd heard her really cut loose and belt out her big laugh? At one time, her laugh had liberated me. Back in college, so bottled up was I that this bellow—and the young woman behind it—had uncorked me. I remember after our second date, she coaxed me to break into the bell tower and climb to the top with her where we unabashedly haw-hawed over campus only to find two security guards waiting for us at the bottom. I looked at Devil Schwartz and a smirk bubbled up in me, a chortle, and finally a belly laugh. Nancy gave me a hug.

Then Otto jumped off stage and came over to give me a hug too. Despite her piercings, dark eye makeup and tattoos, she was a cute little chipmunk of a thing, and she pulled me down for a quick congratulatory kiss and ran back to her art-school friends.

"Who was that?" Carol asked.

"That's what I'd like to know," Nancy said, but she laughed about it. She threw her arm around me and uncorked her big laugh again. It petered out with an infectious grin, which called for a kiss, and I bent to her lips.

I wondered what Jack thought of all this. He hadn't said anything since coming in second. Did the day's events leave him thinking the whole enterprise a folly?

Chapter Twenty-Two

Back in Indiana

The morning after failing to win the pumpkin weigh-in, I stood in the kitchen looking out at the pumpkin patch, fingering every bead on my bracelet, and I knew I wasn't cut out to be an entrepreneur. Maybe Nancy was–she was smarter and tougher. I lost sleep worrying about the vast number of decisions I didn't know how to make. Even, making easy decisions paralyzed me now. Selecting socks in the morning stifled me. Did I really want half-and-half in my coffee? And how much? When I pondered the vast details of starting a multi-million dollar business, marching on Moscow in winter sounded easier.

The risks, the liability my ignorance and incompetence posed to Jack as a business partner, I was a lame duck. Worse than a lame duck–I longed to be a lame duck.

Jack came into the kitchen and said, no offense, but he needed a Starbucks fix, but not the one in Concord. So we drove his Porsche west to Acton, opposite the rush hour traffic. I tried to open the subject of my lameness, but Jack held up a hand. "Coffee first. No business before coffee, at least not today." Before Jack ordered his elixir, he requested the best barista in the shop. The young man handed him off to a woman, and he turned to help the lame duck. Jack's order rolled off his tongue like some sort of foreign language and included more ingredients than my secret fertilizer–it also took the enthusiastic barista about as long to make. For me, I studied the big board with all its choices, turning the beads on my bracelet, and defaulted to a drip coffee, but a bold Venezuelan, half–decaf, grande, with room for half–and–half–but just a little.

Finally ready to talk, I confessed to Jack he had a bad business partner.

"Everyone gets that notion from time to time," he said. "That's part of the deal, John. If it wasn't scary and hard, every jerk from here to Cold Point, Idaho would do it. Remember, we're not the first wizards to think of pumpkin seeds as a snack. But we can do it." He paused and looked at me. "Hey, man, I've been to the rodeo a few times, and I still quiver with uncertainty. Some wins, some losses, but you have to do your homework and you have to believe. As Colin Powell said: 'Perpetual optimism is a force multiplier.' That's a good mindset for a startup. That and don't come to bunt."

He assured me we had a good idea. He and his researchers in Texas had done the homework, and he believed in the plan. Even with potential pivots (whatever that meant, and I didn't interrupt to ask), he felt confident. Now, Jack quickly laid out the strategy to start small in a couple of test markets. "Don't expect to be in every Kroger or Walmart anytime soon," he said, "but wins beget wins."

Then he explained his real vision. What Jack had in mind was not to build a business to last a hundred years, but to form a clear exit strategy. To sell the company. Build it, shine it up, sell it. In five, maybe seven years. Cash out and move on to the next thing. We would have to work hard to build it up enough to make the big guys feel a little sting–so they would want to buy and bury the pain or capitalize at scale on the opportunity we'd seized upon. In time, Jack thought, we might sell it for $100 million. "That's the target," he said, "a one, followed by eight fat zeros," ($100,000,000).

It sounded insane to me. But Jack had already talked to people at a few large food companies, not saying much but trying to gauge interest in a new and different snack product. "There's interest," Jack said. "Trust me. It's going to be huge."

In addition, he had pursued my brainstorms about pumpkin health products–using its fiber for a laxative or paper pulp, using its color and oils for makeup and lotions–and initiated discussions with university and independent laboratories to get quotes for research to develop some of these products. "Dude, I'm personally funding the seed round and, if the government will let me, maybe the A–round," he said. "Not to make you happy–I don't give a shit about you!" He laughed hard. "No, seriously, not because you're my friend, but because it's a good business opportunity." He tapped me in the chest with the back of his hand and said: "By the way, you being happy? That's your responsibility."

Again, I told Jack I wasn't sure I was up for building a company. For some reason Carol came to mind. Would she join us? And would she fall for Jack in the glow of his confidence, his competence?

"Hey, Big John," Jack said, "we'll do it together, and we'll get help, a lot of help." He laughed. "You're the dreamer, the cheerleader, remember? Leave the rest to me."

His "Leave the rest to me," made me itchy, despite his experience and past success. Somehow it recalled his CFO and the tax fraud at Mesa Tech. In the teeth of the thrill, I still hesitated. The idea of creating something, of building a company with my friend, of selling it for a hundred million dollars and getting rich. Even selling it for a tenth of that amount meant fully covered college funds for my kids, walking away from things I didn't want to do–like bake sales, decorating committees, and meetings with deacons–to buy a summer place on Cape Cod, overlooking Wellfleet Bay, European vacations, maybe trying out a luxury car (so I could relate to Jack's complaints about our rental buggies).

In the end, Jack sold me his dream as I had once sold it to him. I was in. Back in.

* * *

A week later, Jack coaxed me into a second visit to the Indiana farm–he'd already set up the flyover. Jack and I had called my dad, and Jack convinced him he'd negotiate something with the farmer for two hundred acres, starting in the new year. I was happy to step back from all of that. I think Dad was too. In the end, Jack sublet the land from the farmer for $40,000, due in quarterly payments with an out clause in case of disaster. It sounded like a lot of money to me, especially since it was basically my land, but Jack waved it off. "Don't think about it," he said. "Cost of doing business." After a pause he said, "It's in line with going rates. Actually a little low. Your dad was getting screwed." In appreciation, he sent Mom and Dad a thank you note in the form of a $5,000 check.

* * *

The day after Jack and I talked, I came back from an afternoon meeting to find an envelope at the church. Handwritten address. Return address: Arizona. It was a check for $60,000 from Dad. My father enclosed a short letter in a shaky hand reminding me of his age:

Dear John,

I was impressed by the business plan for your pumpkin venture. Looks like you landed a good business partner. (I checked out Jack Corbett on the internet–his tax problem notwithstanding, he seems very successful.)

I also wanted to say you and I are different people, and I should not stand in the way of you becoming your own man. You've toiled in my shadow long enough. So I decided to loan you the money you asked for. After you make your first million, pay it back–with a little interest. Ha. Ha.

I wish you all the success in the world, Dad

How crazy was that? Mom's check just passed through the bowels of the banking system, and here came Dad's. Clearly they hadn't agreed at first, so Mom took it upon herself. Then Dad did. I wondered how their discussion went.

But the key here was Dad–a man of great judgment–believed in the pumpkin project. It must have been a good business plan. (I still hadn't read it.) Or my mother's argument persuaded him after the fact, and he didn't want her to know she won.

Whichever. I carefully folded the check, put it in my wallet, and walked toward home.

What if I just deposited the check? Maybe my folks kept different checking accounts. I didn't know.

What would I do with the extra money?

Feather the college funds?

Buy that BMW and roll like the executive I hoped to become?

Put it toward building a house on Pretty Prairie Road in Indiana?

* * *

Back again in Indiana just a week after Schwartz set the new world record–and lost it–back with Jack for a second trip to fly over the family farm on Pretty Prairie Road. We rented another car, and to Jack's further disgust, it was a Chrysler. For twenty miles, he moaned about its inadequacies. The car rode fine to me, but who was I to judge? I drove a fourteen-year-old Ford Taurus and dreamed of a used BMW. Anyway, the car got us where we were going. Jack had arranged the flyover from the Lafayette airport, but we were a couple of hours early, and since it was a nice fall day, we drove to the farm.

"Hey, I have a question for you," Jack said. My nerves tingled. "How about offering Nancy a job?"

"No."

"No?"

"No."

"Look," Jack said. "She's smart, and she's good with people. Excellent negotiator."

"Yep," I said. "But no, because we spend too much time together now. If we both worked in the business, it would be way too much. Besides, she wants to go back to classroom teaching."

"Being a good manager is all about teaching."

"And good teachers are good managers," I added.

"Exactly!"

"Jack," I said, "trust me, it would cause problems. She can be an advisor, but not an employee or manager."

We drove on in silence.

"Because she'd be a good manager," Jack said.

"Yes, she would. Now shut up," I said.

We drove on for about two more minutes in silence. I knew his relentless gears churned.

"Just sayin…"

"Jack," I said softly, "don't make me kill you before we even get to the farm."

"Mmmm, that would be bad," he muttered.

* * *

On our way we passed many broad corn and soybean fields, some picked clean, some waiting, some in the process with insect-like combines combing grain from the fields.

About then Jack started singing that old folk song again, a Woody Guthrie song, about a guy escaping the chain gang. "I'm Long John, I'm a long time gone, boy. Like a turkey through the corn boy, with my long clothes on ..."

When we got to the woolly ground near the river, we saw two green and yellow combines picking and shelling corn, the hoppers filling with golden grain. A pair of tractors with two wagons each waited to haul corn to a grain elevator. We watched for a few minutes. It was impressive, agriculture on an industrial scale. Which is what we hoped to bring to the art of pumpkin growing.

* * *

After watching the combines and discussing where to put a pair of football-field-sized irrigation lagoons laying up next to the river, Jack and I headed for the Lafayette Airport, which was also Purdue University Airport.

Jack had hired a plane from a guy named Johnny Walker, and I made sure it wasn't a nickname. Last thing we needed was a drunk flyer. Anyway, we found Johnny, a little elf of a fellow with a giant lumberjack beard, about thirty-five years old. He sized me up and said there might not be room for all three of us in his plane. Turned out Johnny Walker was an associate professor in Purdue's famed aeronautical engineering program. Before our flight, Johnny gave us

a tour of the research hangars packed with weird–looking test aircraft, some covered with an inch of dust from
decades of abandonment, and dozens of gleaming drones
ranging in size from a dinner plate to a jet–driven dart
about the length of a school bus. On the way to his plane,
Johnny talked about how it had once been used in pylon
racing. When we got to it, I saw the little red package ("Yep,
Johnny Walker Red," he said), and I knew I wouldn't fit. The
interior space resembled Jack's vintage Porsche, with two
tight seats up front and something like a footstool behind.
There was no way to fold my frame into the dragonfly. Jack
and Johnny tried to figure out a way, and Johnny offered to
see if he could borrow another plane. In the end, I passed,
offering to take the car and watch them fly over. Jack promised to take videos with his iPhone.

Jack was jazzed to learn about the plane's racing history. When I took the keys and headed for the car, I heard
Jack asking all about top speeds and agility. Before I got to
the car, I heard the small plane with the big engine roar to
a start. I turned to watch it shoot down the runway and
spring into the air.

After two trips out to the farm, I knew the way and
drove fast. But I slowed near Battle Ground because Dr.
Mike had warned us local cops loved to write tickets. By
the time I reached the farm ground, I saw the red plane in
the distance flash among the fall trees, swinging back and
forth, no doubt tracing the winding path of the Wabash
River. I pulled over, two wheels in the grass, and parked
just past the long, one–lane, iron bridge crossing the river. I
walked out on the bridge to watch them coming. The spans
of the bridge met over an island in the river. It was a fine
old bridge. A metal plaque read, "Erected 1912."

I looked for the plane again. I could hear it, but I couldn't
see it. Then suddenly it appeared, rounding a bend, flying
low and fast over the water. It was headed right for me. I

started running to get off the bridge, but before I went far, it zoomed *under* the bridge and soared high over the trees and circled over the bluff, sunlight glinting off the bright red. Johnny Walker was crazier than Jack–I could imagine them egging each other on. The plane circled over me and waved the wings. I waved back, and the plane dove fast and low over the corn field. The farmers stopped to watch the air show. The plane rose over the fencerow trees and dipped again into the next field.

Again, the little red plane soared up and did a barrel roll. Then it banked into a sharp turn and headed back. It dipped and rose over the tall trees lining the river, but not high enough.

It clipped a tree.

It hit a tree.

I thought it would crash, but it didn't. The strike tore off the landing gear and a piece of the tail. With a wobble, it fluttered over the field. It was coming down. You could see Johnny Walker struggling to flatten it out just before it plowed into the field, slashing a path through the standing corn.

I was running across the bridge again, down the embankment and into the field–self-aware of my huge, loping strides. The farmers ran too. I tried to sprint in the field but fell in the corn stubble. Scrambling up–another gaffe by the giraffe–and ran again, stumbling forward, falling a second time, back up and running slower in more control. The plane was down. Jack was down.

The teenage kid got to the plane first. Then me. The old farmer was still crossing the stubble.

"Jack?" I yelled, out of breath. I pulled open the door, he was still belted in. "Jack?"

No answer.

I reached for his neck seeking a pulse. I felt nothing but warm wet. I drew my hand back, covered in blood. I pulled his head back, blood flowed down his face. Again I reached for a pulse. It was there, weak perhaps, but a clear pulse.

The boy was saying to Johnny, "Mister, Mister? You okay? Can you hear me?" I heard a moan from Johnny Walker, awake but stunned. "Mister, where you hurtin?" the boy said.

I kept my attention on Jack, tracing the blood up his face into his hair, fearing a crushed skull, and found a nasty gash bleeding like crazy. I pulled off my jacket and then my sweatshirt and pressed it gently to the cut to slow the bleeding. Jack was out cold.

The boy continued trying to talk to Johnny Walker. The grandfather spoke into his cell phone, "... yes, out by the old iron bridge on 225, Prophetstown Bridge, yeah, Bovine's Bridge. We're here, but they better hurry, it don't look good. Two men, both injured."

No, it didn't look good.

I couldn't tell what was wrong with Jack. Other than the cut on his head. He hadn't come to yet. I pulled back his eyelids. Pupils dilated, tongue lolling in his mouth. I wanted to smack him to bring him around, but knew better in case of a spine or serious brain injury. Gently, I pressed around his ribs, arms too, legs–all intact.

He was breathing. The pulse was still there, a steady pulse, eerily calm and even.

Johnny Walker came around. He said, "Get back from the plane. Now! It could explode."

Sounded like something from TV, but the aeronautical engineering professor clamored out of the plane with the help of the teenager. I reached around Jack and unbuckled his seatbelt. As I did, he slumped forward across my back, which made it easier for me to heft him into a fireman's carry and lift him out of the plane. The corn stubble which tripped me earlier threatened to topple me again and this time with Jack on my back. The strong, hard hands of the old farmer helped stabilize me and kept Jack on my shoulder.

As I carried him away, this whole adventure came to light for the absurdity it was. What were we doing in the middle of an Indiana corn field? Jack badly injured; how did it come to this? I could've been in the plane too, and killed. I could've lost everything–Nancy, Gordon, Megan. For all I knew, Jack might die right there on my back. I began to pray as I stumbled forward in the corn stubble. But a thought kept creeping in–this was all my fault. My stupid, crazy ambitions had caused this surreal disaster.

Then, I heard a hoarse voice: "Put me down, you big goof."

Chapter Twenty-Three

Hospital Visit

As a minister, I've visited a lot of hospital patients, but when I walked in and saw Jack the day after the crash, it shook me. He was asleep but much more bandaged up than I'd expected. Both eyes blackened like a raccoon and swollen. One side of his head was shaved where they'd stitched up a nasty gash, a broken leg with a cast topping his thigh, three ribs broken, and a concussion to top it off. He was a mess, but not as bad as he looked. Other than the concussion, no internal injuries. Doctors assured us all his injuries would heal in eight to ten weeks, a couple of months, a full recovery. Back to Jack.

After a time watching my sleeping friend and turning the beads on my bracelet while in prayer, my thoughts drifted back to the folded check in my wallet from Dad for $60,000.

I knew what I had to do. I found a quiet place to call Mom and tell her about Dad's check.

"I've been waiting for you to call about that," she said.

"So you knew," I said, thanking God I hadn't deposited it, or worse, blew it on a BMW.

"He and I had quite a wrangle about the money, a regular donnybrook. I decided to give it to you without his consent. Then he came around after reading your business plan and announced he'd sent you a check."

In the pause that followed, I could just picture my father strutting into the kitchen waving the business plan in the air before my mother and explaining the news of his well-researched decision to support our business. She had more to say.

"You know, it's pointless to tell your father that I'd defied him and already sent you the money. I figured you'd call me. Just tear up his check—I take care of our checkbook anyway. Just write him a nice thank you letter."

I fished the check out of my wallet, and tore it in half and quarters by the phone speaker. "Step one, done," I said.

* * *

I stayed in Lafayette, Indiana with Jack at a hotel near the hospital. After a week, his headaches and vision problems eased enough for him to move back to Boston, to Concord. Jack couldn't get around, so we converted my first-floor study into a guest room, and he stayed with us. Saint Nancy tolerated Crabby Jack and patiently nursed him. The kids and I helped too, of course. Jack kept a flow of books and magazines piled by his bed (even though he could only read for short periods), sending the kids off to fetch something at the library a few blocks away and paying them five bucks for every errand. For weeks, Jack couldn't drive, and when he could, his vintage Porsche was off-limits because of the clutch. Here came another American-made rental, a little Ford automatic of some sort. Believe it or not, Jack kind of liked the little car.

The doctor's prediction of a full recovery was off a bit.

* * *

I stopped in Jack's room to see him one morning and to grab a folder on my way to the church. He sat in the rented hospital bed turning an empty coffee mug in his lap. His eyes on the window. I excused my intrusion and went to my file cabinet. Faint smell of hospital. I wondered if his headaches were better.

"Hey, John, do you have a minute? To sit down and talk?" he asked.

I sat on the side of the bed. "More coffee?"

He looked at the mug in his hands as if he'd never seen it before. "Huh? No. But thanks." He took a shallow breath and continued to look past me out the side window. I glanced out that way. An overgrown bush blocked most of the view.

"How are the headaches?" I asked.

He met my eyes now.

"A little better each day. I can read for more than a half hour without getting nauseous," he said. "What I wanted to talk about, what I've been thinking about, is our pumpkin business."

A dread flashed in my heart. I hadn't missed planning and scheming. I'd focused on getting through my days as a minister in Concord and on supporting Shelly Andersen, who'd covered for me in my mental and physical absence.

"I can't do it, John. While healing, I got honest with my-self," he said. "I had to admit the truth of what Nancy said before. I don't know food or consumer packaged goods. I'm a software guy. The more research I did, the thinner the ice felt. It's a good business opportunity. For the right person. I'm just not the right person."

Relief overwhelmed me. We both looked at the tangled bush out the window.

Jack filled the silence parked between us. "The other thing is, I could've died in the plane crash, and it woke me up. Woke me up from the pumpkin dream, but also to the reality that life can change in a second, and I need to contribute with my best skills, which means working in tech. Those guys at Blue Ox Drones keep calling, so maybe that's next for me." He paused. "I'm sure you're disappointed," he said. "I'm sorry."

"No—," I said, but before I could finish my thought of *no, it's okay*, Jack pounced.

"I know it was your dream, your way to escape the church," he said. "But I just can't. I wish I could. Maybe I can help you find another partner."

My escape from the church? Was that it? Did escaping the church drive my pumpkin passion?

Jack was still talking. "—and they'll send your father a check for the $60,000. Then I want to pay you something for all your time and effort."

"Wait. No—" I said still trying to collect my thoughts.

"John, I know it's a blow. Sorry I misled you. And I want to make it right. I owe you—"

"Stop!" I said. "Please, just stop talking, Jack. Wait. Wait." I took a long, deep breath and let it out slowly. "Just listen a minute."

I paused to unscramble the mess in my head.

"Look, Jack," I said, my voice hitched, and I sensed my color rising in blotches, "I love you. You're half as big an idiot as I am, and I love you anyway." I had to wipe a tear away. I charged ahead: "Without you, this nutty, fantastic dream, this adventure in what might be, would've made me 'Crackstone, the Crackpot of Concord.' It would've sputtered out in my backyard. Even with your help, I was terrified about creating a business—I was way beyond my depth. But I never felt more alive. I'm going to miss that part. I'm going to miss hanging out with you and learning so much. And you don't owe me anything. There's nothing to make right."

"I was afraid too," Jack said, and he lifted the empty mug to his lips. "I kept trying to hide it. The bigger it got, the more scared I was."

"I'm glad it's over too," I said. "Sad, but glad."

"I want to pay you for all the time you put in. Especially since you didn't win the pumpkin prize money."

"I didn't win first prize, but a guy offered me $40 per seed for all 527 seeds, so I made over $21,000. After all, Schwartz was the second-largest pumpkin ever."

"That's awesome. But I still want to do something for your family."

Finally I told him if he insisted on helping my family, he could contribute to Gordon's and Megan's college funds.

* * *

We discussed something else that morning, Jack and I. Without knowing how to broach the subject, I just stumbled ahead. I figured our vulnerabilities were laid bare already, so I just said: "Hey Jack, I have to ask you something."

He waited.

"It's about Carol Baker," I said.

He waited.

"Do you have feelings for her?"

Jack laughed, "Do I have *'feelings* for her?'" he said and laughed again. "John, you sound like a middle-school counselor."

Now I waited. Although I grinned at my goofy phrasing and accepted his poke.

"In a word, NO. We just flirted around a couple of times, maybe three times. But none of it mattered. It never went farther than me giving her a stuffed animal at the fair. It was just playful flirting, something people do. Maybe you've never done it." He paused.

I waited.

"What I think, John"—and here his voice fell to a whisper—"is that you have a monster crush on Carol, an infatuation. That's what I think. And your jealous mind is making something of nothing. Because–hand–to–God I have no *feelings* for her."

I could see the plain honesty of his words. And I saw the wisdom of his assessment of my infatuation and my jealousy. He knew. I knew.

Jack wasn't finished. "But let me say this, John. I'd like to ask you to step back and look closely at what you have with Nancy. The two of you have been good partners for a long time. Don't discount the value of it. Most of us aren't so lucky to have a great partner."

* * *

As evening approached, I sat at the kitchen table waiting for Nancy to come home from work, out of earshot from the study where Jack read another library book. She came in, dropped a heavy tote bag on the floor, and plopped her over-sized purse on the counter before she turned and saw me.

"Hey there, I thought you were still at the church office." She stepped forward and kissed me on the forehead.

"I came home a little early so we could talk."

She draped her coat over the chair, her brow knitting. I told her about Jack calling off the pumpkin business.

She stepped around the table and hugged me tight before saying, "Oh, Honey, I'm sorry. Are you okay?"

I thought about it for a moment. "Yeah. It's okay. It's good."

But it didn't feel that way. The thing I'd dreamed about had vanished. The thing to make me rich like many of my neighbors, like my deacons. The thing to let me collaborate with Jack as a partner and build something big. Maybe it was crazy, but it was my crazy, my big crazy. And my big crazy just blew up. Now what? Go back to Concord Congregationalist? Really? Something had to give.

"It was a huge dream, John, an exciting one," Nancy said. "Hard to lose a big dream. But part of you must be relieved it's over." She hugged me again, drawing my head to her soft breasts. "With any big loss, there's a sense of relief. The big thing you wanted was going to turn your life upside-down."

She waited, then went on. "It scared me, your pumpkin-business idea. I feared losing you to the business, or to something else. Even last summer, I felt you slipping away, pulling away from me. I knew you needed a change. Part of me wanted the pumpkin business for you, and part of me didn't. I stayed quiet and gave you room, mostly because I wanted to be supportive, but some things just got out of whack. Neither you nor Jack had ever done anything like it."

"That's what Jack said, and he gives you credit for pointing it out. The plane crash woke him up and made him realize he wanted something else."

"You both wanted change, but in the end, not as extreme as becoming full-time pumpkin farmers and food manufacturers," she said and gave me a contorted grin.

I had to laugh at how absurd it sounded. How stupid.

"Nancy, something has to change in my life."

"Okay, let's figure it out. But can we agree it's not centered around pumpkins?"

It struck me to think it was all gone. My passion for pumpkins. "Right, not pumpkins."

And a gray funk descended on me.

* * *

That night I lay in bed. Though laced with sadness of loss, plenty of relief filled the void for dropping dreams of a pumpkin empire. The vast tangle of details, a Gordian knot of complexity to build such an enterprise staggered me and had already robbed me of too much sleep—despite leaning on the business acumen of Jack Corbett. Even a small, farm-to-table consumer-packaged-goods operation spanned dozens of people, from farmers to partner businesses to millions of dollars in facilities and equipment. I'd never done anything more complex than assemble a small conference, manage my calendars, massage the egos of my deacons, and speak to the congregation on Sundays. That feeling of imminent failure–the one sitting on my shoulders at the midway of the Topsfield Fair–had swelled in me. Now Jack's decision let me off the hook.

Yet, in the back of my mind I wondered if I could build a seed business. With just Schwartz, I'd made over $21,000. Not bad for a summer hobby, and the buyer was going to mark the price up for resale. What if I had six or eight giants–could I contract with that buyer to deliver seeds next year? What if I sold directly online myself? I didn't really need Jack's help to sell seeds online. How much business acumen did it require? Maybe it was best as a hobby that yielded side cash. Or maybe like Jack had said, I could build a job for myself. Jack lived the ambition to create jobs for as many people as possible, not me.

The next morning, I came down to leave for the church, and Nancy, while assembling the kids' lunches for school, said: "You know, on my Grandad's farm–" She interrupted herself: "No eye rolling." She wagged an index finger at me. "Grandad said in a storm, the cattle stand together and face the storm. Out front stands the largest among them. Honey, you're the largest. Step to the front."

"Thank you for sharing bovine wisdom." I kissed her. "Moo," I said and walked out the back door.

But I did think about what Nancy said. What did it mean to face the storm, to step to the front? I'd struggled to get out in front of my church for a dozen years. And where had it gotten me? I had expected to be working in sync with Concord's deacons and congregation long before now. Instead, every week brought some sort of skirmish. Some sort of negative judgment befell me.

At age forty–eight, I knew I'd never fit in.

* * *

I sat in the study watching Jack sleep. He looked better. Lousy, but better. How responsible was I for his condition? My pumpkin dream? Our pumpkin dream? Like a dream, it ended when we awoke after the plane crash.

On the nightstand next to Jack were a half dozen get-well cards. I picked them up, one from Nancy. Two hand-made ones from each of my kids. One from Shelly Andersen at the church. Two from friends in Texas. None from Carol. She hadn't visited him either. This was more evidence of my imagination—or of my infatuated imagination—which had spun a romantic web between Carol and Jack that never existed. Spun from my jealousy, spun from a couple of playful, meaningless flirtations.

Over those weeks at our house, Nancy brought Jack breakfast, helped him to the bathroom if I wasn't around. She read to him when his concussion limited his reading. Every few days, she picked up fresh flowers for Jack and kept them on the dresser at the foot of his bed.

One afternoon when Nancy returned from the church to make lunch for Jack and carried a small bunch of flowers, mums cut from the church flowers, I asked why she did so much for Jack. She said, "Because he's family, the brother you never had." She paused, getting things out of the refrigerator, and then continued as she prepared lunch for the three of us. "Better than family in some ways, because you chose him, you kept him."

Brothers-by-choice, I thought.

Nancy went on, "You kept each other as brothers." She was quiet while she built sandwiches. We both were. Then she added: "And, John, if he's your family, your brother, then he's mine too." She cut and stacked the food. "Could you grab three plates, please?" After I handed them to her, she neatly arranged the sandwiches, cut in triangles and opened out with fruit in the open angle, and she continued,

"It's what I'd do for my brother or sister, for Shelly, for Dennis, for you, for the kids. We're family. We take care of each other. Right? That's what love is."

That's what love is.

I stopped her in her work and hugged her very deliberately. She started to pull away, but I pulled her back tight and held on. She understood why. She knew. When I finally let go, I kissed her forehead, and she looked up for a kiss on the lips.

I held her again for a long, lingering hug. Something inside in my brain flowed out to smooth things, as if sanding off rough edges, lifting me. It was so pleasant. Again, I didn't have to explain this long hug, and she didn't have to ask.

When I let go, she patted my back softly. "Now, go check on Jack. You might need to wake him up for lunch. We'll eat together in the study."

I thought yes, she's right, of course, as she was about so many things. Jack was the brother I never had, brothers-by-choice, a pain in the butt, a best friend, someone to challenge me, always there when I needed him, and sometimes when I didn't.

But it was Nancy who had made it clear. I went to wake him up, my heart so full for my brother, Jack—and for my wife.

* * *

In the study, Jack was asleep as Nancy knew. I looked at him, my brother, sleeping. The dramatic plane crash and the many quiet reflections that followed from the hospital to the emerging awareness of the love in Nancy—these awoke me from another dream and re-grounded me. My nutty infatuation for Carol Baker—like the tide ebbing silently from a Cape Cod salt marsh—moved gently away, almost imperceptibly, without drama, but real and undeniable. I became aware of its absence. It was gone. I crossed to the window with the overgrown bush, and looked out at the empty bird feeder. Not much of a view. The lovely Carol floated as out of reach as a movie starlet. I got honest with myself and admitted the thought of us together had never crossed Carol's mind. What she wanted and needed was a friend and confidant—not a lover.

I say this simply here, but that doesn't mean it was easy. It was hard. Because I did love Carol. Inappropriate, unrequited, misdirected, imaginary, foolhardy—whatever. Despite all that, I loved her. The more my early assumptions about her had vaporized, the more I yearned to comfort and be with her, this military kid, this lonely girl from the North Dakota Indian reservation. Now it flitted away like the wishful chickadee bereft of nourishment at my long-empty bird feeder.

I heard Jack make a noise and looked over. Still sleeping. I looked back to the window. It was November. I should buy seed and fill the feeder.

What about the plane crash shattered my infatuation for Carol? It made me pause. My family, my kids, I didn't want to lose them. And I didn't want to lose Nancy either. I recalled how her laugh had pierced the crowd noise at the jack-o-lantern contest, how it connected me back to a time when my love for her shined brilliantly clear and compelling and natural. It wasn't so much Carol was wrong for me, though she was, what brought me back to Nancy was how she possessed what she had always had, a spirit that captured me from the start. The generous and compassionate spirit she had shown for Jack as well as a toughness and intelligence—but more, the essence of love in her which had formed a safe place where I could be me with all my flaws and weaknesses and fear—where I could let my guard down as nowhere else in my life (especially nowhere in Concord) and simply be.

It was Nancy, because she was Nancy.

We could make it work. We could recapture what was lost, or enough of it. Was it too late? Had I already lost her? Increasing remoteness had let us drift apart for years. And what had I done to stop it? I'd adopted a position of indifference. It was on me to fix it.

Everything I touched over the year had turned to crap. Pumpkin plans, Concord Congregational Church, Carol Baker, my relationship with Nancy and my kids, Jack Corbett and pumpkin dreams. What went well? Was I headed for a major Crackstone crackup? I knew enough of depression to see dark clouds mounting. I didn't know how to talk to Nancy about any of this, certainly not about Carol. I didn't know where to turn for guidance. Then I sat quietly, breathing, turning the beads on my bracelet. Yes, I knew where to turn.

I needed to visit Dennis Cliff–my mentor, my touchstone, my friend–for his sage advice. Besides, I hadn't seen him in over a year. We were past due for a beer and a walk. But no cheese Danish.

"Hey big guy," Jack said. "You okay?" He was awake now.

"Just came in to see if you're ready for lunch, but you were asleep."

"Lunch sounds good, brother."

Brother.

When Nancy came back with three plates, Jack was asleep again. "Hey, brother," I whispered hand on his shoulder, "how about some lunch?"

I helped him sit up and brought him the plate Nancy had prepared, and the three of us broke bread together in the study.

When we finished, I took the plates back to the kitchen and called Dennis Cliff.

Chapter Twenty-Four

To See Dennis

On Wednesday morning, as soon as Megan and Gordon left for school, I snatched up my overnight bag, fired up my fourteen-year-old Ford Taurus and took off for Worthington, New Hampshire. It takes two-and-a-half hours, sometimes three, to get there from Concord, and I took my time to enjoy the last vestiges of fall foliage, the vestiges of nature's annual spectacle.

Along the route, I turned off the radio to ride with my thoughts. I had plenty of time to think. I looked forward to seeing Dennis Cliff–my life-guide in so many ways. But why now? Beneath the surface, the visit felt urgent, but why? What did I expect?

I pondered this question as I drove. There was no one in Concord, other than Nancy, who I could talk to about how challenging life had grown in my church. And I could only tell Nancy part of it because I didn't want her to worry about how soul crushing it had become, and she couldn't really do anything to help. So I sought Dennis's council about Concord and how I had struggled for twelve years without ever accomplishing a sense of success, just facing a drought-of-joy and a feeling of futility. Perhaps I wanted Dennis to give me permission to walk away from all I'd been told I must hold onto and must strive to achieve. For me, John Crackstone, the striving was hollow, the prize hollow, the goals hollow. I really had to go. While the pumpkin enterprise fizzled, perhaps I could sell seeds. At least until I figured out something else.

Then there was the need to unburden myself about Carol. I knew the Carol foolishness connected back to my church issues, my hunger for fulfillment. Though my infatuation had faded, I now carried the weight of it, the shame of it.

My recent sadness threatened to return, and I feared it might become a full-blown clinical depression. To talk it out, to own it, was the first step, and the person I thought most able to understand and help was Dennis Cliff.

Further north, I-93 ribboned along the Pemigewasset River valley, crossing and re-crossing the river as it curved around mountains of scrub pine and gray granite–and near Franconia Notch the season passed into winter with the taller mountains snow-peaked.

I arrived in my former hometown in time for lunch. I met Dennis at the church, found him in his office, which he'd occupied for forty years. The pile of papers and books on his desk threatened to avalanche over his laptop in the middle. All of that met expectations. What I didn't expect was how Dennis had aged in the year since I'd seen him. Though twenty years my senior–he was now sixty-eight–I couldn't believe how time had slowed my elfin friend. He rose ponderously from his chair, with a grunt as if his back hurt, to deliver his familiar, though gentler, bear hug. Memories of his heart attack, more than a dozen years ago, rolled in. He'd had a couple of ailments since, and it showed.

"Ready for lunch?" he asked. "Have you tried Siam Delight?"

"Siam Delight?" I said. "No."

"It's Thai and pretty new and very good. Opened in the old Kathy's Kitchen."

"I remember Kathy's Kitchen on the millpond. That was one of our staples."

"Yeah," he said, screwing up his face, "I never liked her, but the food was pretty good."

"—and cheap," we said simultaneously with a laugh.

Turned out the young couple who owned Siam Delight attended Dennis's church, and he introduced me to them. The Saelims, husband Somsak was the chef, and the wife, Anong, ran the operation. I ordered a yellow curry with chicken, and Dennis got a pad Thai with shrimp.

"The food is fantastic," I said, "and not much more expensive than Kathy's Kitchen."

"Yeah, the restaurants in town have gotten a lot more interesting. In addition to this place, we have new Vietnamese, and Mexican places.

During our long lunch, I summarized my adventures over the last eight months. Could it be just eight months? I paused over my Thai lunch to calculate the time from the Easter snow and BHAG failure to early November.

When I told Dennis about the pumpkin growing, including the short-lived world-record and jack-o-lantern contest, it gave him a big laugh.

I also told him:

About the dreams and plans with Jack for the pumpkin enterprise;

About my visit to my parents in Arizona and getting $60,000 out of my mother, then a second $60,000 from my father;

About the trips to Indiana to see Old Isaac's Land Warrant, and the plane crash;

About my sense of loss and relief when the business dreams unraveled.

(But not about Carol and Nancy—not yet.)

After lunch, we strolled the Millpond path to the dam and then along the river. We paused to watch a couple of day hikers climbing on rocks by the water.

"That's quite an eight months, John," Dennis said and nodded to the dam. "Overflowing." We walked on, and he added, "So what do you want to have happen next?"

"I'm not sure," I said. "The pumpkin business with Jack excited me, but it also terrified me. Still, I trusted Jack to lead the business. Then the plane crash put an end to all the dreams. It gave Jack pause to realize he was a software guy. I had the idea of creating a pumpkin seed business by myself–it might work as a money-making hobby, but probably not a job."

"And your church?"

"That's a sore subject. After twelve years, I'm still not comfortable in Concord. Never got comfortable and relaxed as a kid. Never will as an adult." We walked along the trail quietly. I picked up a rock and threw it in the river before going on. "Is it a crisis of faith? I don't think so. But over the last seven or eight months, I didn't think of the Lord much. And when I did, I thought differently."

"What does that mean?" Dennis asked.

"Faith and action were always married up in my head. To live and act on faith. But that created conflict in Concord. My deacons pushed me to accept where the community stood first–embrace the good people of Concord and all they'd done to earn their prosperity–then layer on the message of love and such. Never question the good people of Concord. That was the overriding message. It came from Dad too. I bent to the pressure. I shut off that part of my brain for a long time. But it always nagged, and now it's back. Either you live it or you don't, Dennis."

We walked farther, and I knew he waited for me to finish.

"I know people are at different places in their lives, and I don't want to create a cult-like following. But when the organization deliberately divorces faith and action, I have a problem with that. And I've lived with it too long."

Dennis said, "What about the last eight months?"

"It began on the snowy Easter. Something cracked in Reverend Crackstone. An obsession sparked that day. Two obsessions. That was the night I planted my pumpkin seeds."

"And your second obsession ...?"

"Ah, that," I said reluctant to give voice to it, fearing judgment. Then I plunged in. "Carol Baker, my neighbor, and wife of a deacon." I told him about my attraction to her—my infatuation—how nothing more than a hug ever came of it physically, but how emotionally I got lost. I told him how my infatuation and the pumpkin empire ended with the crash of the plane, and near death of Jack, which woke me up. I told Dennis I felt ashamed for violating the trust Carol put in me as her minister. Along with all of that, I recognized I still loved my wife and wanted to stay with Nancy. And wanted to raise our kids together.

"But, Dennis," I choked on my words, "I may have ruined it with Nancy. Like everything could break apart." I turned each bead on my bracelet. "The pumpkin business, the crazy infatuation for Carol, the asking my parents for money, neglecting my job, neglecting my marriage—all of it. I might have ruined everything."

"Were you happy before?"

"No, but I had something. I guess I still do, but is it all slipping away? It's like I'm tumbling toward a depression or something. The next steps are not clear to me. Dad told me I have a broken moral compass. Maybe he's right."

"Your dad ..." Dennis shook his head. "He cares about you and wants the best for you, but he's not always right. And I'll say right now, he's not right about your moral compass. Let's talk about him later.

"First, John, I want to say I'm not trying to fix any-thing for you, but let me play back what you've told me.

You still have a job leading one of the most prestigious Congregationalist Churches in the country. That's a big deal. Sure there are bumps, but you still have the job. And you have the support of a great associate minister. Next, you have a family. With a wife you still love, and while there are bumps, you want to make your marriage work. And it appears she does too. You have two wonderful, healthy kids you love. And you want to protect the family." He paused. "Man, you have a lot going for you."

Dennis stopped to tie his shoes, clunky-brown Rockports. First one, then the other. I took the moment to ponder Dennis's summary. When he stood up, he said, "Do you see it, John? How blessed your life is?"

"I do. But there are troubles and downsides."

"Reverend Crackstone, there are always troubles and downsides." He slapped me on the back. "So you pursued a lark in pumpkin growing. And you had the guts to start a business. How many startups fail? I'd say you got lucky to fail before you lost a lot of money or quit your day job."

"Right," I said, smiling and shaking my head.

"So what would you say to a member of the congregation in your position? I mean it. Honestly, what would you say?"

"I'd say, 'Give yourself a break. Be gentle with yourself. It took courage to try what you tried, and you never put your family at risk, never put your career at risk.'"

Dennis nodded. "That's good counsel." We walked on a few yards. "Can I say something?"

"Of course."

"Give yourself a break, John. Be gentle with yourself. It took courage to dream big like you did. You never put your family or job at risk." He patted me on the back. "John, can you take your own, sage advice?"

Is it any wonder I loved that guy?

Indeed, I would try to follow the advice.

We walked along quietly, enjoying the river and the mountains. Then Dennis said, "I know you well, John. There's a reason Concord has been hard for you. And it's not because you're wrong or broken in some way. It's not that you have a defective moral compass. You know that."

"Thank you, my friend. And, yes, I know that. But I feel worn down, defeated."

About a mile and a half outside town, the trail rose to the overlook where we often rested on the bench. We sat and enjoyed the view while my fingers turned the beads. The river wrapped around the foot of a small mountain and disappeared into the woods. In the distance, peaks of the White Mountains rose high and gray, the tallest topped with snow. Looking back toward Worthington, the white spires of the Congregationalist and Methodists Churches spiked above the gray trees. I'd been to this spot many times, alone and with Dennis.

"Beautiful here," I said.

"Physically beautiful, yes, but things have changed since you left. I'm sure you've heard about New Hampshire's terrible opioid crisis. Not as bad here as Manchester, but terrible. I did funerals for six overdose victims two years ago, ten last year, twelve so far this year." He shook his head. "Casey Bates, who now runs EMT for the fire department, told me his team deals with an overdose almost every day. Sometimes more than one a day. It's just crazy."

"Any positive developments?" I asked.

"We have a growing immigrant population. Central Americans mostly, but also Southeast Asians, especially Vietnamese. They've been great for the community–they're responsible for the new ethnic restaurants–and most people who resisted them have come around. Worthington lost population for generations, and the immigrants have filled the gap. So that's been really good. Despite the opioid crisis, it's still a good place to live and raise a family."

We enjoyed the view in a comfortable quiet. Then Dennis said, "Any chance I could get you to move back to work with me? I figure I'll work about two or three more years. Retire at seventy, maybe seventy-two. Then it'd be yours."

Whoa. This was a total surprise. It hadn't even occurred to me. I'd thought I'd leave the church altogether. But working alongside Dennis, in a town I knew and loved, which had even added international diversity, it could be great. Being here with Dennis made sense. My heart did a little flip at the idea. What would Nancy think? The kids?

Dennis was talking: "I'd have to take it up with the deacons, but I'm willing to do it. If you're interested. You talk to Nancy, and get back to me."

"I will," I said. "I appreciate the thought, more than you know. I'd love to work with you again."

"I'm pretty sure we can make it happen. But let's not talk about it a lot right now. Sit with it. Talk to Nancy. It would be a big change from Concord and Boston. For you and for your family."

I didn't call Nancy that night, but the more I lay in bed thinking about it, the more I wanted it. Maybe this option had been here all along but I hadn't seen it. It didn't matter. The opportunity was here now. I'd talk to Nancy tomorrow.

* * *

In the morning Dennis's wife, Amy, tapped at my door so kindly, so gently, that it eased me out of sleep the way a mother's kiss on the forehead eases a child awake. "John?" she whispered through the door. I could smell coffee as I came around.

She'd brought me a strong cup of joe in a stout, plain white mug. Dennis had run over to the church to finish a couple of things, so he and I could have breakfast, she said.

I took a quick shower and headed to the church. Though I wanted to stop at the bakery for a couple cheese Danishes for old times' sake, I followed doctor's orders. Tiffany, who worked at the Bluebird Bakery, tapped on the window as I passed and gave an enthusiastic wave. And she wasn't alone, several people in the few blocks to the church called out a hello or a welcome back, recognizing me from my days here. It was like a homecoming. It felt like home.

* * *

I found Dennis at his desk, dressed for a hike, and at his elbow—what else but two cups of coffee and a white bag with two cheese Danishes.

"Dennis, you're not supposed to eat these anymore," I said.

"Special occasions call for special treats, my friend."

I commented on his boots, some seriously broken in Asolos, which showed every step of twenty-plus years on granite and dirt trails.

"I figured we'd climb Mount Worthington if you're up for it," he said. "If you don't mind a slow pace because it has been a few years for me."

"Been a dozen years for me," I said. "But I brought my boots." I hoofed it back to the house for my Merrells. When I drew them out of the trunk of my car, they showed almost as much punishment as Dennis's boots. I slipped in my size-seventeen kickers, and they fit like an old glove, like an old shoe, and I walked back to the church to more high-handed waves from locals who recognized me.

Dennis was stretching leg muscles on the side stairs when I arrived to meet him. "Let's walk to the trailhead to get warmed up," he said, and I took up the day pack. He seemed more energized, more like himself, charged up to hike.

At every block we were stopped by some friend of Dennis's or someone who remembered me, so it took nearly an hour just to walk through town to get to the trailhead. We took the King's Trail, so named because once upon a time, the tall, straight timbers on this slope were marked by King George's men for masts of British ships. Anyway, Dennis and I knew this trail well, but there's always something new to note.

We made our way easily on the old logging road which ended in a single-track trail rising on Mt. Worthington. I let Dennis set the pace. He did well—steady, strong even. Though sunny, a cool November breeze foreshadowed the coming winter. When we paused for water, a chill shook me, but Dennis was sweating. He said he felt fine, but I doubted it. I asked if he wanted to turn back. No way. So I told him I needed to slow down. His look suggested he didn't believe me either. Couple of lousy liars.

In truth, I was out of shape for climbing and neither of us talked much over the huff and puff. We went on up, slower now, climbing the first of a dozen steep boulder climbs. Dennis clearly struggled. It was hard for me too. Really hard.

We stopped at the top of our first boulder climb. To catch our breath, grab a gulp of water and enjoy the narrow view into the valley. "Hey," I said, "maybe our climbing days are behind us."

"Nope," he said and knocked back his water bottle. He wiped his mouth with the back of his hand. "I've been afraid to try it since my heart attack."

Now it was my turn to wait him out. We sat in silence.

"But I'm stronger now, not afraid now," he said, "and I want to see the view from the top one more time. I'm willing to go slow, but I'm not willing to quit."

"Okay. Slow works for me. But so does turning back. No failure in playing it safe. Remember a lot of startups fail." He chuckled at that, and I went on, "We're not kids any more. No need for bravado."

At our next stop, Dennis said, "Last time I climbed this mountain was with you. About fourteen years ago."

"That was my last time too," I said. I knew it was false. I remember a few hikes to the top after our last together. The first came when Dennis was in the hospital, and I went up to ask God why. And to ask for the courage and competence to lead the church in his absence.

The climb was a slow go. Almost like those movies of people climbing Everest. Step, pause. Step, pause. Step, pause. Painfully slow. More than a few young hikers motored past us. In both directions. But we kept at it.

Eventually, we reached the summit. Bald, gray granite, crystals sparkled in the sunshine. It was cold. I'd almost forgotten how beautiful the views were from there. Although Mt. Worthington is not one of the four-thousand-footers, it sits in a broad valley and is completely bald, rewarding the climber with unobstructed views for miles and miles in any direction, east to the snow-covered Presidential Range and west into Vermont.

In fall and winter, downed foliage allows a summit view over the small city of Worthington. Dennis and I stood looking down on the town he'd served for forty years. "The promised land," he said, and I couldn't detect a note of irony.

The bald summit of Mt. Worthington resulted from a lightning-strike fire in the early 1800s. For a hundred years after, a manned fire tower took advantage of the clear views. Now there's just a camera on a tall pole to scan the horizon, and someone far away watches video monitors for smoke.

"I am so happy to be here," Dennis said, "and to be here with you."

We sat in a low spot out of the wind and ate a little food and drank some water. Dennis held up his sandwich and declared, "Best peanut butter and honey sandwich ever."

"Best ever," I said holding mine up to his and tapping whole-wheat as if clinking wine glasses, but in my mind those words stood for best mentor, best mountain, best place, best friend.

We stood on the highest point together and some college-age kids took pictures of us with my phone. Standing side-by-side, more than a foot difference in our height, I was always stunned how this man, a giant to me, could be so much shorter.

We sat quietly on the granite enjoying the view a bit longer before heading down. And then, as we stood up, just then, Dennis stumbled. I thought he'd just lost his balance. But he fell hard on his chest. I grabbed him and rolled him over. He'd hit his head and was bleeding. I rummaged in my daypack for a sweatshirt to hold to his head.

"It's not my head," he whispered. "It's my heart."

"What?" The wind in my ears or an unwillingness to register what I'd heard, I don't know. I could see he struggled to breathe.

"John, it's my heart. My heart."

He's going to be all right, I thought. He had a heart attack before and made it. I pulled out my mobile phone and hit 911. Nothing. No coverage.

"Help." I yelled. "Help! HELP!" But there was no one there. Different people up on the mountain top with us almost continually. But now, no one.

Please, Lord, help this man, I prayed with all I had. *Lord God, few people are so beloved and so giving in your cause. Help Dennis through this. Please.*

I fished Dennis's mobile from his pocket. Weak reception, but something. I called 911 and a woman said she'd dispatch an emergency team from the Worthington Fire Department right now. In the meantime, I should keep Dennis warm and monitor his breathing. I hung up, then wished I'd told her it was Dennis Cliff. But it dawned on me the rescue team was probably led by Casey Bates, and he'd sprint to the aid of his worst enemy. Except he had no enemies.

I took off my coat and wrapped it around Dennis. Breathing shallow but steady. This reminded me of Jack and the plane crash. Jack pulled through. So would Dennis. He had to. His eyes were open, but he didn't seem fully alert, suspended in time. Breathing there? Yes. I held him in my arms to keep him warm. Breathing shallow but steady. I whispered to him. I rocked him gently. I hummed a couple of hymns. I said the Lord's Prayer.

God, I am here, I prayed, *please help Dennis Cliff. I have never wanted anything more, and I have never asked more directly. Lord, save this man.*

Some life flickered into Dennis's eyes, "John?" Then he said: "Why does granite have to be so bloody hard?"

"And cold," I said, and we both smiled. He would be okay, I told myself.

Dennis went on: "You know, it has been a good life." He paused again, I could tell it hurt to breathe and talk. "Tell Amy and the girls I love them. Tell the congregation I love them too."

Part of me wanted to say the movie cliché of "Tell them yourself," but I didn't. I couldn't.

Instead, I simply said, "I will."

I was about to tell him I loved him, but I heard voices. "Hey, are you okay?" The three college kids, the ones who took our pictures, must have heard me yelling and came back up. No doctors among them. One noticed me shivering and gave me a jacket, a fleece, which was absurdly short on me, but it helped. The other two decided to go down the trail to help Casey's team. The other college kid, a young woman, stood a few feet away, wanting to help but not knowing how. I didn't know how either.

I held Dennis and waited quietly. He rubbed his boots together, the way a baby rubs his feet together as he's falling asleep. One of his boots came untied. His breathing was rough, faint, struggling. We'd both been in this situation before, with someone dying, but I'd never been there with someone so close to me. My fingers turned the beads. Another silent call to the heavens: *Do you hear me Lord? Save this man, the best man I've ever met. The world needs him.*

All I knew to do was to be quiet and peaceful. Then came the final exhale, the death rattle as they call it. And I knew he was gone. I wasn't going to give him mouth-to-mouth resuscitation or CPR, it was time to let go. We both knew it.

We sat there quietly, me holding him. Feeling the hard, cold granite on my butt. I cried a little. My dearest, truest, deepest friend was gone. Quietly, peacefully gone.

How could you? I silently scolded God above. *Of all people, how could you take Dennis? How could you take this man now? Here and now in this beautiful place? Are you there? Can you hear me? Do you care? Do you exist?*

Soon, I heard Casey and his team making their way up the mountain. I wanted to call out or tell the girl to inform them to take their time. No rush now. No rush.

* * *

When I told Amy Cliff that Dennis had died on the mountaintop, she just sat down. Right on the slate floor of the entry. Not a collapse, but a sit. I helped her to her feet and guided her to a chair.

"I knew this was coming," she said. "We both did. The doctors said he needed to be careful, lose weight, easy exercise." She stood and looked out the window. "What was he thinking? Did he have to climb the mountain? You know what he told me? He told me you two were walking the River Trail, an easy walk on the River Trail." She paused. I said nothing. She went on: "It was a lovely day for the River Trail."

"He wanted to climb Mt. Worthington one last time," I said.

"Well, he got his wish, didn't he?" she snapped.

"The last thing he said was to tell you he loved you and the girls, and he loved the congregation."

"Yes," she said and sat down again. She curled her hand into a fist and lightly pounded the arm of the chair.

"I'm so sorry," I said.

Though those meager words are never enough, in difficult times, there's nothing else to say.

We sat. Nothing left to say.

I wanted to offer her a prayer, to pray with her, but right then, I didn't believe God was listening. He was of no comfort to us, to me.

For a long time we sat.

Finally she said, "Perhaps you should go now, John. We can talk tomorrow."

This was a little awkward since I'd spent the night there, so I went upstairs and gathered up my bags. I considered trying to drive home but reconsidered and drove to the other end of town and took a room at The Long View Inn.

Chapter Twenty-Five

A Second Coming?

The next morning, Amy called and asked me to conduct Dennis's funeral. I had expected this and called Nancy to ask her to bring me clothes and take the kids out of school. Then I phoned the church and told Shelly Andersen what happened and asked her to cover my schedule for the rest of the week.

The first thing was to meet with people who knew Dennis, to get their stories and experiences. Usually I held two meetings with three to five people. But with Dennis, it was another matter. I set two meetings of eight people, and they both ran three hours. Then more people heard and tracked me down at The Long View Inn, including immigrants from Latin America and Vietnam. This led to a series of impromptu interviews, and two more group meetings, stretching into the night. Not only did people want to share their experiences and appreciation, they asked if they could speak to the congregation. Several were townspeople unaffiliated with the church. I knew Dennis was beloved far and wide, but this outpouring threatened to spin out of control.

* * *

On the topic of out of control, during the endless interviews, I told folks I needed a fifteen-minute break to stretch, get coffee, and prep for more talk. I went upstairs where Nancy and the kids were in the nice suite the church had provided. When I walked in, Nancy pulled me into our bedroom to talk.

"You didn't make a contribution to the kids' college funds yesterday, did you? Or your folks? I just got an email about one."

"No. But Jack wanted to do something for the family to assuage his guilt about the end of the pumpkin business and you taking such good care of him."

"Well, that explains it," she said.

I thought he might be generous enough to put in $500 for each of them.

"Jack put in $50,000 for Gordon and $50,000 for Megan."

Crazy generous. Yeah, he could afford it, but it was very generous. I shook my head and smiled. "That's him," I said, "No-holding-back Jack like we called him in seminary. He doesn't like to bunt. Quintessential Corbett."

"John, this is too much. How do we thank him?"

"Honey, it's Jack," I said. "We just thank him. He didn't have to do it, but he wanted to. He can, and he did. If there are any strings attached, it would be that he expects us to raise our kids well enough to take advantage of the gift and make the world a better place."

"So generous," she said.

"He's a great friend. A great man."

Then I gave her a quick kiss and said I had to get back to my intake process for the funeral.

* * *

After three non-stop days of intake, I had to shut it down, so I could think.

Normally the process, the mechanics, of a funeral chug along, and I can plod through it, checking the boxes, laying the bricks. But this was Dennis Cliff. Not normal for me. Or for the town. I had to hold their pain as well as Amy's, their daughters', and my own. Then function.

The Long View Inn kept a steady fire going in the living room, and I kept a steady flow of thinking, writing, note-taking, and pondering. But people kept stopping in to tell me what a wonderful man Dennis was.

While uplifting and inspiring to hear the regard for my mentor and friend, I tried not to dwell on his death and my own loss as I consoled others, nor on my guess that Amy blamed me, and that I blamed God. How could his death be better for the world, for this community, for me (me, the petty, little giant)? When I asked these questions of the heavens, my queries vanished into the void. No return.

The flicker of hope to stand with my friend and work alongside him for the next two or four years–to learn from him and reintegrate with this community, and to serve God together again as we did during the most spiritually fulfilling time of my life–all of that died with Dennis too. It left me to go back to my spiritual desert of Concord, Massachusetts.

But I couldn't. There was no way I could return to the pulpit in Concord. My opportunity here in Worthington had perished on a mountaintop, and my pumpkin pipe dream crashed in an Indiana cornfield. What next?

* * *

Finally, we were ready to begin the funeral. There'd been a delay because Casey, head of Worthington's EMT and volunteer technical director for the church, had to set up speakers outside for hundreds of people who couldn't get into the sanctuary. The music director continued a flow of appropriate music and singing from the choir. I had waited in the back, reviewing my notes and preparing. Trying to keep from having it out with God.

When Casey gave me the thumbs-up, I moved from the wings toward the pulpit, looking down and reviewing my notes once more.

Then I looked up. And without thinking, I stepped back.

A wall pressed against me, a wall of pain, of emotion. I'd never felt anything like it or seen anything like what I saw. The sanctuary had a capacity of four hundred, but on that day every space, save the center aisle, was packed. People stood shoulder-to-shoulder in a silent reverence around the pews. There had to be a thousand people inside. My eyes went to the windows, and there stood a crowd of hundreds and hundreds of people gathered all the way around the front and sides of the old church, spilling into the streets, at least another thousand outdoors. This church, perhaps no church in the region, had ever seen such a gathering. Two things came to mind: first was why didn't this many people show up for church; second was how the crowd demonstrated Dennis's reach and greatness, extending far beyond his congregation.

Everyone inside had seen me step back. I paused for a deep breath and stepped back up.

I decided right then that all the time I'd spent preparing would carry me forward. This was no time for a script.

I took another deep breath and spoke: "I expected to face a crowd and to face my own emotions but not such a large crowd. And not such deep emotion. We reverends are trained to lean on process, tradition, and mechanics to get through hard funerals, and I've done some hard ones. But none harder or more personal than this one."

I looked down at the casket, a simple but beautiful form in black walnut, handmade by a local craftsman and void of any frills, so perfect for my friend. I looked back up to those gathered and said, "Dennis Cliff was my mentor and dear friend. Obviously, he was a friend to many of us here, and I'm sure to many more who couldn't join us here today. Welcome to you all as we come together to remember and celebrate this great man."

With that I offered a brief prayer, and then I signaled the organist who played "What a Friend We Have in Jesus" with a soloist from the choir.

I came forward again, pausing as the last chord evanesced into the air of the old chapel.

"During the week, I spoke to more than two dozen people in town about Reverend Dennis Cliff, and even though I knew he was among the most beloved people in Worthington, the breadth and depth of admiration for him surprised me."

This was true. During interviews, you expect some old cross to surface, someone angry, someone with an ax to grind, someone slighted. But not with Dennis. Not from his wife or daughters. Not from his friends or staff. Not from a single townsperson. Remarkable. "Another thing was how many people asked to speak on his behalf." Amy and their daughters preferred not to speak. They just couldn't do it. "I wish we could hear from everyone, but here are a few of the many volunteers."

* * *

Jenny McGrath started. She told what happened after her husband died from an overdose of pain medication, following a sawmill injury. Jenny worked at Walmart but couldn't get enough hours to join the health plan—or to make ends meet for her and their two sons. Dennis offered food and clothing, but she wouldn't take it. Then, about a week later, Dennis announced the church was opening a free breakfast program and asked Jenny to volunteer five mornings a week before school with her sons to help run it.

"You know how Dennis was." She laughed and lifted a tear. "He asked in his way that left zero wiggle room to say no." People chuckled because they knew. "We needed the help and wouldn't take it. So he created a situation where he needed my help and wouldn't take no for an answer–classic Reverend Cliff. It meant me and my boys got a big, hearty breakfast every morning." She wiped her eyes and nose. "That's the kind of person Dennis Cliff was."

Next up was Ethan Campbell. For generations his family managed to eke out a living farming the harsh New Hampshire land while others moved to the prairie states. The Campbells had given up crops and scratched out a living on dairy production, sheep, and a mid-sized apple orchard. Ethan wore khaki pants and a worn navy-blue sport coat, and his work shoes with mud on the heels. He told how a couple of years ago the federal government cracked down on undocumented migrant workers and there was no one to help bring in apples.

"Next thing I knew, Dennis had stitched together an army of volunteers, including half the high school and many of the folks in this room. Well, I gotta say, you were a rag-tag group." People laughed. "Not nearly as good as them hard-working Mexicans. But without Dennis's help, and yours, we might've lost the farm."

Finally, Mayor Fredericks came up and spoke. A native of New York City, he had long ago become a part of Worthington, raising four kids in the public schools while running a local insurance agency before running for mayor. He and Dennis were old friends–most of the time, he said.

"I remember after I lost the election for a second term, Dennis told me to listen." Fredericks paused. "We were walking the River Trail at the time, and I thought he wanted me to hear some bird or something, so I stopped to listen. Dennis laughed at me and said, 'Not now, Stupid.'" People laughed and nodded. "Dennis went on, 'Well, yes now. And always.' Dennis explained to me: 'Freddy, you lost the election because you didn't listen to people. Listening is the key in life, especially in a life of service. If you really listen, the answers are much easier.'"

The mayor paused again, as if he were hearing the advice again, as if he were listening to Dennis. "What I learned from a master was the value of listening—to nature, to people, and to the whisper of God. That's why I've won reelection six times since my early failure. I learned from my great friend, the great listener, Reverend Dennis Cliff."

At that point, I signaled two local musician friends of Dennis's who came up with guitars and played a solid imitation of Van Morrison's bluesy version of "Just a Closer Walk with Thee, Part II." It was a nice contrast to the choir and the organ, and it was a fitting example of how varied Dennis was.

When they finished, I reached down inside the pulpit and pulled out Dennis's battered hiking boots and put them up on the pulpit. There were a couple of chuckles. "Many of you will recognize these beat up old boots. Lot of miles on these boots. Our friend and leader walked among us, crossing every walk of life, listening to everyone as the mayor said. As a man who wears oversized shoes, I look at these size-9 boots and think: 'These were the shoes of a giant.' Dennis Cliff was a giant to us, certainly to me. He mattered to so many of us. But more importantly, we mattered to him. He had a huge capacity for love.

"Though we have lost him and his beacon of light, we can all learn from him. He set forth a brilliant, lasting example of the power of love."

As people filed out, the local Van Morrison cover band followed up with his "Have I Told You Lately That I Love You?"

* * *

After the funeral, riding to the cemetery, I thought again about how crazy life had been over the previous summer with my pumpkin dreams and infatuation with Carol Baker. It seemed so long ago. The death of Dennis brought me back to reality, back down to reality.

We pulled up, followed by a line of cars–dozens and dozens of cars, from junkers to Jaguars. The graveside service floated past in an emotional fog for me. An oversized crowd huddled against the cold. What I remember most was watching his beautifully simple walnut casket lowered into the hole. I said goodbye to many people and thanked them for coming. I told them it meant a lot to the family and Dennis would've appreciated it. When finally the crowd was gone, I looked back, and the cemetery staff arrived to finish the work. I walked to the graveside and held out a hand. One of the men surrendered his shovel, and with the sound of cold steel on soil, I heaped the first few loads of dirt into the hole and handed back the tool.

As I walked away, I heard the sound of soil on cold steel again and again, now moving at the pace of two professionals with a job to do.

* * *

After the graveside services, we headed to the church for a memorial reception. Nancy stayed briefly before taking our kids back to The Long View Inn. One of Amy's friends walked her home. I lingered until most everyone was gone and helped with the cleanup until Carl Neeman and Mike Smithson, two of the senior deacons I knew from my days as Associate Minister, asked if they could talk with me.

We went upstairs, me following on the worn, red carpeted stairs, into the conference room where the other deacons sat waiting. They all stood when I entered.

"Reverend Crackstone, please take the seat here at the head of the table."

It had always been Dennis's seat.

"Thank you," I said and sat.

Everyone sat. All twelve deacons were there, and I scanned the faces, seven men, five women–including Anong Saelim the woman owner of Siam Delight–two Latin Americans, one Asian, ages ranging from twenty–eight to eighty-two. I knew most of them, and had met the others over the last few days as I prepared for the funeral.

Carl Neeman broke the quiet: "Reverend, we want to thank you for spending the last several days with us and with the community here. Your excellent work captured the spirit of our dear friend Reverend Cliff beautifully and has already helped the healing process."

Several of the deacons chimed their agreement and gratitude.

"Reverend, there's something else," Sandra Norse said. "We would like to offer you the job of Senior Minister, re-placing Dennis Cliff." This surprised me. It was so sudden. My left hand went to the bracelet on my right wrist. Sandra was still talking, "We know Dennis would want this. He spoke to some of us the evening before your hike, seeking permission to offer you the role of co-Senior Minister." She paused to glance around the table. "For those who don't know you well, Dennis's endorsement is enough."

One of the other deacons, Rachel Lancing, the youngest among them, said, "Reverend Cliff also told us he men-tioned this possibility to you, so we assume you've begun to consider it."

"And we all support this offer," Bihn Dao, the Vietnamese man, said.

Holding her hand forward, Ana Maria Lopez added, "We want you here."

"Unanimously," Mike Smithson said with a nod.

All heads around the table were nodding.

These people wanted me.

And I wanted them.

I noted the contrast to the twelve, wealthy, older, white, male faces around the polished conference table in Concord–those who had made my life difficult from the start–who'd never expressed a desire to have me there, who had regularly held out my father as a role model for success.

It was clear the Worthington deacons were waiting for a response.

"First, let me say I greatly appreciate your offer." I took a deep breath. "Before I can respond, I need to discuss it with my wife." I had not told Nancy about Dennis's idea of me returning as co–Senior. "And, of course, it would help to know details of the offer."

"As chair of the Finance Committee, let me speak to that," Mike said. "We have prepared an offer. Without the salary amount."

He paused, eyes scanning those at the table, visibly uncomfortable. One thing I'd learned from my businessmen deacons in Concord, and from observing Nancy's negotiation with Jack, was that in financial negotiations, the one who spoke first usually lost. So I remained quiet and waited.

Mike said: "Would you mind disclosing, in confidence, of course, what your current salary is?"

I told them.

Eyebrows went up around the room.

Mike Smithson, silently looked from face to face of each deacon. Each nodded, a few with an angled nod. Then he turned back to me. "We'll match it."

This stunned me. I wondered if it was wise of them to offer me this amount but said nothing. The salary went a lot farther in Worthington, New Hampshire than in Concord, Massachusetts. I took a deep breath and looked around the room, a somewhat shabby room. Cheap paneling, worn red carpet, battered chairs around the original table, which had a patina that spoke of many meetings since 1813. It was a far cry from the polish and posh of Concord Congregational.

I asked about the financial strength and the congregation size and makeup. They were prepared for these questions, and shared the numbers. The financial strength impressed me, as did the budgets for community outreach programs. The congregation size had grown over the last decade with the diversity of the congregation mirroring the one around the table. Dennis and this team had done a great job.

Mike Smithson returned us to the offer. "The benefit package is pretty standard," he said, "and I'd like to agree to the salary for a five-year period. As you might guess, it's higher than we've seen before."

I held my tongue. Though I found this acceptable.

Mike went on to explain how they'd take care of moving Amy Cliff out of the parsonage in the next sixty days, and then they'd work with us and a designer to renovate and update the house to suit our family. They would set us up in an apartment in town until the house was ready.

Then Mike wrote the salary amount on the papers before him, signed the bottom line of both copies, and handed them to the Chairman, Carl Neeman. Carl also signed and then handed the copies to me.

"Do you have any more questions, Reverend Crackstone?" Carl asked.

"No," I said, "I think it's pretty clear, and you've been very forthcoming. I'm grateful for the offer and the opportunity. I'm excited about sharing it with Nancy tonight."

"Speaking of Nancy," Sandra Norse said, "there will be a full-time teaching position for her if she wants to come back in the fall. Or she can work part-time teaching English as a second language, starting this winter."

"Oh, that's great," I said. "May I have a couple of days to get back to you with a decision?"

"Two days would be ideal," Carl said, "and feel free to call me or Sandra if you or Nancy have any questions. I put my cell phone number below my signature." He placed both hands flat on the beautiful, old table. "If there's nothing else ..." Carl checked with everyone at the table. "Then we look forward to hearing from you in the next couple of days." And he reached out to shake my hand as we both stood.

"Thank you, Carl," I said, then to the table, "Thank you all."

Each deacon came forward to shake my hand and say how pleased they were to offer me the position.

* * *

I knew what I wanted before Nancy and I sat down to talk. She listened carefully looking in my eyes as if watching for some kind of doubt from me. I felt truly seen. She asked if I had reservations, and when I said no, she had her answer ready.

"It's terribly sad to lose Dennis," she said, "but somehow this all feels like it's meant to be, John. Like you're honoring him and his memory."

We were moving back to Worthington.

Now I had to say goodbye to Concord.

Chapter Twenty-Six

Worthington Homecoming

A rollick in the mud might describe how Concord received the message of my departure. No one believed I chose "Cow Hampshire" on purpose. One deacon said: "Over Concord? Why would anyone in his right mind make that choice?" A neighbor said when Nancy assured her it was our choice: "But what about your children?" As if we planned to live among a band of headhunters–and I don't mean the type who live in Lexington and recruit for Fidelity Investments.

In truth, I did worry about my kids. Not about the quality of their education but about their ability to adapt to the White Mountains, far from a major city, and removed from a level of sophistication. Concord was the only home they'd known, our parsonage the only house they'd lived in, the schools, the friends, the neighbors ... It would be hard. It would test their resilience.

Around me, the Concord rumor mill churned out a narrative saying the board had squeezed me out–Reverend John Crackstone, booted over some misconduct or short-coming. I didn't care.

Sitting with Jack Corbett at a table under the Wayward Tavern's ancient and low–slung beams–beams upon which I'd bumped my head, or at least my hair, many a time–with a cooling bowl of beef stew, I mustered the courage to break the news to him. Instantly, Jack's first question hit me, "Did the godless bastards of Concord Congregational throw you out?"

Why did people assume I got sacked? Once I explained how it came about, he wondered out loud if this move flipped me from one mistake to another by not leaving the church: "Out of the frying pan, into the fire," he said. It pissed me off, but I let it go as a kind of idiotic stream of consciousness from a guy recovering from a head injury. As we talked, I relayed how Worthington had always been home to me, and how my crisis of conscience, of Christian faith, lay more in my inability to reconcile the lives of my wealthy Concord deacons, neighbors, and congregants than in my core belief. But Jack had to badminton this back at me: "Just be careful, Big John. You know how it is, when one thing doesn't work out we can convince ourselves another thing is perfect. Just sayin'."

Just sayin', my keister.

I explained the ministry was still my life's work. But where one worked mattered too, as did the boss (the deacons in this case), the culture fit mattered, and for me, for us, the culture fit in the White Mountains was better. For me it was better.

"And the weather sucks," Jack said. "First snow comes, what, late October?"

"Usually."

"November, December, January." He was counting on his fingers. "February, March, and a little in April?"

"A little in April."

"Dude," Jack said, "you're looking at five months of winter. Maybe six. Followed by Mud Season." He shook his head. "So you got half a year at best of good weather."

"Winter is not bad weather. Cold and snow is not bad," I said. "I grant you mud season sucks."

Jack nodded. He didn't say much, but his eye spoke of doubt. Then he changed the subject and said he was heading back to Texas, to help launch the drone business for agriculture–as a partner and Chief Operating Officer. "Blue Ox Drones, Johnny, it's gonna be HUGE," Jack said, arms wide and grinning.

He shipped his vintage Porsche a few days later and flew back to Austin to take the reins of Blue Ox Drones, Inc. I don't know if the world is ready for it, but Jack Corbett never shied from a challenge, and I wouldn't bet against him.

* * *

To tell Carol Baker about our pending move, I asked her to go with me to get coffee at Java Jazz. When I picked her up, she wore an oversized sweatshirt hanging down over her butt and jeans–baggy jeans. If she wore any makeup, it was minimal, and her hair hung in a low pony hugging her neck. This was probably her the most casual since finals week at North Dakota State.

Yet she looked beautiful.

We skirted the couch–of–no–return, and took a table by the windows and watched a light November rain roll in. She had a latte, me hefting an extra–tall. When I told her about the move, I imagined she might cry at the end of our "emotional affair," but instead she said, "I'm happy for you, John. Happy for your family." She swept a loose strand of blonde hair behind her ear. "Concord weighed on you. I'm sure it's hard to leave, but whenever you talked about your years in Worthington, you lit up, and had this easy smile, you were lighter. It sounded like home."

Home. Yes, it was home, the often–troubled, quirky town in the mountains.

"I'm going to miss our talks," she said. "It has been fun to have a friend."

"For me too. And you'll find another friend." Though I wondered if she would. Then it occurred to me: "You should talk to Shelly Andersen. She's a great listener, smart, and caring."

Other than Jack and Carol, I found myself just doing a dump-and-run announcement about our leaving. I slowed down enough to properly thank the deacons and the con-gregation for their years of support—blah, blah, blah. And held my tongue on the torment I'd experienced and how freeing it felt to leave, but I didn't care much about what the people of Concord thought. I just wanted to move on. As I crossed the chapel one last time heading for the side door, I heard a voice. It was old Joe, the volunteer who was always there when you needed him. It was years before I found out he lived in a studio apartment on the edge of West Concord. His clothes were worn and a bit tattered.

"Reverend, I hoped I'd catch you. I just wanted to thank you for letting me be of service in your church. I'll help Reverend Andersen, but I'm sorry to see you leave. I'm gonna miss you."

"Thanks, Joe. I appreciate how you're always here to help and take on the worst jobs with a smile. Thank you for your years of service helping me and helping others."

Joe smiled as he often did. Then he softly added: "Anyone can share themselves to help others. It doesn't take money to help others … we are all poor."

Yes, in the end, we're all poor. "Those are some of the wisest, most Christian words I've heard here in Concord," I said. "I'm going to miss you too, Joe."

With that, I slipped out the side door, reflecting on Joe's words of wisdom.

One of the good things about living in a parsonage is how you can move as fast as you can pack your bags. But first I had to find my replacement, an interim Senior Minister. Obviously, Shelly Andersen was the answer. She'd proven herself beyond doubt after nearly ten years as an Associate Minister. She had Concord-worthy credentials and intelligence. Some of the deacons would want to bring in a big gun from a big church. Some might resist a woman as Senior Minister. But Shelly Andersen was ready to take over permanently.

First, I went to Shelly and asked her if she wanted the role.

"I want the job," she said, "but I don't want the house."

Before I could ask why, she went on, "Your parsonage is too big for one person. What would I do with a four-bedroom house, John? And even if it weren't too big, the trend is to provide a housing stipend, so ministers can live where and how they want. My condo in Arlington is perfect for me. Just a few minutes outside Concord, beyond the watchful eye of nosey congregants, and closer to friends in Boston and Cambridge."

As usual, Shelly had thought it through.

"Besides," she said, "your house is worth over a million, even with the upgrades it needs. The money could be put to good use for the Church. Part of it should be set aside and invested to provide a housing allowance for the Senior Minister."

I went to Matt Baker and asked him to support Shelly and her housing plan. He agreed. Together, Matt and I went to Caleb Bradstreet and a few of the other old guard. One by one, we leveled support for Shelly, enough to assure a winning vote. It marked the first time Matt and I collaborated like allies on an important issue.

By unanimous vote in special session, Shelly Andersen became the first female Senior Minister of Concord Congregationalist Church in its two hundred years, with roots going back to the 1630s. I took pride in my role of writing that bit of history. There was no on-boarding required since Shelly knew all the players and had helped build the organization.

Afterward, Shelly took me to the Wayward Tavern for a glass of wine to celebrate. She ordered a fine bottle of cabernet. Over wine, Shelly articulated her appreciation of me and what I'd done for her. When she finished, I returned the favor, and I finished with the truth: Shelly Andersen had surpassed me, certainly for a place like Concord. She had the intellect, the wisdom, and the street smarts to survive and thrive there.

That hour with Shelly was my only long goodbye to anyone in Concord.

Within a month, by mid–December, we had moved to Worthington.

* * *

Nancy relished working with a designer to plan the new kitchen and bathrooms, picking colors and preparing our new home as well as preparing to teach ESL. The kids learned to ski. Gordon loved exploring the woods with a couple of neighbor kids–and wanted to join Boy Scouts after being invited to make a winter climb of Mount Worthington with the Scout troop. Megan explored the woods with a couple of girlfriends too and was learning to ski race with a new friend from school. Both of them flourished from the start. Meanwhile, I met with just about everyone in town, everyone associated with the church, the city, and the local paper, all the while planning my first sermon.

My return to the Worthington pulpit would be Christmas Eve. The evening service always shined a light on the joy of the season, short and to the point, a lighthearted one–including a traditional children's Christmas pageant–all to reground people in the meaning of Christmas before ripping into ribbons and wrapping paper. While poring over the meaning of Christmas, I eventually hit on how to end the sermon–something I would never try in Concord.

When Christmas Eve came, I was leaving early to check on everything and to go over my sermon. Nancy and the kids were getting ready. I buttoned my black overcoat and pulled my red scarf around my neck. I turned to say good-bye, and there stood Nancy next to the Christmas tree, waiting for me. Oh my, she wore an emerald–green wool dress with a cream yoke across the shoulders which came together in a V-neck and formed a tapering panel down the front where it parted again to encircle a high–low hem. (She had to tell me it was called a high–low hem.) Nancy also wore pearl earrings and a pearl necklace, and her blonde hair had grown out to shoulder length. I'd never seen her look more beautiful. I went to her and said, "You look gorgeous."

She smiled and did a turn to show off the full skirt of the dress. "You don't look so bad yourself, big boy."

I laughed and shook my head. "You are a wonder. Thank you for standing by me."

"We stood by each other," she said. "Took care of each other. That's what love is."

I gave her a quick kiss and started for another, but she stopped me with a thumb to my mouth. "You've got lipstick on you." She chuckled. "Now go on, we'll see you at the church."

I walked from our temporary digs in an apartment above the Bluebird Bakery. A light snow fell through the streetlights, forming a quiet, classic New England Christmas Eve. When I rounded the corner, there was Casey Bates from the Worthington Emergency Team putting salt and sand on the steps and sidewalks for us. I thanked him, wished him a Merry Christmas, and entered the church. I'd expected quiet to gather my final thoughts, but the chapel buzzed with giggling kids and the director and parents of the children's pageant, making sure every costume and prop found its place and preparing a final walkthrough.

I climbed the dark stairs to Dennis's office, now my office, and went over my notes for the hundredth time, turning the beads on my wrist. My approach was a gamble perhaps, but it felt right for Worthington.

Up in front of the standing-room only gathering, I thanked everyone for coming and expressed how happy we Crackstones were to return, especially for Christmas, and shared our gratitude for the warm welcome we received. I also said I was so sorry my return came after the loss of Dennis Cliff, a dear friend to me and most everyone in Worthington, an irreplaceable spirit we all missed. Finally, I turned to the sermon. Without pressing, I spoke of Mary and Joseph's pain and fear as they searched in the dark for a place to stay, but also seeking their place in the world—and they found it in the most humble location, in a barn where Mary gave birth to Jesus.

The children's pageant followed, as it has in this church every Christmas Eve for more than a century. Then I took the stage to close the evening.

"A couple of weeks ago, like many of you, my family huddled around the TV to watch *A Charlie Brown Christmas*. What a classic it is, with the kids practicing for the Christmas pageant." I paused to look at our cast. "Though I don't think we had a Lucy angling to be Christmas Queen." They laughed. Thank God, they laughed. They were with me. On I went.

"For me, as I'm sure it is for many of us, the greatest moment is when Charlie Brown cries out, 'Isn't there anyone who knows what Christmas is all about?' And in a humble voice, we hear Linus say, 'Sure, Charlie Brown, I can tell you what Christmas is all about.' Then Linus moves to center stage."

At that point, I stepped away from the pulpit and picked up a blue blanket as I moved onto the kids' center stage. Like Linus I called out, "Lights please." And right on cue, a spotlight hit me as the rest of the lights went down.

"Then Linus recites verses from the King James Version of the Gospel of Luke. And it goes like this–"

Like Linus, I spoke the lines from memory:

> And there were in the same country shepherds abiding in the field, keeping watch over their flock by night.
>
> And, lo, the angel of the Lord came upon them, and the glory of the Lord shone round about them: and they were sore afraid.
>
> And the angel said unto them, Fear not; for, behold, I bring you tidings of great joy, which shall be to all people.
>
> For unto you is born this day in the city of David a Savior, which is Christ the Lord.
>
> And this shall be a sign unto you: Ye shall find the babe wrapped in swaddling clothes, lying in a manger.
>
> And suddenly there was with the angel a multitude of the heavenly host praising God, and saying,
>
> Glory to God in the highest, and on earth peace and goodwill towards men.

I let the scriptural passage settle over the congregation as I eased back to the pulpit and put down the blue blanket before continuing, "Then of course, Linus turns to his friend and says, 'That's what Christmas is all about, Charlie Brown.' And I suppose it is. For all the noise, and stress, and distractions this time of year, that's the timeless spirit of Christmas. May all of you pause to give thanks and enjoy this Christmas season with loved ones and pray for peace on earth and goodwill toward men and women and children as we celebrate the birth of our savior, Jesus Christ."

In closing, I signaled the children from the pageant and other children from the congregation to come up and sing "Hark! The Herald Angels Sing" just like in *A Charlie Brown Christmas*, and then the adult choir came in behind the children. I moved to the door as the kids rejoined their families.

As people filed out, I stood at the door shaking hands and exchanging warm holiday wishes with my new parishioners. Many of them stopped to welcome us back to Worthington and to say how much they enjoyed the sermon. I stood tall and straight, feeling only slightly the oddity of being the tallest man in the Granite State.

Outside, softly, gently, snow continued to fall through the lights of Worthington.

Acknowledgements

Writing a novel sometimes feels as crazy as trying to grow the world's largest pumpkin. In this slow-growing effort, I received encouragement and guidance from many friends and family. In this, I am a rich and grateful man. Topping the list is my wife, Lauren Hall Young, for her steadfastness—as well as my kids, Nick and Tess. A special thank you to Nick Young for his graphic design and illustration on the cover and how well it captures the crux of this novel.

Editorial encouragement and suggestions came from the writers Caroline Leavitt and Don Tassone. For guidance on the life of clergy, I thank two friends and "men of God" David Burstein and Eric Miller.

No book reaches a reader without a publisher and an editor. For this I appreciate the thoughtful collaboration with editor Scott Walker and publisher Michael Mirolla and his team at Guernica Editions.

A final note of appreciation to all who dream big, whether in growing giant pumpkins or writing a novel, and to those who support them.

About the Author

JOHN YOUNG is the author of the novel *When the Coin is in the Air* and the collection *Fire in the Field and Other Stories.* When he was eight years old, Young told his mother he wanted to be a scientist or a clown. So he went into advertising and figures he got pretty close. Born and raised beyond the suburbs in Indianapolis, Indiana, he graduated from Indiana University and earned an MFA in creative writing from Emerson College, Boston. Young also taught English and writing at the high school and college levels and spent many years in advertising as a copywriter and creative director, mostly in Boston. After 20 years in Beverly, Massachusetts, he now lives in Cincinnati, Ohio.

You can learn more at: www.johnyoungwriter.com